RETURN TO
GLORY

SARA ARDEN

RETURN TO GLORY

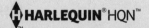

Recycling programs
for this product may
not exist in your area.

ISBN-13: 978-0-373-77930-7

Return to Glory

Copyright © 2014 by Sara Lunsford

Printed in U.S.A.

www.Harlequin.com

Dear Reader,

I'm so excited to share my new series, Home to Glory, with you. These are stories that prove that love really does heal all wounds by teaching us to heal ourselves. In this series, it happens in the small town where they grew up—in the town where *I* grew up. There's something both cathartic and terrifying about healing in the town where you were raised. It's much harder to show your scars to people who already know you. But that's definitely where the magic happens—you can't get to the castle until you go through the haunted forest.

I can't begin to thank everyone who helped me with with my research. The SEALs, rangers and private contractors I spoke with helped me bring these characters to life both as soldiers and as people. They chose to remain anonymous, as some of them are still in theater, but I thank them for their help, their courage and their service.

I hope you enjoy Jack and Betsy's story.
Do stop in and let me know what you think at www.facebook.com/saraardenbooks.

Thanks for reading,

Sara Arden

PROLOGUE

IT WAS DURING the predawn hours on a Saturday morning when former navy SEAL Jack McConnell donned his dress whites and pressed the cold, hard barrel of his .357 Magnum to his temple. With only one bullet in the cylinder, he had a one-in-six chance fate would right the wrong it had so grievously dealt him eighteen months ago.

Jack was supposed to be dead.

He'd sacrificed all he had to give, and now he was nothing but a broken weapon of war. No use to anyone, or anything. If he'd had even a shred of honor left, he'd have made sure every slot in the cylinder was full when he played his little game with fate every Saturday.

But something wouldn't let him, and for that, he cursed himself for a coward. Death was no stranger to him; it'd been a warm friend at his back for every mission. So why couldn't he meet it with certainty?

Jack took a deep breath, hoping it would be his last, and pulled the trigger on the exhale. The hammer made an impotent little click that echoed like a gavel in his ears.

It occurred to Jack that maybe the first time he'd played this game, he'd won and this was actually hell.

Today, Glory would welcome him home, the returning hero. Welcoming him back to the town where he was born, back to the house that had stood empty since his parents' deaths and back to the corpse of a life that was no longer his.

And he was expected to stand up in front of them all and happily accept it as his due with all eyes on him, his ruined face and his new leg made of metal and gears rather than flesh.

A loud bang exploded into the silence and Jack dived to the floor, his hand curled around the .357. The racket repeated and he realized it wasn't an explosion. It was only someone knocking boisterously on the back screen door. Jack realized it was a paradox that he'd just held his own weapon to his head, but any sound similar to gunfire caused him to take cover. To try to protect himself.

He swore as he struggled to pull himself up onto the couch. Jack could walk on his leg, he could even run, but he still had a tough time from a prone position. The knocking banged again and the handle rattled.

Jack had a good idea who it was this early in the morning. He didn't want anyone interfering in his business, and the best way to ensure that happened in a town like this was to act as if there was no business in which they could interfere.

"If this isn't the zombie apocalypse or you're not Salma Hayek," he began as he finally pulled himself up and grabbed his gun, "you're about to gain ten pounds of lead."

Why had he come back? If he'd never— He cut the thought off. He'd come back because even though he was ready to die, he still had affairs to put in order. Jack was a man of his word and he'd told *her* he'd come back. It had been visions of her, of his promise, that had kept him alive, and while part of him hated her for that, he'd been the one stupid enough to make the promise.

"I've got your ten pounds and I'll raise you another ten," Caleb Lewis, one of Glory P.D.'s finest, said with a grin and his hand on his gun. "Saw your light on and thought I'd stop in."

Jack had been in town for only a few days and he was glad their reunion was private. It meant more that he wasn't just one of the rubberneckers.

"I could have left it on because I'm afraid of the dark. You might have interrupted my beauty sleep." The words felt hollow to him, and this easy banter that had once been the hallmark of their friendship felt forced and awkward. At least for Jack. Although he did put his gun down.

Caleb snorted. "I hate to break it to you, but you're not getting any prettier."

"That's because you woke me up." Jack forced the corner of his mouth that could still hold expression to curl into a half smirk. He appreciated the other man's frank observation. It was something Caleb would have said to him before the explosion.

Silence reigned for a moment and the air was

thick with expectation. It snapped when Caleb spoke again. "You know Betsy will want to see you."

This was the collision of past and present Jack had been waiting for—the debt he'd come back to settle.

A tidal wave of memories hit him hard and fast. *Betsy.* Caleb's sister and the girl he'd left behind holding only his dog tags and a childish promise to return. The way she'd looked at him at the bus station, as if her whole world hinged on the very air he breathed. He'd have done anything to keep that adoration in her eyes. Jack had never been anyone's everything, and after he saved her from drowning, he'd become her hero and he'd allowed her to hoist him up on a pedestal.

He'd almost knocked himself off that pedestal when he came home after BUDs. She'd been so beautiful....

"Jack?" Caleb prompted, stemming the flow of memories.

"Yeah, I know."

"I don't think you do. She's still half in love with you."

"She'll get over it." He looked at Caleb pointedly.

"Hey, you know her better than that. She doesn't care what you look like. In fact, she'll hoist your pedestal even higher when she sees the sacrifices you've made."

"So what is this? Warning me off your sister? Really?" He scowled. "I've never taken advantage of her." He'd come precariously close to crossing the line, but he hadn't. Instead he'd given her his tags and a promise to return.

"You've never sat in the dark alone in your dress whites with your weapon in your hand, either. I won't pretend to understand what you're going through, but you're as much a part of my family as she is."

"Then what are you saying?"

"That I see you. Maybe you should see you, too." Jack opened his mouth, but Caleb cut him off. "And that's all I'll say. I gotta go, man. Maybe we can catch up over a few beers later."

He should've known that Caleb would see through all of his carefully constructed walls and chimera within seconds and that he'd call him on all of his bullshit.

Especially where Betsy was concerned.

The best thing to do with her was settle up, just as he'd planned to do. Then he could leave and he'd never have to think about this town, the people or the weight of a hero's mantle that Betsy had so artfully pinned to his scarred shoulders.

CHAPTER ONE

BETSY LEWIS NEVER planned on staying in Glory. There was a big world out there with so much to be seen, done and most important, tasted. For one brief year, she'd escaped to the Institute of Culinary Education in New York.

If anyone were to ask her, she'd say freedom tasted like New York. Specifically, coffee and cheesecake from Junior's before class. Sometimes, after class, too. For a city that was supposed to have horrible water, coffee didn't taste the same anywhere else. Neither did the pizza crust, but that was another matter entirely. Her mouth watered just thinking about it. New York was freedom, success and happiness.

Paris, on the other hand, Paris tasted like Glory. A brew of bitter failure and broken dreams. She had gone there after graduation from the institute, one of the few chosen to be mentored by the famous Chef Abelard. Instead of being the jewel in her crown and the beginning of her career, it was a black stain. For her first dish, she and the other students had been told to prepare mushrooms bordelaise. They had to hunt for the mushrooms themselves, and rather than paying attention to what she was doing, she'd been too busy soaking up the countryside, the culture and Marcel to notice that she'd gathered death cap mushrooms. If not for Chef Abelard's highly sensitive caninelike sense of smell, she might have killed someone.

After the incident, she'd told herself she never wanted to cook, she never wanted to be a chef, she was a baker. An artist who wrought beauty out of sugar and flour. Not someone who worried about brisket.

So she'd returned to Glory and the small-town life that always seemed too small. But after the incident, New York was too big.

Except for Jack McConnell. Yeah, she'd rather think about him than how she'd blown her dreams out of the water with both guns blazing. He was the only thing about Glory that was big-screen.

Jack. Even thinking his name made her insides flutter like a thousand butterfly wings. Of course, that fluttering nonsense had been cordially invited to stop when his letters stopped. The butterflies didn't take the hint, but she hadn't found a way to effectively serve them an eviction notice.

They were the reason she hadn't slept. Or more accurately, Jack was the reason she hadn't slept. The butterflies were hosting a rave at the prospect of seeing him again. Jack had come home and as of this particular moment was barely three blocks away. The knowledge they were even in the same zip code had each nerve ending on high alert. Betsy was sure her eyes were open so wide she looked like some kind of speed freak.

She'd replayed every memory over and over again until the edges seemed tattered like an old quilt, and just like that old quilt, she'd wrapped herself in those memories—especially of his kiss.

Betsy hadn't been kissed like that since—an electric current she felt all the way through to her toes. Not that many had gotten close enough to try. Betsy didn't trust easily. She was friendly and warm, but few were invited to her inner circle. Almost drowning as a child had been a hard lesson. When it had happened, Betsy could see the people who were supposed to be her friends through the heavy wall of water that held her down. They'd simply stood immobile and watched as her life slipped away. The EMTs said inaction associated with fear in that kind of situation was common, but rather than offering comfort to Betsy, it drove home the idea people weren't to be trusted.

All except Jack. He'd rescued her. That memory replayed itself more often than his kiss.

This constant cycle of thoughts had been set to "spin" since she found out Jack was coming home. Now he was here, and today they'd welcome him home in the same gym where they'd said goodbye.

She rolled over and over, trying to get comfortable, but sleep was elusive. Betsy gave up trying. Her bakeshop, Sweet Thing, would open soon. While she loved her shop, it was still the consolation prize because it was in Glory. She had a small staff, but

Betsy still had to finish the cookies she was taking to the ceremony. She wanted to do those herself. They were Nutella cheesecake, Jack's favorite.

She slipped into the dress she'd made just for today. White with a bright red cherry print sewn in her favorite pattern. It accentuated her assets while kindly camouflaging her flaws. Betsy draped a crisp apron over the creation and headed downstairs to the shop.

The scent of glazed donuts and maple coffee greeted her when she walked through the door. Betsy inhaled deeply and exhaled slowly, as if she could keep more of the scent with her. There was a kind of Zen for her in the bakeshop. Simply walking through the door was a tonic for Betsy that eased her hurts and soothed her mind.

A blond head poked out from the walk-in cooler. India George was a newly minted addition to the Glory P.D. and her brother's partner. India was supermodel gorgeous, with high cheekbones, long legs and wide blue eyes. But she'd never been one for dresses and frills; she was rough-and-tumble all the way. She'd been back only for a few months, but it was as if she'd never left. This morning she'd agreed to be Betsy's minion and help run the shop while Betsy handled the orders for the ceremony. In return, Betsy promised no cop/donut jokes for at least a week.

"Didn't sleep, did you?" India asked as she pulled out a tray of donuts ready for frosting and set them on a prep table.

Betsy grabbed some icing bags and handed one to India. "Sleep is overrated."

"Have you seen him yet?" India didn't look at her as she accepted the bag and began icing a donut.

India wasn't only her brother's partner, she was also his best friend and had been since the first time she made him actually eat dirt on the playground after taking her ball. India was the big sister she'd never had.

"No," Betsy admitted. "I almost went to see him the day he came home, but I thought he'd need some time."

"That was smart. Adjusting to civilian life is hard, even without his challenges. His parents' deaths..." She shrugged and kept icing.

What India hadn't mentioned, but left hanging in the air like a contagion, was the stark reality of Jack's injuries.

"I remember when I got the call last year," Betsy said quietly. "After his parents died when he was first deployed, I was his emergency contact. The nurse asked me if there was anything I wanted her to tell him. She thought he was going to die."

India had a donut halfway up to her mouth but put it down. "I didn't know that. What did you say?"

"He promised to come back to me, India." Betsy nodded silently as that last and most hated memory churned to the surface. She'd been avoiding that one, pushing it out of her head every time it struggled forward. She'd rather drown a thousand times than ever take that call again or remember how it felt. She found her voice and lifted her chin. "I told her to remind him of his promise."

"Oh Bets." India covered Betsy's hand with her own. "That was a long time ago. Maybe even another person. He—"

"It's not like I spent the last five years waiting for him." Betsy turned back to her work.

"Isn't it?" India asked in a careful tone.

"No, that would be stupid." Or maybe just pathetic. She hadn't waited for him, but Jack McConnell had the set the bar by which she measured a man pretty high.

"When was the last time you went out with someone?" India had latched on to the idea that Betsy had waited all these years for Jack. Like a rabid dog, she wasn't going to let it go any time soon.

"Scott Meyer."

"Not who, *when?*"

Betsy cringed at the answer. "Last year."

"And before that?"

"There was that guy in Paris." She thought about Marcel and how he'd broken her heart right after she'd broken her own dreams. She sighed. Marcel didn't matter. What would she have done with him anyway? Stayed in France? Married him? And never been good enough, smart enough, pretty enough or talented enough? She'd always be the wide-eyed girl from America who liked to play in the kitchen. Why had she ever put up with that from him?

"Right about when Jack stopped writing and calling?" India eyed her. "You still have his dog tags, don't you?"

The tags were in her nightstand. "I still have my yearbook, too. That's not especially significant." Now, Jack, he was the one she would've married. If she were with him, Glory wouldn't be such a bad place to end up. In fact, when she was a little girl, she didn't dream of France. She dreamed of him and Glory.

"A yearbook is nowhere near the same thing as a soldier's dog tags."

Betsy could admit India was right about that, but Betsy didn't think there was anything wrong with keeping his tags. He'd been a big part of her life. The breath in her lungs was there only because he'd given it to her. Keeping his tags didn't seem above and beyond reasonable.

"Look, I know Jack isn't the same guy who left. He couldn't be. But that guy made me feel like a live wire and see stars where I knew there weren't any because my eyes were closed. If someone makes me feel that again, then I'll go out with him. I won't settle for less."

"Honey, if Scott Meyer didn't make you see stars, you're a lost cause," India teased.

Betsy could admit Scott was a catch. He was a fireman. It was some unwritten law that all firemen had to be sexy. He was smart and funny, country-boy sweet with a pair of shoulders like Atlas. Betsy had kissed him on their third date. It had been nice, but it had reminded her of chocolate. Godiva to be exact. She liked Godiva and enjoyed it, an excellent product, but it didn't do things to her senses the way André's Confiserie Suisse did. Having had André's, she was spoiled for anything else.

"Didn't you go out with him a few times after you got back? I don't see any follow-up dates that you had, either. You must be a lost cause, too," Betsy deflected.

A haunted look flashed across India's features, only to fade into a brittle smile. "I am at that, Bets." She nodded.

"India," Betsy began haltingly.

"I'd rather deal with your mess than mine." India's expression softened. "I know you and Caleb love me. If I need you, I'll ask, okay?"

There was so much Betsy wanted to say. India was just returning to civilian life after deployment as a military police officer. While she'd come home physically whole, something catastrophic had happened to her that was more than just the reality of war.

"Okay," she agreed softly. "But you better hurry up in the dating department. Otherwise you're stuck with my brother." They'd made an oath at fifteen that if neither of them was married by thirty, they'd bite the bullet and marry each other. Betsy's mom had been thrilled and suggested they start dating as a practice run.

"More like he'd be stuck with me." India managed a real laugh. "Don't you have cookies to bake?"

Betsy let it drop. "Are you sure you can handle the counter? The morning rush is kind of crazy."

"I'm a cop." India shrugged. "How bad can it be?"

"You're tempting fate with that question."

"She can go ahead and *bring it*." India screwed up her pretty features into an expression that said she was indeed ready for anything that came her way.

That was old-school India, and Betsy was happy to hear it. "If you're sure. If you need me, I'll be in my *laboratory*." She pronounced the last word with what her brother had come to call "evil genius inflection."

Betsy had to admit that baking sometimes made her feel like a mad scientist, or a witch brewing spells and potions. It was part of what she loved about baking. Quality baked goods were all about chemistry and reaction, but not just of the ingredients themselves. It was about how those things interacted with the people combining the ingredients and those who would partake of the results.

Betsy tried to stay calm and happy while she worked. In the early days of her shop, she'd taken out her frustration on bread dough, and even though she'd done nothing different, when she was unhappy, the bread tasted like a scoop of used kitty litter.

As she mixed the dough for the cookies, Betsy let go of everything that weighed her down. She surrendered to the initial feelings that always enveloped her when she walked into the shop. Peace. Joy. Home. She kept each one on her mind and in her heart while she formed every cookie.

It was a blessed respite until several hours later. When all the batches had cooled and she packaged cookies for Jack and some for the ceremony, it occurred to her that maybe Jack wouldn't want to see her at all. Her heart twisted in on itself, the cruel hands of possibility wringing it out like a sponge.

She crushed that thought beneath her vintage high heels. It didn't matter if he wanted to see her or not. With all he'd lost, he needed someone. Even if it was only to let him know he wasn't alone. It was possible and even likely he'd changed more than she could ever know, but underneath it all, he was still Jack. Betsy owed him her very life, and if he needed her now, nothing would keep her from repaying the debt. She might not be able to make mushrooms bordelaise, but she could help Jack.

Betsy kept her focus on that determination while she closed up Sweet Thing, loaded the bakery van with India and even after she'd taken her seat inside the community center.

But then her first sight of Jack obliterated all her good intentions. Any notion of debts and repayment quickly morphed into a familiar hunger. Her breath caught and time stopped.

A tsunami-like surge of emotion crashed over her now. She devoured the sight of him, as if any second he'd disappear and she'd have only these few precious seconds to remember him.

He was harder now, aged in a way deeper than skin. His shoulders were wider, his chest thicker and his jaw harder. His close-cropped hair now accentuated the high-angled sharp lines of his cheekbones and cinder block jaw. His mouth was set in a grim line, scar tissue crisscrossing in a haphazard melee across the left side of his face. When he turned his head, she saw that the scars ran down his neck and disappeared beneath his uniform.

Tears welled up in her eyes for him, but not because of how he looked. Even with the scars, he was as handsome as he'd ever been. Maybe even more. His scars were proof of his strength—of his courage. The spray of white-ridged marks across his skin, and tributaries and valleys of twisted, ropey sinew and puckered flesh, horrified her not because they were ugly, but because she couldn't imagine the pain he'd suffered.

Betsy tried to look away. But try as hard as she could, there was nothing else she could focus on but Jack. Just as it had always been.

CHAPTER TWO

JACK WOULD HAVE known her anywhere.

Betsy Lewis was a lush caricature of the lovely girl he remembered. Her ethereal beauty had become earthier. That pale skin had turned to cream perfection and her rounded curves had become full-on dangerous. A tumble of black hair hung over her shoulder to curl against her cleavage, and she looked every inch a vintage pinup queen, right down to her matte red lips and the matching cherry print on her white dress. Everything about her blared sex, and his body answered, painfully hard, at just the sight of her.

Or maybe it was just because he was a twisted bastard? That was more likely. She was a beautiful, kind woman who deserved better than him imagining her to satisfy himself during the long, lonely nights. He'd thought that part of his life was over, that need. Either the shrapnel or the whiskey had taken it from him, and until now, he hadn't cared. He didn't want to look at himself, or touch himself, so he was under no illusions that anyone else would want to.

Especially not her. She couldn't even look at his face.

He tried to block out the memory of her kiss, that innocent touch of her lips against his, begging him to be her first—and what inevitably came next. His patient, tender refusal. The look in her eyes now when she'd had to turn away was much the same. As if something inside her had been crushed.

What the hell was he thinking anyway? Even if he'd come home whole, he still wasn't good enough for Betsy Lewis.

God, but he wanted a drink. He wanted to silence the voices in his head, the memories and the pain. He consoled himself that this would be over quickly. The townspeople would get their look at him and then they'd leave him alone.

That's what this recognition ceremony was all about—they wanted their look to satisfy their curiosity. They'd go home and talk about what a shame it was what happened to Jack McConnell and then they'd leave him in blessed peace.

The mayor continued to drone on and Jack managed to tear his gaze away from Betsy. "And with that, we'd like to present you with this award," the mayor finished.

Jack stood slowly, his prosthesis working with him and straightening as the rest of his body did. He still couldn't move too fast or it would throw off his balance.

He was expected to speak, but he had nothing to say.

"It's an honor, sir," the mayor said, shaking his hand.

He leaned over the mic and fixed his stare on a point against the far wall. "The honor is mine. Both to have served my country and to be part of this community. Thank you." Jack accepted the plaque and headed for the exit, trying not to choke on the bile in his throat.

Betsy was suddenly standing in front of him with one of the purple boxes—just like the ones she used to send him. "Hi, Jack." She thrust the box into his hand and flung herself into his arms.

She clung tightly to him and he couldn't stop himself from clinging back. The scents of vanilla and sugar washed over him. She smelled so good, so wholesome, and she felt even better with her full breasts against his chest. She fit against him as if she'd been made for this moment—for him. Her hair was so soft against his cheek, like black silk. Jack could have stood there forever simply holding her.

But like all breakable things, he knew every second he touched her was dangerous.

"It's so good to see you," she whispered against his ear.

Her breath was warm on his skin, tingling. The sensation caused him to remember what it felt like to want. To need. Jack couldn't help himself. He tightened his embrace and crushed her solidly against him. "You smell like cookies." He hadn't seen her in five years, and the first thing he said was that she smelled like cookies. Stupid.

What else was there to say? *Don't tell me it's good to see me when you can't even look at me?*

She laughed, the sound musical and light, but she made no move to release him and he found he didn't have to the courage to pull away from her. Right now it was just a hug. They could be Jack and Betsy. When he released her, she'd have to look somewhere and it wouldn't be his face. He couldn't blame her.

Or at least that's what he told himself.

Instead of letting go, he wanted to touch her more thoroughly. To see if she was really so soft and perfect everywhere. Only being this close to her made his skin feel too tight, itchy. Made him think if he could just scratch deep enough, he could peel off what he'd become, but he knew better. So he pulled back from her, but she stayed in his embrace.

"That's because I was baking all morning. They're Nutella cheesecake."

He looked at her blankly.

"Your favorite." She had yet to focus on his face.

Jack couldn't remember what his favorite was, but if she said it was, he'd believe her. He hadn't been able to taste anything but ash, or remember anything before the char consumed his nose, his mouth and his lungs. She pulled farther away from him slowly, and he let her go.

It occurred to him that she was as beautiful as he was ugly. No, that wasn't even the right word. She was like the sun, warm and bright, but she would scald him through to the bone if he let himself bask in her rays for too long. He needed to take cover, and in this case, distance and darkness would be his shield.

"Thanks." He held up the box in his hand. "I guess we should settle up."

"What do you mean?" She looked at a point past his cheek, not focusing on his face.

"I owe you. For taking care of the house. My parents." He swallowed hard. "Being there to take the call when I was injured."

"Oh Jack. You don't owe me for anything." She looked down and smoothed her hands on her dress to straighten an imaginary wrinkle. "You came home. That's all I wanted."

Before this moment, he hadn't been able to admit he wanted Betsy to look at him the same way she had done those years ago when he left. She wasn't that girl anymore and he certainly wasn't that boy. "My parents left you something in their will. I wouldn't feel right if you didn't get it." That was a damn lie, but it had to be done. After everything she'd done for him, he owed her. Jack was a man who paid his debts.

"Come by tonight after you close the bakery." It would be dark then and she wouldn't have to see his face. He didn't wait for her to respond but abandoned her there by the stage. Jack didn't want to hear her say no.

Hours later, with a bottle of whiskey in hand, Jack was wishing he'd stayed to hear her refusal. Then he wouldn't have been sitting there rotten with hope for just one more look at a woman who wasn't coming.

What the hell had he been thinking anyway? He could have the papers to the account drawn up and have them delivered. Jack didn't have to be here. He could leave her the house, too. He took a long pull, finding comfort in the fact that oblivion was only a bottle away.

He was almost all the way through the amber bliss when the front bell rang. Jack didn't jump half out of his skin this time, because he'd reached that plateau where his constant fight-or-flight reaction was a distant discomfort. Jack would've just let the bell ring, but there was still the faint hope it could be her.

She smiled at him when he opened the door, another purple box in her hands. "Sorry it's so late. I've got Halloween orders to fill, so I've been working late."

He held the door open to allow her inside. She was wearing a different dress. This one was vintage as well, yellow-checked gingham with pockets in the front and a neckline that had to be illegal.

The sound of an old engine backfiring on the street outside elicited an immediate response: *take cover.* He hit the floor, dragging Betsy with him and shielding her with his body before he could process that it was just another shitty car in a small American town. He wasn't in Iraq anymore.

A cool hand on his cheek brought him into the present. "It's okay. We're safe," she whispered to him.

Shame, hot and putrid, washed over him. "I'm sorry."

"You were protecting me. There's nothing to be sorry for."

He recoiled from her, pulling himself off her and

leaning his back against the wall. "I, uh, what my parents wanted you to have, it's on the table."

"Jack," she began. Her presence was overwhelming, smothering. She seemed to burn up all the oxygen in the room.

"Just take it and go." He struggled to get up, but he couldn't get his balance with nothing stationary to which he could anchor himself. The prosthesis bent at an awkward angle and he crashed back to the floor. Jack cursed, more determined than ever to get up now. He had to. She couldn't see him like this.

At least at the ceremony he'd been upright and in his uniform. Wearing a symbol of something that mattered. Now he was just Jack.

Broken.

Useless.

He tried again to stand but failed. Rage filled him and he didn't care if he broke the thing, he *would* stand. Jack attempted to claw his way up.

"Jack," she said again, horror shading her voice.

"I don't want your damn pity," he roared.

She reached for the crushed purple box and put it up on a nearby table and then moved next to him, pulling his head down into her lap.

Even as it was happening, Jack knew it was wrong. He wanted to tell her to leave. No, now he was lying to himself. He didn't *want* to tell her to leave, but he knew he needed to. Her touch was tender and sweet, stroking over the good side of his face. "Pity and empathy are two different things."

She still smelled so good—of all things sweet

and wholesome. While he stank of Old North Bend whiskey.

"You should go, Bets." His actions betrayed his words because he'd wrapped an arm around her thighs.

"Not a chance. It's not you who owes me, but the other way around. Did you forget that you saved my life?"

"That was a hundred years ago and another life."

"Maybe. But men aren't the only ones allowed to have their honor. I pay my debts, too."

"There's no debt. Your life is yours, free and clear." He didn't want her to be here because of some imaginary debt.

"I'll never forget opening my eyes and seeing you leaning over me." She stroked her fingers through his hair. "The streetlight made a halo around your head and I thought you were some kind of angel."

"What utter tripe," he said without conviction.

"I have never been so terrified. When I realized I wasn't going to make it back up to the surface, I was so angry. I wasn't ready for my life to be over. Especially not for some stupid childhood prank. I didn't want to die. And it hurt, it was like my lungs were on fire while being pressed under a million pounds of solid rock."

He didn't speak but pulled away from her and the intimacy of the position.

"Then there you were, Jack. While everyone else watched and did nothing, it was you who saved me. You gave me everything I have. So if you think for a minute I wouldn't do the same for you, you've got another think coming."

"I'm not drowning, Betsy."

"Yes, you are. You're drowning yourself in whiskey. I smelled it on you at the ceremony, and your house reeks of it."

"I'm already dead, sweetheart. It's a wasted effort. So take what my parents left you and go."

"Shall we see about that, Jack?" She pulled away from him and stood.

"What?"

"Get up."

"I can't." He might have expected this from someone else, but never Betsy.

"I said get up, soldier. You made me a promise. You said you'd come back, but this isn't you. This isn't Jack McConnell."

"You're right. I told you, Jack McConnell is dead and I just brought his body back for you to mourn."

"I don't accept that. I said get up."

"How!" he roared again, and it wasn't a question.

"Ask me to help you." Her voice was calm and steady.

"I didn't beg when I was captured in Mosul. I'm not begging for anything here."

"I don't want you to beg. I want you to ask. There is no shame in that." Her voice, while sweet, was braced with steel. "Ask me."

"No."

"Unacceptable." She nudged him with her foot. "Ask and I'll make it worth your while."

"How could you conceivably do that? I can't taste the sweets you make, and my dick doesn't work. So what could you possibly offer me?"

"Right now I'm offering to restrain myself from kicking you. The Jack I used to know would knock your teeth down the back of your throat for talking to me that way."

He sighed. She was right. "I'm sorry, Betsy. Just go."

"Not a chance." Her voice was softer now and she leaned down over him. "I *will* help you. I'm not leaving until you're at least in that chair."

"Fine. Help me."

Seemingly satisfied she wasn't going to get any better from him, she helped haul him upright. It was an effort, but she managed. He should've expected her strength; she carried around fifty-pound bags of flour all day and kneaded loaf after loaf of fresh bread for hours.

She didn't try to help him to the chair. Instead he found his back against the wall and Betsy on her tiptoes, her matte red lips pressed against his with no care for the ruined part of his face. She kissed him wholly, completely.

It was as if those years had never passed and they were under the stars again the same as the night he'd left. Pieces of himself he thought long dead sparked and flickered—a bulb in a faulty socket. He tightened his arms around her, pressing her more firmly against him.

She felt so good. It had been so long since anything felt good. She even tasted like vanilla. That had to be his imagination because he hadn't been able to taste anything but ash since he'd awakened from the burning hell of his nightmares into a real world just as awful.

Jack deepened the kiss, tasting more of her, storing up the memories of vanilla and sugar. Betsy broke the kiss all too soon and pulled away from him, and the new bud of light that had taken root grew dark. He'd have given anything to turn it back on.

"I'll see you tomorrow, Jack."

He didn't respond, only watched her go.

She turned halfway out the door and light from the street lamp pooled around her. "In case you were wondering, *everything* seems to be working just fine." She shut the door behind her.

CHAPTER THREE

BETSY'S LIPS TINGLED from the passionate kiss. Her body burned with need, and those fireworks she'd been talking about with India had burst to bright and heated life. Even tasting the whiskey on his breath, even scarred as he was, his mouth was still the only thing that had ever lit a blaze so hot. Being pressed against his hard body… Yes, everything was in deliciously proper working order.

Except for the most important spark. The flame that was inside him that made him Jack. There was a darkness in him now that was so heavy it threatened to smother all the light.

Betsy refused to allow that to happen. She'd meant what she said. She would save him whether he wanted her to or not. When she was drowning, she'd had no way to ask for help, and she figured that analogy couldn't be more spot-on. He was drowning in the dark.

Jack had taught her that life was meant to be lived. He'd shared part of his spark with her, and that was why she had to ignite that inside him again no matter what it took.

She cast a glance back at the house over her shoulder as she headed to her car. Jack was at the window. Betsy knew he would be—he'd watch over her until she was safely locked in her vehicle.

She held up her hand in a gesture that wasn't quite a wave, but more of a thank-you as she unlocked the door and slid inside.

She drove the short way to her mother's house on Westwood, and the memory of the night he left crashed over her. Betsy pushed it away; she didn't want to remember. It was too much like holding on to a dream that could never be real.

Except it had been real and it was over. Time marched forward, their lives changed, but she'd never forgotten how he made her feel.

And the night she'd said goodbye to a dream.

Jack McConnell had been all-American perfect.

The boy who'd been an Eagle Scout, volunteered at the homeless shelter in the city, an all-star quarterback and a straight-A student had graduated from BUDs. Jack was officially a navy SEAL, the best of the best.

And just as he'd come home from BUDs, Betsy had had to say goodbye again. But before he left to serve his country, there was something he had to know. Something that couldn't wait.

Betsy was in love with him.

Nothing else mattered but making sure Jack knew he had a reason to keep himself safe—to come home. Her mind flashed back to that night.

Her heart was so full of him, it actually hurt. Sometimes she wondered if it was possible to love someone so much a heart could burst.

The party Betsy's parents organized in the community center gym to send him off in patriotic style was in full swing. Couples moved on the floor to a high school band that supplied melody while others scavenged the potluck buffet. Veterans and active-duty service members shook Jack's hand. They thanked him for his service. The man who ran the military memorabilia store teased him and said even though he'd chosen the navy, Jack was still okay in his book and guffawed.

Jack took it all in with a good-natured grin that was his trademarked expression. He turned to her, as if he felt her eyes, and gave her a smile that was only for her. He excused himself from his well-wishers.

"Hey, sweet thing. Did you have a good time?"

She smiled. "The party was for you." Betsy didn't know how she could be expected to have a good time when he was leaving again.

"No fun at all?" He raised an eyebrow.

"Not a single bit." She gave him a conspiratorial look. "You can make it up to me, though."

"Oh can I? Who says I want to?" he teased.

"You never tell me no."

"And now I'm paying the price." He slipped his arm around her waist.

Betsy couldn't help the thrill that jolted through her at the contact. His hands were so warm; his whole body radiated heat and the sensation stole nearly every thought in her head. "You can let me go with you to the bus station."

"Bets. We talked about this. You're still in high

school and you shouldn't be out by yourself that late at night. It's dangerous." He held up his hand to silence her when she would've interrupted him. "And I don't want my last memory of tonight to be you red-eyed and snot-nosed."

Betsy had other plans for his memories of tonight, but she had to get him to agree to the bus station first. "I promise I won't cry until you're gone, and Caleb said he'd bring India to ride home with me so I won't be alone." Betsy bit her lip. "Please? I need to tell you something and I don't want to tell you here."

"What's this about?" His confusion looked genuine.

As if he didn't know how she felt or what she could possibly want to tell him. All the more reason this was so important.

"I'll tell you if you come with me. You've had enough of the party, right? Wouldn't you rather have some of my mother's fried chicken and my Nutella cheesecake cookies down by the river?"

"Sometimes I think you know me too well. The party, your parents, it was great, but—" He shrugged.

"They know that. My mother packed the picnic basket in my car."

"I'm going to miss Lula's cooking."

You could have it every day if you stay. *Of course, Betsy didn't say that. This was the life he'd chosen, the one he wanted. Either she could behave like an adult and support him, or she could be a selfish child worried only about her own feelings. She was trying very hard to be the kind of woman he needed.*

Tears pricked at the corners of her eyes, but she blinked them away. "Come on, then." She grabbed his hand and led him out to the parking lot.

Betsy was so nervous her knees shook and she considered herself lucky she was able to walk upright and didn't fall on her face. Not only did Betsy plan on telling Jack she loved him; she planned on showing him, too. It would be perfect. Moonlight and stars, the smells of the grass and his cologne would be indelibly marked into her memory. The taste of the homemade blackberry cordial she'd smuggled out of the pantry on their lips.

Or so she'd read in the books her mother kept under her bed. Of course she'd heard things from friends, but Betsy preferred to think it would be like the books rather than sweaty grunting and strange faces with a gearshift digging into her back.

Whatever it was, she decided it would be perfect because it was with Jack.

The community center overlooked the Missouri River, but there were still too many people around for what she intended. Betsy drove to a small campsite close to the riverbanks and parked. They walked a short trail to a secluded spot where she spread out the red-and-white-checkered blanket.

"It's been a long time since we've been here. I thought you forgot."

When she was younger, after he'd saved her from drowning, Jack had brought her here to show her the river wasn't something to fear. It was powerful and should be respected, marveled at, but never feared. She always felt so safe with him, which was why this was the perfect spot. Something else new to experience with him.

A small voice niggled at the back of her brain asking what if he said no? What if he didn't want her? Betsy refused to think about that. Fate was never wrong, and she knew with a certainty as deep as her bones that Jack McConnell was her fate.

"How could I forget, Jack?"

She pulled out the cordial and offered him the bottle.

"Does your mother know you have that?" he asked.

"I told you that she packed the basket." *A teensy, tiny lie. Infinitesimal, really.*

Of course he could see straight through it. "You're a horrible liar."

"What she won't know won't hurt her. It's just a little bit and it's just tonight."

"Only one sip if you plan on driving me to the bus station," *Jack admonished.*

A four-letter word clanged in her brain like a gong. She hadn't thought of that. "Like I said, just a little bit. My grandmother calls it her tonic, so it must be good for us." *Betsy grinned.*

"So, what did you need to tell me that was so important?"

No! Not yet. She had to let him relax into the moment before she pounced. "In a minute. Right now I *want to lie back and be still with you. We'll make our own constellations in the stars like we used to when my brother was playing Ghost in the Graveyard and wouldn't let me play. How was it you always got stuck with little sister duty?" Betsy laughed and reclined on the blanket, close enough to touch him.*

"I volunteered."

More sparks burst in her stomach and Betsy swore her fingers were numb. Simply being this close to him and knowing he wanted to spend time with her, too, it short-circuited something vital.

"That one, over there." Betsy pointed, leaning so her head was almost on his chest. "It looks like a lollipop."

"You see sweets everywhere. In clouds, stars, and probably when you sleep."

"I do," Betsy admitted. "I dreamt about spring cake last night."

"What's spring cake? Or do I dare ask?"

"You'd love it. It's going to be yellow cake with lemon. Just enough for a bit of tart, but otherwise sweet with key lime frosting, I think."

"You're going to make some man very lucky someday, sweet thing."

Her heart thudded so loud for a second, she couldn't hear anything else. It was now or never. "What about you, Jack?" she asked quietly.

"No, I doubt I'll make any man happy."

Was he being purposefully obtuse? The night was suddenly still, a calm before the storm, but Betsy

*wanted the storm. She needed it more than her next
breath. "Would I make you happy?"*

"Jesus, Bets."

*That was not the response she'd been looking for,
but she forged ahead. "What I wanted to tell you is
that I'm in love with you."*

*He propped himself up on his elbow and he stud-
ied her a moment before he spoke. "I know you think
you feel these things, but it's only because I'm going
away. You're scared because things are changing,
and that's okay. I may be leaving here, but I'm not
leaving you."*

*"Things have already changed, Jack. I will admit
that I'm scared, but it made me realize I want to
spend every day with you. Every night."*

*His face was unreadable. "You don't know what
you're saying, what you're asking for."*

*He was determined to be the good guy. She'd
known this part would be difficult, but that was part
of why she loved him. Even if she had to work harder
to get what she wanted—happily ever after with Jack
McConnell. "Don't I?"*

*Being bold was easier now that she'd already
said she loved him. Betsy looped her arm around
his neck and pulled him down to her. She tilted her
mouth up to kiss him, and as soon as their lips met,
lightning coursed through her veins and she swore
that for the briefest millisecond, the spark between
them stopped her heart.*

*His kiss was everything she'd hoped it would be.
Strong and sure, but passionate and tender. She*

knew the stars burned brighter and hotter because she could see supernovas behind her eyes.

He became the aggressor, shifting his hard body on top of hers, his fingers tangled in her hair. Betsy loved that he was touching her, but she wanted him to touch her everywhere. *Not just her hair. The fire of her need burned her from the inside out.*

This was sheer bliss and just as she'd imagined, she committed every sensation to memory. The exploding stars, the scent of him, the texture of his shirt under her palms and the taste of the cordial on his mouth, which was more potent than she could've imagined. They'd drink this at their wedding.

His hands wandered down to her hips and slid beneath her dress and up her thigh. Betsy couldn't breathe, couldn't think; she could only feel. He broke the kiss, his mouth trailing down the column of her throat.

This was actually happening. "Yes, Jack. Please," she urged.

He stopped all the delicious things he was doing and stared at her as if she'd morphed into a two-headed dog.

"Betsy! I'm so sorry." *He scrambled away from her, his breathing ragged.*

"Don't you dare be sorry!" *Betsy straightened herself.* "I have my own brain, which works just fine, and a mouth to say what I do and do not want."

"You're only sixteen."

"I'm not a kid anymore, Jack. I may be a young woman, but I *am a woman.*"

"I'm not talking about your body. I'm talking about your life. Your experiences."

"So give me some," she blurted.

He closed his eyes, his jaw clenched. "You can't say things like that. Someone will take advantage of you."

"Obviously not." She eyed him expectantly and all of her bravado melted away as that tiny voice whispered doubts in her head. "Unless you don't, you're not..." She pursed her lips and shook her head, unable to finish asking if he wasn't attracted to her.

"You're beautiful, sweet thing. Your letters during basic and BUDs kept me sane." Jack paused. "I'll admit I thought about you more than I should have. In ways I shouldn't have. But, Betsy, you're Caleb's little sister and where I'm going, I can't put that life on you."

Betsy accepted what he said, but it wasn't surrender. Fate didn't make mistakes. She grabbed his hand. "Then I'll wait for you. Just promise you'll always come home no matter what it takes."

He took off the tags from around his neck and pressed the warm metal into her hand. "I promise."

She knew there was nothing else to say then but goodbye.

They drove to the station in silence, and when it was time for him to board, Betsy gave him a fierce hug.

Rather than tell him she loved him again, she whispered in his ear, "Don't forget your promise."

"I won't." He brushed his lips lightly over the

*crown of her head and boarded the bus without look-
ing back.*

   *Betsy stood alone in the pale, sodium light of the
station with his dog tags clutched in her fingers and
kept her own promise. She didn't cry until the bus
was gone.*

   That was the last time she'd seen him, before tod-
day.

   Now he was back and her stupid heart didn't understand how much things had changed. How much
he'd changed.

   Betsy knew the only way this could end was
badly—that was one thing her heart did understand.

   And it didn't care.

CHAPTER FOUR

JACK COULDN'T FACE HER after what had happened.

He'd been so weak, so powerless, so *broken*. His failure had been splayed wide in front of her like an autopsy, but she hadn't turned away from him, which was worse somehow. Maybe because it was obvious she thought he could be fixed.

But some things, once broken, couldn't be pieced back together—parts were missing.

Like Jack. He wasn't whole, and he never would be.

Despite what had happened last night, he had to face her again, if only to make her take that check. Jack knew he owed her, and the money was the only thing he had to give.

A small voice reminded him that wasn't quite the truth. He had his wreck of a body, and if her kiss was any indication, she seemed to want it. She couldn't look at his face, but she'd pressed herself up against him, her sweet, lush curves so inviting.

He knew she was still in love with the idea of him, still wanted the golden boy he'd been when he left. Maybe that was what she needed—the ugly truth to crush the fantasy.

So maybe she'd let him go. The fire in her eyes, the determination...

Now he was lying to himself. He wanted Betsy, and as far as he'd fallen, if she'd have him, he wouldn't be able to say no. Touching her was bittersweet because it was the only time he could feel anything more than pain.

He eyed the whiskey bottle on the table, and when he would have reached for it, he stopped. Next to it was the envelope that held Betsy's check, and it sat there like an accusation.

Jack swore and picked up the envelope instead of the bottle. He'd need it when he got home anyway.

It occurred to him that rather than see her again, the embodiment of the life that was lost to him, he could simply give it to Betsy's mother and leave. He'd promised Betsy he'd come back, and so he had. Their accounts would be as even as they ever could be.

Yes, he'd leave before he shattered the image of the hero she believed him to be, and the heart of the girl who'd loved the man he'd been.

His decision made, he grabbed the envelope and headed to his car. Driving with the prosthesis wasn't a challenge, and he knew that he'd fared better than most with the cutting-edge technology of the endo/ exo implant—the titanium mesh implanted in his femur having actually become part of him. He'd had less downtime, fewer struggles, and logic told him that he had a lot to be grateful for.

But logic wasn't there with him in the dark. It should have been; he'd been a SEAL—the best of the best. He stared death in the face and dared it to come take whatever it thought it could, and yet, when the flames came and he could smell the stench of his own burning flesh in his nose— He pushed the thoughts away, unwilling to face his cowardice.

When the house came into view, a sickening wave of nostalgia washed over him and turned his stomach. He remembered every night he'd spent in that house. The tree house at the back of the property where he and Caleb had hidden out from India when she was on a tear, his first real kiss in the closet in the downstairs family room during a middle school party, and Lula Lewis's fried chicken on a Friday night after a home football game.

The house lived and breathed with memories that were better left undisturbed.

A sudden dread hit him. As if, if he took those last few feet, everything would change, but that was stupid. There was nothing behind door number one that could change what he'd come to do—what he had to do.

He moved forward, one foot in front of the other.

The brightly painted red door opened, and rather than Lula, it was Betsy standing there.

Her features were drawn and tight, some heavy burden tugging her shoulders down, the corners of her mouth, and the weight extinguished the light in her eyes.

Seeing her like that tore at him with sharp claws. That was exactly what he feared he'd do to her. He realized Betsy wasn't the only one attached to an ideal. Jack needed to believe nothing could touch her, that she was safe from all the bad things in the world. Especially him.

"I came to give you this." He thrust the envelope at her.

She drew her gaze up slowly, her regard burning him through to his bones. Suddenly he felt even worse about offering her the check than he did not reading her letters. She hadn't said anything, hadn't been angry, but it was all there in the pools of her eyes. The acknowledgment of everything he hadn't wanted to say to her, but somehow she knew.

"I don't want your money." Betsy turned away from him, but he grabbed her wrist.

Jack found himself watching the scene from a place outside time. A place where his rational mind could protest what his body wanted and no one would hear it. Instead of releasing her when she turned, he pulled her into his arms.

She came to him easily, all soft sweetness. Betsy clung to him like a life raft in a hurricane—and he thought the description apt because he was ravaged by the storm the same as she was.

Touching her felt as if all of his nerve endings were on fire at once when before, they'd been numb. It was pain, it was bliss. It was everything he wanted and everything he feared.

If he could feel all of this from a simple embrace, what would it be like if he kissed her again?

The moment hung between them, gravid with everything they'd left unsaid and undone. The weight of a semi crushed down on his sternum, and the envelope burned his fingers.

She pulled away from him slowly as if moving through water. Betsy slipped her hand into his. She led him inside and toward the stairs.

Toward her bedroom.

Toward something he knew was wrong but wanted more than his next breath.

If he'd taken her that night under the stars with whispers of love and blackberry cordial on her breath, it would have been more forgivable than what he was about to do.

She pushed the bedroom door open silently and he followed behind her.

The room was still pink, her sheets still white, just as they'd been when she was a girl, but all of the pictures and posters had been taken down and there were boxes stacked in the corner. Two lone pictures had been stuck to the mirror. One of Betsy with two friends with the Statue of Liberty in the background, and one of Betsy with a man. They were standing behind an array of pastries, both of them with a certain glow to their cheeks. Accomplishment. Camaraderie. Something else Jack didn't want to name.

Betsy reached up and wrapped her arms around his neck again and he looked away from those pictures of another life, turned his mind away from the questions that bubbled up inside him. If he spoke, he knew the spell over them would shatter.

It was the right thing to do, to stop this before

it went any further, but Jack was tired of the right thing.

Even though it was on the tip of his tongue to tell her she didn't want this with him and all of the reasons why:

That he was broken.

That he was ugly inside and out.

That he had nothing to give her.

That even these moments would only be a hungry shadow of what she deserved.

He said none of them. Instead he kissed her. Jack crushed his mouth to hers and he wasn't sure if it was because he needed to taste her again or if he was punishing them both.

Her for making him feel, making him want, and himself for not being able to deny the pull between them.

She melted under the onslaught, her body molding against his. There was no shy confession from her, no demure invitation like before. She was bold, her hands moving under his shirt, over his chest, his shoulders, his back.

While scarred, he knew that part of him was well made and pleasing. He was strong; he had to be to lift himself. He could lift her, too. Jack remembered that was something Betsy had always liked, to be picked up. To be shown that her curves weren't too much for a guy to handle. To be reassured that petite wasn't the only definition of *sexy*.

When he would have hauled her up and wrapped her legs around his waist, she was too busy tearing his T-shirt off him, her fingers on the button fly of his jeans.

Stark terror coursed through him and he stumbled away from her.

Because she'd see. The ugliness would be right there in her face. There was no hiding it under a pant leg; there was no pretending he was whole.

What the hell had he been thinking? It was the middle of the day, the sun high overhead, and there was no darkness for him to hide in, no shadows.

His dick withered at the thought. He couldn't let her see.

Yet his eyes were drawn to her mouth, the rise and fall of her chest as she struggled to catch her breath.

She still didn't speak but turned her back to him and pushed her hair to the side, exposing the zipper on the back of her dress. Betsy stepped out of her vintage shoes and nudged them out of the way with a stocking-covered foot.

Everything about her was seductive, every gesture and every breath.

Against his will, he found himself drifting toward her, his hands on her zipper, sliding it down the length of her back. He drank in the sight of her creamy skin, her bra and panties a splash of delicate pink lace against perfection.

He pulled her back against him hesitantly, his arm around her waist, and fastened his lips to the swan arch of her neck. Even her skin tasted sweet. If he thought he was broken before, Jack knew she was going to wreck him.

He could still stop. He could pull away from her; he could—

Betsy drew his hand up from her waist to cup her breast. He could do none of those things because he was lost in the undertow. Instead of drowning in the dark, he was drowning in her, in the inky black waves of her hair, in her creamy skin. He never wanted to surface; he wanted to fill himself up with her until there was nothing but Betsy.

She was warm, safe—she was all things good.

Until she tried to turn in his arms again.

"I don't want you to see," he confessed in a harsh whisper, sure that the spoken words would rip like daggers through the haze of need over them.

Betsy turned anyway and for a moment, he thought there would be pity on her face, but there wasn't. Her dark eyes were half-lidded, her lips swollen from his kisses, and she was the embodiment of desire.

"There's so much you don't want, Jack. Tell me, what is it that you *do* want?"

"To stay lost in you," he answered honestly. "But I haven't touched a woman in two years."

"What about yourself? Have you touched yourself?"

"Bets—" He was torn between being even more turned on that she asked, that she thought of him like that, and the shame that he hadn't had the desire since his injury. He couldn't stand to look at himself, let alone bring himself pleasure.

And the whiskey…he was surprised he could maintain an erection.

"This isn't going to be good for you." Another confession torn from him. He meant for more than the here and now, more than just fleeting bliss he might have been able to offer once upon a time, all those years ago.

Her hands slid down to his button fly again. "Yes, it will. You're good at everything. You're Jack Mc-Connell."

When her fingers closed over his length, he still had his doubts. "This is going to be over before it starts."

"And yet it still will have happened." She tilted her face up to his and feathered another kiss across his mouth. It was nothing like his cruel mastery, but it punished him all the same.

"Why do you want it to?" He breathed against her lips.

"Because if all we have is ashes, we should at least get to burn in the fire."

He could understand that, process it. Her words made much more sense than the idea that she actually wanted him. He didn't know where things had gone wrong for her, but obviously they had if all she had to do on a Sunday afternoon was him.

She was right. They both wanted this and it didn't matter that he wasn't whole, that he couldn't spend hours worshipping her body, bringing her off time and again, even though he wished he could. This was about the moment, about burning to nothing. About feeling something more than pain.

For all that he thought she didn't understand, with that simple sentence, he knew that she did.

If she could lose herself in him the same way he could be lost in her, he could give her that.

He tangled a hand in her hair and surrendered.

BETSY DECIDED THAT was nothing compared to what it was like to have his hands on her body, his mouth on hers, and the sure knowledge that she'd finally experience this with him. It was the culmination of a fantasy, of a schoolgirl crush, but it was something more, too.

This joining was a haven against everything wrong in the world, against all their shattered dreams.

It was only right that the first time would happen in this room where she'd spent so many hours dreaming of him. Of course, when she'd imagined giving herself to him, it was all fey bubbles and breathy sighs. He'd been kind and patient in her fantasies— gentle and tender.

The reality was nothing even close to that. His hands were rough and calloused, his kisses were more like a battle than a seduction, but it was still everything she wanted because it was real.

She angled him back on the bed, still stroking him. Betsy didn't want him to think about anything other than how good this felt.

Part of her was still afraid he'd try to be noble or

maybe that he just didn't want her. Even with the hard evidence of desire in front of her, that fear was still present that he'd said no all those years before and used her age, her brother, his nobility as an excuse so he didn't have to tell her that her stomach wasn't flat enough, her face not pretty enough...

Marcel's face bloomed like a rancid flower in her mind. *You could be so lovely if—*

No. She wouldn't do this to herself.

"It's okay if you changed your mind." His voice was ragged and low, as if every word cost him something vital to speak.

Betsy realized she'd stopped her caress and was leaning over him with his jeans halfway down his hips. Low enough to reveal only what he wanted to share, but would still hide what he didn't want her to see.

He thought that was why she'd stopped. Nothing could be further from the truth—it was only her own insecurities, but she was determined to face them.

"Just a bad memory."

"Then I'll give you a better one." He slipped the straps of her bra down her shoulders and made quick work of the thing, discarding it on the floor. Her panties were next and she shivered with anticipation.

When she straightened to step out of the lace, she reached into the nightstand to grab a condom but found her fingers closing over his dog tags. Betsy didn't want him to know that she still had them, and she snapped the drawer shut as soon as she found the foil packet. They'd been there for a few years, the condoms. She'd stolen them from Caleb's room in hope that some day, she'd be exactly in this position. Alone with Jack, and he'd want her.

Even though they were here in this room, in this tribute to days gone past, the tags belonged to the man who'd left. She knew they didn't belong to the man in front of her, and she didn't want him to doubt that she did.

He took it from her but dropped it on the bed next to him. "Oh no, sweetheart. Not yet. You can't burn with only kindling."

The expression on his face was familiar, the look he always wore when he met a challenge he was sure he'd defeat. From silly bets to when he told her he was going to be a SEAL.

To have all of that intensity focused on her made her bite her lip.

"You did say you wanted to burn, didn't you?"

She nodded, breathless.

"Then come here."

Betsy leaned into him, suddenly shy. When she'd been pursuing him, it gave her focus and made her forget everything but the goal. Now the goal was in sight and she was afraid to reach for it. She wanted to hide from him and her own desire.

His arms closed around her waist and he dragged his stubbled cheek across her skin. She shivered again and pushed her fingers through his close-cropped hair. He turned his face into her and kissed the soft curve of her stomach.

"I haven't been able to taste anything, Bets. Not

for so long." His tongue darted out against her flesh. "Except your skin. Your mouth. You taste as good as you smell." Jack's hands wandered the curve of her hip, the dip at the base of her spine, the round globes of her bottom. "And I can't help wondering if you taste as good *everywhere*."

His words sent shudders through her body and she clenched, imagining what it would be like to *be* tasted everywhere.

"Show me," he said as he leaned back on the bed and dragged her with him. Jack splayed his hands on the backs of her thighs and pulled her forward.

She obliged him, sliding up his body until her knees were positioned on the outside of his shoulders. Betsy felt vulnerable, exposed, and she kept waiting for him to say something about needing to adjust their position because of her weight, but he didn't.

He didn't say anything at all.

Jack tightened his grip and anchored her against him, his mouth too busy to form words.

At the first caress, Betsy cried out and fisted the duvet. A myriad of sensations bombarded her. The intimacy of their position, the feel of his tongue curving around her swollen nub, and the sure knowledge that all of her fears had been for naught because he loved this. If there was one thing Betsy understood, it was the palate. No one could use their mouth so diligently if it wasn't the most decadent of delights.

His touch sent her spiraling higher and higher until she was up in the stratosphere with no way down and begging for more anyway. She fought the sensation he wrought in her until she was mindless with bliss. Something hot and sharp exploded into thunder and lightning through her veins, and that ecstasy shot through her body.

But he wasn't done. While she shuddered and quaked, the rip of the foil was a distant sound. He maneuvered her easily with his great strength, shifting her down his torso until she was positioned over him, his erection poised at her channel.

Jack pulled her down so that his lips were a breath from hers. "You were sweeter than I ever could've imagined. And believe me, Betsy, I imagined it time and time again." He kissed her hard and gave her no time to process his words, his actions.

All she could do was feel.

Then he was inside her, and even though she was on top of him, he was still very much in charge of their encounter. He set the pace by rolling her hips to meet his thrusts, moving her as he would.

Nothing had ever felt this good. Not getting accepted to the institute, not getting out of this town, and not even her first time with Marcel. Only this.

The aftershocks of her orgasm still ricocheted through her even as he continued.

How he'd ever thought this thing between them could be anything but magic, she'd never know. He hit the core of her with every tilt of his hips.

It was heaven, but it was hell, too, because Betsy knew no one else could ever make her feel this way.

Jack wasn't looking for forever, and he'd as much as told her that he didn't have it to give.

When his body tensed and he found his culmination, it was bittersweet for Betsy.

She knew the spell that had led them here had been broken.

Betsy buried her face in his shoulder because she didn't want their idyll to be over. Part of her wondered if she could just hide inside him, inside this moment, and make it last forever.

He stroked her hair, fingers tangling in the mess of curls almost lazily, as if maybe he wanted to stay in the moment, too.

Or maybe because now that it was over, they'd have to come up with something to say, some action to take that was both the same as it had been before they'd done this, but different, too.

The only action she wanted to take was to do this again—be touched by him, utterly consumed by the fire. Burning once just wasn't enough.

CHAPTER FIVE

"Why did you come back here?" he asked as he continued to comb through her hair.

"Who says I left?"

"The pictures on your mirror."

"Maybe it was a vacation." Betsy didn't want to talk about this now. Anything she could say would make him feel guiltier for not reading her letters, and this wasn't supposed to be about guilt or duty, only passion.

"Betsy, if you're still pissed I didn't read your letters and you don't want to tell me, it's okay. I get it. But that guy you're with, the body language between you speaks of more than a vacation. There's intimacy there."

"Is this really the best time to be asking about other men?" Betsy giggled.

"Yeah, the bastard was looking at us the whole time," Jack teased.

She couldn't help it, she laughed again. "If only."

"I didn't know you were *that* kinky," he teased some more, and Betsy was grateful he hadn't gotten too serious, too heavy. It somehow made it okay to tell him what had happened with Marcel.

"No, he was just… It was over with him when Paris was over." It would have been over anyway; moving was an impetus. Marcel didn't do the things a lover was supposed to do. He didn't make her a better person. He didn't make her want to be better, and she didn't do those things for him, either.

His fingers stilled. "Why was Paris over? It wasn't because of me, was it?"

Betsy closed her eyes. "No, it was because of me. Because I failed." It was the first time she'd said it out loud. Betsy had replayed it over and over in her head, said it to herself again and again, but she'd never articulated those exact words before. She'd always said she made a mistake, a dangerous mistake, but just a mistake. She'd never owned her failure. Now she was burning again, but it wasn't with the heat between them. It was with shame.

Everyone had had such high hopes for her.

Especially herself.

She wasn't ready to examine that too closely.

"Rather than beat it to death, maybe we could go back to the singing my praises and giving me orgasms. I like that better."

"Don't we all?"

"Do you really?" She lifted her head and met his gaze.

So much for not beating it to death. Why couldn't she leave the hows and whys of this thing between them alone and just enjoy the moment? She'd been managing so well for about five minutes.

She saw from the look on his on his face that she didn't really want the answer.

Betsy reluctantly peeled herself from his arms. Their idyll was over. Whatever spell they'd been under had unraveled. "I know Mom would like it if you'd stay for Sunday dinner." At his stricken look, she added, "Caleb and India will be here, too. No big deal if you can't."

"I don't know if that's a good idea, Betsy."

She tried to convince herself that the sharp pain that stabbed through her was just because she was hungry and craving her mama's fried chicken.

"Okay." Betsy hated how forlorn and sad she sounded at his refusal.

"I came to give you that check because I'm leaving," he added. "I can't stay here."

"I said okay." She wouldn't look at him as she slipped into her dress. "Will you zip me up?"

"It doesn't sound okay."

What did he expect? "You want me to tell you it's okay that you're leaving again to go somewhere no one knows you, no one loves you, only to drink yourself to death alone? That's not going to happen. So go. I can't stop you, but it won't be with my blessing."

"That's a little overdramatic, don't you think?" His breath ghosted along her neck as he helped her with her dress.

After he'd zipped her, she turned to face him. "No, I don't." She studied him hard for a moment that seemed to stretch out into eternity. "I think you decided that you came back. You showed your face so you fulfilled your promise to me, and now you can go off and do whatever it is you want to yourself in peace. I know you, Jack. I know how your mind works. And I can't stop you. But you should consider that no one knows how much time they have and you may not want what you've got. I can see it in your eyes. But would you rather spend it drinking whiskey and choking on the ashes that we've talked so much about or have more days like today?"

"You can't save me. I already told you that." He shook his head.

"Only because you won't let me."

"You don't understand." The defeated expression on his face was killing her.

"Maybe I haven't been to war, but this—" she gestured at the space around them "— isn't what I wanted, either."

"I'm supposed to be dead." His voice was low and gravelly.

"You told me last night that you already were. That you just brought back a body for me to mourn," she reminded him.

"Yes."

The one-word answer infuriated her. He was being purposefully obtuse and drowning himself not because he couldn't break the surface, but because he just didn't want to. "Dead men don't talk about the taste of sweetness, Jack. And they sure as hell don't move their tongues like you just did."

"When I'm with you is the only time I'm not dead, Bets."

His confession cooled her anger. "So be with me." She didn't understand why it had to be so complicated. One plus one equaled two. Betsy plus Jack equaled happy. It wasn't so difficult a prospect.

"You don't know what you're asking for." He wouldn't look at her, and this conversation sounded very much like the one they'd had the night he left.

His answer wasn't good enough. "People rarely do. That's not specific to me. Stay for dinner."

"And eat food I can't taste, laugh while I can't breathe and surround myself with everything I can't have?"

Part of her softened at his words, but she knew him too well. That's what his words were designed to do, to deflect her attack. Even if they were true. "You're not even trying. You don't know. Give living a chance. No matter what you think, you're not dead," she cried.

"No, Betsy. It's you who doesn't know."

"Maybe not, but I dare you to have dinner with us and find out what I do and do not know." She put her hands on her hips and lifted her chin in defiance.

He raised his gaze to hers again, something dark there. "Fine. After dinner you come home with me and spend the night."

Anticipation and expectation curled in her belly. Another night like today? She'd take it. "How is that a chore?" She rolled her eyes and slipped into her shoes.

"You'll see what it's like to be me."

"Fine." She lifted her chin another notch. Yeah,

spending the night with him was some kind of punishment. "I'll see you downstairs."

Betsy waltzed out of her room as if she'd just one-upped him, but as soon as she was out of sight, her shoulders sagged. She'd practically bullied him into staying. The same way she'd bullied him into letting her take him to the bus station.

Why couldn't she just leave him alone? He didn't want her help.

Well, that was too bad, because he was getting it.

She needed to do something to get her mind off what had just happened, and what was going to happen again later tonight.

And inevitably, what was going to happen in the morning. His regret, his— No. She wasn't going to think about that. There were potatoes that needed peeling and oil that needed heating for the fried chicken.

"Hey, Bets. Is that Jack's car in the driveway? Am I setting another place for dinner?" Caleb asked as he barreled through the door.

He was still in his policeman's uniform. It made him look taller, more imposing. As if he needed it. He was already a big guy, but there was something about the uniform that made his jaw look harder, his eyes brighter, and his black hair shinier. When Betsy was little, she always thought he looked like Christopher Reeve. Except he had brown eyes instead of blue.

"You better take off your gun before you sit down to the table." She looked pointedly at his duty belt.

"You know Mama doesn't like to have it in the house. Let alone at the dinner table." She took down the cast-iron skillet her mama used for the fried chicken and started making the preparations.

"Didn't answer my question."

"Yes. Jack is having dinner with us tonight."

"How did you swing that?" Caleb smirked.

"The promise of sexual favors." It wasn't a lie, if she boiled it down to the basics, and she liked to rattle him.

"You're not funny, Betsy." He scowled.

"Why do you always think I'm kidding?"

"I don't want to know." Caleb shook his head in denial.

"Then why did you ask?"

"Before I thought better of it." Caleb peered down at the oil over her shoulder. "Did you add a little salt to the oil? Because—"

Betsy was quick to interrupt him. "Mom's frying the chicken."

The Great Chicken Debate had raged in the Lewis household for years. While Betsy was the baker, Caleb was an expert when it came to main dishes. Before the army, he'd considered going to the same school Betsy attended in New York.

"Well, I just think that she should—"

"Caleb," India said from the doorway. "You know you never win this. Your job every Sunday is to be the dish boy. Deal with it." Her blond ponytail swung as she nodded her head to accentuate her point.

"I'd think you'd be on my side, India. You love my fried chicken." Caleb eyed her.

"At *your* house when we're watching the Chiefs with a cold beer. This is your mother's thing. I fancy keeping my head where it's attached to my neck, thanks." India nodded sagely.

"I don't know how you stand him," Betsy teased her.

"Me, either." She shrugged.

"You're no picnic yourself, George." Caleb grabbed a beer out of the fridge.

"I am a paragon of virtue," India retorted.

"Whoever told you that was lying like a rug." Jack wandered into the kitchen.

"Shut up, McConnell. I've got a pair of cuffs and I'm not afraid to use them." India indicated to her duty belt with a grin.

Jack arched an eyebrow. "Why doesn't that surprise me?"

"You always were the bad influence," India tossed back, and grabbed two beers out of the fridge. She handed one to Jack.

"You just didn't like it that Caleb and I would hide from you in the tree house. Your mom didn't want you climbing trees, so that was the only place we were safe."

Betsy watched the easy flow between them. Yes, things had changed. The three of them had gone away to war, and two of them had come home with pieces missing.

But she knew that India's pain was Caleb's, too.

If she was wounded, it twisted something in him, as well. Caleb and Jack were as close as brothers, but his bond with India was something different.

Something Betsy always thought was more like love. Not a familial love, or even a brother in arms, but deep, abiding happily-ever-after kind of love. Betsy had mentioned it to Caleb once and he told her it was just because she always wanted India to be her sister.

"I seem to remember that time with the firecracker bomb you were not safe at all. In fact, you both screamed like little girls."

"We were ten." Jack raised an eyebrow. "And you blew out the floor of the tree house."

"Hey, man, that's okay. Let her have that. That's the only time she ever got the better of us." Caleb grinned and stiffened as he prepared himself for the impact of her fist into his arm.

"Did you forget that you have to go home with me tonight? I know where you sleep."

It was Betsy's turn to arch an eyebrow. "Oh really?"

India blushed, something she didn't usually do. "His place is being sprayed. The neighbors have roaches, so he's bug-bombing just in case."

Betsy didn't mention the obvious: that he had a room here he could stay in, if need be.

Jack wouldn't leave it alone, though. "Is that what the kids are calling it these days?"

Betsy fled the scene.

She suddenly understood what Jack meant about

sitting around wanting things he couldn't have. All of the easy banter in the kitchen, just like when they were kids. It had been a scene much like this one where she'd planned out their lives. India and Caleb, Betsy and Jack. They lived in Kansas City, far enough away from the small town to have a city life, but still close enough to their parents. Instead of going into the navy, Jack had taken a football scholarship to KU and was drafted to play for the Chiefs. Betsy and Caleb were partners in a successful restaurant, but India, she was still a cop. There was no life Betsy could imagine where India wasn't chasing down the bad guys and giving them what they had coming.

And they spent all their time together. Every night dinner was together at the restaurant.

Betsy knew those dreams were naive and childish, but they'd been born in simpler times. A more innocent time.

JACK WATCHED BETSY FLEE and gave her all of three minutes before he went looking for her. If he wasn't allowed to hide, neither was she. He knew that's what she was doing. He could see the memories crashing over her in some acid wash that wounded her. Why did she think it would be any different for him?

She was leaning against the wall in the kitchen, her arms crossed over her breasts, and he did his best not to let his gaze linger there because he'd forget what he was supposed to be doing. Harsh words brewed on his tongue to remind them both, but when she turned to look at him, she looked so utterly fragile that they withered to dust.

"Outside, Bets." He nodded toward the door to the back patio.

For the briefest moment, he thought she might argue with him, but she stepped toward the door. Once they were outside, she turned to face him.

"What happened just now? Why did you leave?" he asked.

"It was too much like old times. But neither of us is the same person who left."

"That's why this wasn't a good idea."

"One moment of melancholy doesn't mean it wasn't a good idea." She'd gone from vulnerable to determined in less than a second.

He scrubbed his hand over his face. "I'm going to go. I don't belong here anymore."

"Don't go." She wasn't begging or demanding now. It was simply a quiet request that was all the more powerful when she fixed him with the weight of her clear-eyed stare.

"Bets—"

"Maybe you don't need us, but we need you. *I* need you. Okay?" Emotion hung on the last word, making it come out like a question that needed an answer, and he had only one to give her.

He scrubbed his hand over his face. "I'm not a hero. I never was. When you realize that, you're not going to need me. You're not even going to like me."

"Maybe." She narrowed her eyes. "So start making it up to me now."

Christ, but she was like a dog with a bone. He cocked his head to the side. "You never give up, do you?"

"Not when it's something that's important to me."

"Okay, Bets. What do you want?" He'd give her anything if he thought it would erase the guilt, if it would stop twisting up his insides.

"This is about more than dinner."

"I gathered." He might have been weak and broken, but he wasn't stupid.

"That you really give life a chance."

"This again." She didn't know what she was asking of him. Not really. She didn't know what it was like to wake up from a nightmare and find the scenery hadn't changed, that she was still trapped. She didn't know what it was like to be missing a piece of herself, literally and figuratively. She'd always known what she wanted and reached out and taken it.

And of course how could she understand? She'd never had to do the things he had done, witnessed the things he'd seen. Not that he'd want her to. He couldn't imagine what it would do to her, the way it would change her.

"This, *always*."

"I agreed to dinner. What else do you want?" He always felt torn around her, as if he were two people. Part of him wanted to break that air of innocence around her, sully it, so she couldn't taunt him with it. The other part of him wanted to wrap her in a glass bubble and protect her from anything that could ever touch her or take that away from her.

He was a twisted bastard, he thought yet again.

"I propose a trade. Like dinner. You asked me to come home with you tonight, and I agreed. For every new thing that you do, with *minimal complaining,* I will do one thing for you."

The part of him that wanted to sully her, to make her understand, to break that sweet naïveté, reared to the surface. He smirked. "One thing? You should probably specify your parameters." He knew just how to make her back off from this. Even though they'd shared something this afternoon, he was sure when he started suggesting sex she'd change her mind. This would be too sordid for her. Earlier had been about some girlhood fantasy for her and this…this was the real world. He wasn't a hero, or a memory any longer. He was a flesh and blood failure.

"There aren't any. You want me to clean your house? I'll do it. You want me to bake you cookies? I'll do it. You want me to give you one day where I leave you alone? I'll do it."

Jack knew she'd do all of those things for him anyway. Except leave him alone. That was the one thing that would be a concession. Although none of those things were what appealed to him most. Even being left alone, which surprised him, but it shouldn't have.

He'd come over to give her the check because he knew where things were headed and also knew that could only end in a fiery wreckage for both of them.

Yet he forged ahead anyway, his mouth moving, speaking words he had no right to speak. Especially in her mother's house. If he were Caleb, he'd knock out his teeth and leave him to pick them up with broken fingers for talking to his sister in such a way.

But he wasn't her brother.

"What if what I want is you in my bed?"

Twin spots of color bloomed on Betsy's cheeks. "Jack, you could have that anyway."

Her voice was breathy and soft, all sex. He was hard again. His body's reaction to her surprised him, but it shouldn't have. Nothing had ever been able to exorcise his fantasies about her. "No expectations, no strings, and it's *my* time. No trying to fix me," he warned.

"I'm not trying to fix you. I can't fix you. You have to fix yourself."

"And I don't want to, but you're forcing it on me. So I might as well get something I do want out of it."

He hadn't realized how harsh his words sounded until the cycle of expressions played out on her face. First, she'd blushed and a secret smile had curved her lips. It made him remember kissing them and being inside her. Her back straightened and the line of her mouth tightened at the *no expectations* and *no strings*. He expected her to balk then. Although when he told her he might as well get something he wanted, it was almost as if he'd taken a knife and cut her. He'd basically told her he had no use for her but her body, and that wasn't what he meant at all, but he didn't know how to fix it without digging the hole deeper.

Maybe this would be what she needed to see

that he was beyond help, that all he would do was hurt her.

Only he'd underestimated her again. "Okay." Her whisper was barely audible.

His displeasure must have shown on his face, because she spoke again. "What, you didn't want me to agree? Why ask for it if it isn't what you actually want?"

He closed the distance between them. "Oh I want it, all right. But I think about another man saying these things to you and the way you just said yes… I'd kill him, Bets. So would Caleb."

"It's not Caleb's business, is it? Not yours, either. You said so yourself. No strings, no expectations. That goes both ways, cowboy."

He scowled. She'd changed since he was gone. He knew that, but seeing it here in front of him, it startled him somehow. She'd always been headstrong, but this was more than that. This was steel in her spine and more nerve than sense. "Maybe we should set some ground rules."

"You want rules now? I've got some of my own. You will give me until Thanksgiving. You will dedicate yourself wholly to every task. If you refuse a task, then you don't get your night."

He narrowed his eyes. "I thought you said I could have you in my bed anyway."

"I thought *you* said no strings. With ground rules, those are strings."

She had him there. "Fair enough, but if I'm dedicated wholly to this, then so must you be."

"I am." Her eyes narrowed.

"No, you're not. There's a picture of another man on your mirror." He felt small and jealous by demanding she take it down, but it was still in his head. He didn't like knowing that picture was part of a room of memories that should've belonged to him. Once upon a time, that mirror had been covered with pictures of him. He realized he'd taken her devotion for granted.

"Oh for the love of—" She rolled her eyes. "He's just a memory."

"So am I." That was all she was to him, and that was what he wanted her to remember, that he wasn't that Jack anymore. Only seeing evidence that she'd moved on, that someone else had taken his place—no, not his, the place that could've been his in her life—stirred up his guts like a stick in a rotten stew.

"Really?" She pursed her lips. "Marcel Babineaux has more right to that space on my mirror than you do. When I offered him my V-card, he didn't say no."

He knew that she was right, but being right only fueled his rage. Jack pushed her up against the door, and even though he was angry her arms still twined around his neck. "I'm the one that's here," he snarled.

"Are you?" she whispered against his mouth. "Are you really?" Betsy kissed him hard and fast. "Then I guess it's you who'd best remember that when you're talking about living and dying, huh?"

"And you should remember I'm not the same man who said no."

When he would've slammed his mouth back down

for another punishing kiss, the gentle touch of her cool fingers on his cheek stayed him.

"That's not something that I'll ever forget." As if it was a good thing.

His anger dissipated like mist and he found he couldn't even look at her. Jack tried to turn his face away, but she wouldn't let him. Suddenly all of his sins were under a spotlight and he couldn't hide them, but she continued to meet his eyes, unflinching and unafraid of anything she saw there.

"How did you get to be so strong?"

"You," she said simply, and kissed him again. Her mouth was tender and reverent as it moved over his lips. The caress was everything he'd wanted to drive out of her. But he couldn't. Not when she said he'd made her that way.

"Am I interrupting something?" Caleb asked, pushing the door open.

"Yes, and you obviously know you are and don't care," Betsy pointed out, slipping from Jack's arms.

Caleb shrugged. "You're right. Kick rocks, little sister."

"Don't you dare give him the big brother speech."

"Wasn't going to. We already did that Saturday morning." Jack's friend smirked.

"Oh really?" She scowled and put a hand on her hip.

"Yes, really." He was unfazed.

"I don't need you to fight any battles for me, Caleb." Color rose in her cheeks.

"Who said we were fighting? Did you forget that Jack and I are friends, too? Go play dolls with India."

"I'm going to tell her you said that." Betsy and Jack shared a grin. He knew that if India thought he'd actually said any such thing, the consequences would be dire. He didn't know how she did that—switched subjects and emotions so easily. She let each one roll through her—pass over her—just like a storm.

"You do that." Caleb smirked again.

"I know that's just a ploy to get rid of me, but I'm going along with it because I want to see her hand you your hind parts on a platter."

"Bloodthirsty, isn't she?" Caleb said casually as Betsy went inside the house.

"That's tame compared to what's going to happen if India thinks she's serious," Jack warned his friend.

"I know, but it'll be worth it. I love that look of incredulity India gets when I say those things. It just completes my day." Caleb laughed. "You should've seen her last week when we were watching the game and I told her to go get me a sandwich and a beer."

"You live to annoy her."

"I do. It's brought me untold joy since we were kids." Caleb shrugged again.

Silence reigned for a moment that stretched on forever. Jack got the impression that Caleb was waiting for him to fill it with something, but he didn't know what to say.

"So, you wanted to get rid of Betsy. I assume to talk about her?"

"No, I just wanted to rile her up, too. It's a spectator sport."

"Living dangerously."

"No, living dangerously would be to have a few more beers and challenge the girls to a round of Ghost in the Graveyard after dinner." Ghost in the Graveyard was essentially a mashup of tag and hide-and-seek played in the dark.

"Oh yeah, that'll be fun," Jack said in a tone that indicated it would be anything but fun.

"It'll be like old times. Except Betsy's old enough to play."

Jack cut a sharp glance at his friend, wondering if he meant the double entendre the way it sounded. "Man, if you want to chase India around in the dark, you don't need a game of Ghost in the Graveyard. You should just tell her. That way I don't have to fall and break a hip just so you can get into her fatigues."

"You're a crappy wingman." Caleb took another pull off his beer.

Jack was surprised Caleb hadn't argued with him about wanting to be with India. He'd refuted it so many times when they were growing up, his protestation had started to sound like a scratched CD.

"I'm crappy at a lot of things." Jack would be the first to admit it.

"Did you really tell Betsy that we should go play with our *dolls?*" India stood like a raging Valkyrie in the arch of the door, eyes narrowed and cheeks flushed.

Caleb smirked at Jack. "See what I mean?"

For the first time, Jack looked at India and really saw her. She wasn't the tomboy kid who always had a dirty shirt, tangled hair and a scowl on her face any longer. India George was a woman—a beautiful woman. Not as beautiful as Betsy, but Jack could see the appeal and knew why Caleb liked to bring that flush to her cheeks.

"Yeah, I think I do." Jack nodded.

"Oh do you?" India turned on him. "And just what is it that Mr. Soon to Be Dead meant?"

"That you're hot when you're angry." Jack didn't hesitate to dump his friend from the proverbial frying pan into the fire.

Then Caleb did what any sane person would do when faced with the wrath of India George.

He ran.

Caleb took off toward the property line and the tree house that had once offered him protection against her fury, but India launched herself at him the way she would have a perp and took him down.

"They're like puppies," Betsy said, laughing.

"He thinks it's a good idea to play Ghost in the Graveyard after dinner and a few more beers."

"He's still twelve." Betsy shook her head. "It could be fun."

Jack couldn't help wondering if things had been different, if he'd come back whole, whether he'd be chasing Betsy through the grass right now. If he'd be thinking about a few more beers and stalking her in the dark until she was breathless and wanting underneath him.

Instead he had to worry about navigating unfamiliar and unsteady terrain—the very real possibility that he could fall and break something vital that would further impede his mobility. He couldn't think like he was twelve, or seventeen, or even twenty-four. He had to think like an old man who was at the end of his life and whose body had started to fail him.

The sensation that his skin was too tight washed over him again and he wanted to rip it off, along with the mask that told the world everything was okay. It wasn't.

It never would be.

He needed a bottle of whiskey, but he'd have to settle for another beer.

"Come on. Don't you want to chase me? I've been chasing you since we were kids. It's your turn."

"Bets, I can't." He gritted his teeth as he spoke. Damn her for making him say it.

"Yes, you can."

"Don't make me say it again."

"What? Because of your prosthesis? People do triathlons, cross-country and all manner of things. You just have to do it."

"And how do you know so much about it, huh? You go missing anything vital lately?" he snarled.

"Yeah, I did."

He'd had enough of this. "It's not the same thing, and you know it."

"Isn't it? I feel like there's a part of me missing, Jack. I've had to start over. Aren't we in the same place?"

Her face, her innocent determination, it was all just too much. "Only you, Bets, would equate moving back to Glory with fighting a war."

"That's a mean thing to say. You know that's not what I meant." She bristled and straightened her spine, obviously gearing up for a fight.

"Isn't it?" He laughed, but the sound was cold and empty. "I feel as if there's *not* a piece of me missing. In fact, it still feels like it's on fire. So you should really know what you're talking about before you make that comparison."

"You know, Jack, you're not the only person who's ever suffered. Your pain isn't so much bigger and worse than everyone else's. You've got it worse than some, but better than others."

"Really? Who do I have it better than?"

"The ones who didn't come home."

"If I could trade with any one of them, I would." Jack watched as Betsy deflated. All the fight seemed to just wilt out of her, faded away with an exhaled breath.

"I wonder if they'd say the same, if they could speak." Betsy turned and went back into the house, carefully pulling the door closed behind her.

CHAPTER SIX

THE BRIEF GLIMPSE of the old Jack was gone and in its place was this hard, angry man who'd come home in his stead. Maybe Betsy shouldn't have been so hard on him, but she couldn't stand to see him like this. Their conversation earlier had felt as if she was being cruel, but he needed someone to tell him these things. Didn't he? She wished she could just take away his pain, Betsy thought as they ate dinner.

His gaze met hers over the mashed potatoes, and she was surprised to see how unguarded his expression was. His eyes were pools of sorrow, and they were so clear she could see all the way to the bottom.

She wondered again if maybe she was pushing too hard and too fast.

Betsy had to look away first and she cast a glance over at India, who was drawn and pale. Her brother's mouth was set in a grim line and his jaw was clenched.

Lula Lewis, who'd slaved in the kitchen all morning for the family Sunday meal, wasn't the kind to let that go unremarked upon. "Is there something wrong with the chicken?" She arched a perfectly groomed brow and inclined her recently colored, curled and coiffed dark head.

"No, Ma." Caleb shoveled another bite of potato into his mouth.

"The potatoes?" she continued.

"Everything tastes great," India said flatly.

"Well, something's wrong because no one seems happy to be here." She put her fork down, which in the Lewis household meant things were about to get dicey. "I haven't had all of my kids at my table in years." She focused on Jack. "And yes, Jack and India are both mine, too. So I want some happiness to see each other and I want it right now." Her tones were dulcet, but Lula obviously meant business.

Jack was always the best at talking them out of trouble with Lula, but he didn't say anything. It was India who jumped to their rescue. "We're all too busy eating this chicken."

"I call bullshit." She eyed each of them in turn. "But I'll let it slide for now." Lula took a bite of her corn on the cob and after chewing said, "So, Jack, what are your plans now that you're home? Have you considered joining Caleb and India as one of Glory's finest?"

Betsy was on tenterhooks waiting to see what he would say. She hoped he wouldn't be as angry with her mother as he was with everyone else. The old Jack never would be, but he'd made it clear he wasn't the old Jack.

"No, ma'am. I hadn't given it much thought. I really didn't plan on staying in town very long."

Betsy noticed he didn't say *home*. He wasn't planning on staying in town, not home. Glory wasn't home to him anymore.

"We're glad you're home no matter how long you stay, right, Betsy?"

Betsy looked up at her mother and at the quiet understanding on her face. "Yes, Mama." She looked back to Jack meaningfully. "We are."

He didn't say anything but took another bite.

"There was some mention of buttermilk chess pie?" India said in a perky voice, but Betsy could tell the question was forced and hollow. Caleb made it a point not to even look at her. His eyes were focused on his plate as if it were the most fascinating thing he'd ever seen.

Betsy wondered what had happened between them and if it had to do with what had happened to India while she was in Afghanistan.

"I'll get it." Betsy offered to retrieve the pie.

"No, I think India should go get it," Lula said. "And since she can't be trusted with it alone, Caleb should help her."

Caleb grunted and put down his fork, a solemn expression on his face, and dutifully followed India into the kitchen.

"Okay, so what's going on with them? This is ridiculous," Lula said.

As if it was all the tension between India and Caleb and had nothing to do with Jack's silence or hard manner.

"I don't know, but we should leave it alone. They'll

work it out," Betsy advised. She hoped her mother would take the hint. She didn't want any help with her interactions with Jack. Betsy had screwed things up enough on her own.

"They always do," Jack added. He seemed more at ease talking when the subject wasn't himself.

"Hmm. We'll see."

India came back a few minutes later carrying the pie. A piece was already missing and she had crumbs on her mouth. Caleb was right behind her.

"India! You cheat," Betsy teased.

Only India looked a little dumbstruck and Betsy couldn't be sure, but Caleb might have had crumbs on his mouth, too.

"I need to go," India blurted.

"I'll take you home," Caleb offered.

"No!" India cried. She straightened herself and pulled on a casual mask. "I mean, I've got some other errands to run. Thank you for dinner, Miss Lula."

"Of course, honey. I hope we'll see you next Sunday." Lula watched her go and Caleb didn't even excuse himself; he just followed her out. She looked at Jack and Betsy. "She does know it's Sunday, right? Glory rolls up the sidewalks at five."

Betsy got up and began gathering the plates.

"Aren't you going to have pie?" Lula asked her.

"No, but let me cut Jack a piece." She didn't wait for him to agree; she just handed it to him. "Best pie ever." Betsy smiled at him.

And Jack, he accepted the pie, but he watched her

with every bite. There was nothing salacious about his regard, but Betsy still felt naked and vulnerable.

"I'll do the dishes. You kids let your food settle." Lula stood.

"Actually, Miss Lula, I need to be going, as well. Thank you for dinner." He carried his own plate into the kitchen and headed toward the door.

A panic gripped Betsy. She had a sinking feeling that if she let him walk away without saying anything, she'd never see him again.

She intercepted him. "Did you forget that you wanted me to go home with you?"

"I thought you might have come to your senses." Maybe that was what he thought, but his eyes roved her body, and her breath caught in her throat. His body had other ideas, and so did hers.

"I gave my word, Jack. You better not go back on yours."

"I've kept every promise I ever made to you," he growled.

That was the source of a lot of his pain. Everything he'd endured just to keep his promise. Just to come back to her. She softened. "I know. You're the only one who has."

"Stop it," he hissed.

"Stop what?" She didn't know what she was doing that was so wrong.

"Painting me like some hero."

"Stop acting like you're not," she tossed back as if it were the most obvious thing in the world. "And stop telling me what to do, what to think, or assuming you know what I want."

"I do know what you want and it's always been so much more than me."

"This pity-me song is already old. Sing something else." She hated that he felt that way. On the one hand, it was a wonderful balm for all of her old hurts that he thought he wasn't good enough for her. Marcel had only ever thought she wasn't good enough for him. Jack was twice the man Marcel was.

He took a deep breath, as if steeling himself for something. "Why do you think I was always at your house on the weekends?"

Her heart ached for him, but she couldn't let that change what she said to him. He needed tough love, and Betsy hoped she was strong enough to do this. "I know why you were at our house. Your father was always drunk." She reached out to cup his cheek to soften the blow of what she said next. "You're starting to act just like him."

Betsy didn't want to wound him, but she wanted him to know that she saw him. Really saw him, not the painted facsimile the rest of the town saw, but the man underneath. They were so close to the same person. On the face that Jack tried to hide was the one that adopted everyone's sins as his own.

Rather than get angry, Jack said, "That's what I've been trying to tell you."

"No. We make our own decisions about who we are. You choose to pick up the bottle, you choose to drink from it and you choose when you put it down."

"I choose to pick it up," he repeated. "I choose *not* to put it down until the screaming in my head stops and the nerve endings of a leg I don't have stop burning."

"Okay." She exhaled heavily. "It's your time at night and if that's how you want to spend it, then that's what we'll do. Let me tell Mom I'm leaving. I'll drive. You can get your car tomorrow."

"Damn it, Betsy."

"Add to that list to stop trying to scare me off. It's not going to work." She leaned in and kissed him again, savoring the freedom she had now to do it as she wished. "You know why? Because you're still trying to do what you think is best for me, no matter how you feel about it. I will never give up on you and there is nothing you can do that will make me."

"Is that a challenge?" His eyes narrowed and he was suddenly focused on an escape hatch.

"No. A challenge implies that it's something defeatable. In this case, I am the immovable object *and* the unstoppable force."

"That would be a paradox."

"Wouldn't it just?" She wasn't going to argue with that. It would be a paradox, but Betsy would let nothing, not even the laws of physics, get in her way.

"Betsy," her mother called from the dining room.

"One moment, Mama."

"No, no. Just remember what I said. *Country club,*" her mother reminded her.

Betsy flushed, remembering exactly what her mother had said about making her a grandma and asking if she wanted her wedding reception at the country club. She'd been telling her that since she was sixteen.

"Go on, then. Good night, Jack." Her mother said with a purposeful drawl.

"Good night, Miss Lula," he called back, and then dropped his voice to a whisper. "What's she talking about country clubs?"

"Nothing. She's senile," Betsy hissed.

"I heard that, and I am *not*," Lula's voice echoed through to the foyer.

She opened the door and pushed Jack outside in the hopes that her mother wouldn't decide confession was good for the soul and come spill everything about their earlier discussion.

"Does she know you're coming to my place?" Jack asked hesitantly halfway down the stairs.

"It's not that hard to figure out."

For a moment, Jack wore a stricken expression.

"She never did ground me for stealing that cordial." As if that made it okay.

"You said you had it with her permission." His mouth curved into a sly grin.

"And you said I was horrible liar." Warmth filled her at the memory. She'd replayed it in her head so many times, but with a much different outcome.

"You are."

There was something in his voice, something soft, tender. Something he'd been hiding from her.

"Did you ever wonder what would've happened if you'd said yes?" The words escaped before she could think better of them and then she blushed. "I mean, beyond the obvious."

He opened her car door for her. "Beyond the obvious? Did *you?* Before you made your declaration, did you stop to wonder what would happen if you got pregnant?"

She studied him hard as visions of every possible outcome blared through her mind like a siren. All the talk of babies forced her to imagine what it would be like to have a child with him. "I don't imagine my life would be much different than it is now." Only then she'd have a piece of him that belonged wholly to her. A piece that she could keep safe and— God, what was she thinking?

Only what any woman would think when looking at Jack McConnell. Even as damaged as he was, Jack was still what dreams were made of. At least, her dreams.

"That look on your face is terrifying, Betsy," he whispered.

She started the car without looking at him. "What do you mean?"

"It's that hero worship again. When I was a kid, I loved that you looked at me like that. I would have done anything to keep that, but now I'm just waiting for you to realize I'm not who you think. When that goes away, I'm never going to have that look again."

Then it all made sense. Why he pushed her away so hard, why he kept telling her she didn't want him. He wanted to be the one to decide it for them both so it didn't hurt him.

The realization only strengthened her resolve.

"Jack—" she turned in her seat to face him "—I don't expect you to be anyone but who you are. We did have sex, but that doesn't mean I'm assuming we're in a relationship. You just got home and you've had trauma. I get that. The only thing I expect from you is to stick to the parameters of our deal. Give living a chance before you decide that you're dead. That's it. Just a chance. I don't need you to promise me shining armor, or white horses, or some castle in the clouds."

"I don't know what I'm supposed to do," he confessed.

"What do you *want* to do?"

"You keep asking me what I want."

"Well, yeah. Haven't you thought about it?"

"No, not really. It's never been about what I want. It's been about what I'm supposed to do."

Betsy knew exactly how he felt. "Your obligations here are only to yourself. That's something you should think about. Didn't you ever wonder what you'd be if you weren't a SEAL?"

"No."

"You can be anything you want when you grow up."

"I wanted to be a SEAL."

"You were, but now that's passed. It's time for something new."

He seemed to be thinking over her words, and she thought it was a good sign that he hadn't snapped at her. He was angry, and Betsy understood that. She knew he had to mourn the part of himself that was gone—both the physical and the mental.

"See you at the house." He closed her door and went to his car.

Betsy tried not to focus too hard on the flame of hope that burned in her chest as she drove the short distance across town to his house.

She parked on the street and couldn't stifle a yawn when they met again on his porch.

"I've exhausted you already?"

Betsy tried not to think about the ways she still wanted him to exhaust her when she answered, "I keep early hours. I have to be at the shop by four so I can get things ready for the morning rush at six."

Most of the shops downtown didn't open until eight or nine, but Betsy wanted the breakfast crowd. It was where she made the majority of her income, aside from wedding cakes and parties. In fact, it was what kept the business afloat when things got tight.

"Then I guess we should go to bed, if you're still staying."

She followed him inside silently. Betsy didn't trust her voice. She focused on the broad planes of his back, the contours of his biceps and what it felt like to be in his arms. Would he hold her while they slept, or would he—

"There's a guest room upstairs."

"Really?" Betsy asked, arching an eyebrow. She'd sooner sleep naked in Haymarket Square than sleep in the guest room.

He closed his eyes and exhaled heavily. "Look,

when I made that demand about you spending the night, I was trying to push you away. I had every intention of bringing you here and being a special kind of bastard so you'd see how hopeless this is."

Rather than be angry, she was curious. She wanted to know what brought about the change in his thinking. "What changed your mind?"

"I don't want to hurt you, Betsy."

"So don't. You invited me to sleep over. Let's have a sleepover. Remember that week you spent at our house when Caleb was at camp and we watched bad horror movies all night? We could watch scary flicks and eat popcorn."

She was doing her best to link their interactions to good memories of things he could still do. Betsy purposefully avoided mentioning those nights after football games when he'd been the star quarterback. Or the ski trip to Snow Creek.

He sighed. "I can't sleep without the whiskey."

"I bet you can." Betsy used the zipper on her dress as a way to bring contact between them, but she didn't actually need him to unzip her. She had to dress herself in the morning, after all. So she reached behind her, tugged the zipper down and stepped out of her dress. "If you exhaust yourself."

She'd expected he might demur, might make another excuse, but she'd found the one thing he wanted, the one thing worth all of the risks.

He reached out and ghosted the back of his knuckles down her arm and she shivered at the light caress.

Jack pulled her against his chest and she hooked her arms around his back.

"You feel so good." She kneaded lightly, enjoying the feel of his muscles bunching beneath her hand, reassuring her that he was real.

He was really home.

This was different between them. In her room, it had been homage to a dream whose time had passed, to say everything with her body that she'd never been able to give voice to. Now, standing in his house, pressing herself against him, this was about the present. This was for the woman she'd become who still wanted the man in front of her.

He lifted her easily and she wrapped her legs around his waist. Betsy feared he'd tell her no. She'd pushed him so hard she was starting to doubt herself. This was the validation she needed that she was on the right track. Nothing was more life-affirming than sex.

Betsy buried her face in his neck; she couldn't get close enough. The scent of him was intoxicating, something strictly Jack that always made her think of home. She inhaled deeply, clinging to him as she brushed her lips over his neck and the hard razor of his jaw.

"To bed, then?" he asked, his voice low and hoarse.

"Oh yes."

He carried her with ease, making her feel utterly delicate. Something that was a completely new sensation for her. The fact that she trusted him to carry her, didn't ask him if he was sure he could lift her or balance their bodies together, seemed to spur his confidence.

Or maybe it was just that he was so hard for her he didn't have time to battle his insecurities? She didn't know, but he moved with more surety toward the downstairs library he'd turned into his bedroom.

He bent slowly, his muscles straining as he balanced them and carefully deposited her on the bed.

She noticed that even with the duvet, it had hospital corners. Neat and tight. More hope. He hadn't given up on daily tasks—the things her mother's doctors told her to watch for as signs of depression.

Jack wasn't as far gone as he thought, or as he wanted others to think.

"You're so strong," she praised.

"You're lucky I didn't drop you."

You're not a small woman, Betsy. Marcel had said that to her when she was in his lap. She knew that was not what Jack meant, but it didn't stop the words from replaying over in her head on a stupid loop.

Jack was right. She needed to take his picture down. Maybe that would silence his voice.

"Bets?"

She realized she'd pulled the pillow in front of her. How stupid was that after her brazen display, stripping for him twice, and he'd already been inside her? She couldn't hide, but she wanted to.

Betsy suddenly understood that about Jack, too. Why he wanted to hide things from her in the dark, why he didn't want her to see.

For the millionth time, she realized that she was in way over her head.

"You know that I didn't mean it that way."

"I know," she said, unable to look at him.

"Then why are you hiding from me?" He tilted her chin up gently.

Her eyes were heavy, and she didn't want to meet his eyes, but just as she wouldn't let him turn away, he wouldn't grant her that mercy, either.

"You stripped for me in the daylight and now you want to hide in the shadows?"

"You want the light off, so why can't I hide, too?" She swallowed hard.

"Because you're the most beautiful thing I've ever seen." He tugged the pillow out of her grasp slowly and pushed it to the side. "Art was meant to be displayed and admired, not hidden."

From anyone else, it would have sounded like a line. Something whispered hurriedly to assuage her fear so he could still get a piece, but not Jack. From him, it was earnest poetry.

"Hasn't anyone told you how perfect you are?" The incredulity in his voice gave her pause.

"No one is perfect."

"You are."

She didn't know what to say, or what to do. No one had ever told her those things, and for them to come from him...

He leaned down and kissed the inside of her knee, his breath warm and his lips like a brand. "Touching you here—" he kissed her again "—makes you shiver and squirm in the best way." Jack didn't stop there but moved higher up her thigh. "And right here is all strength and feminine softness." He clasped her hips. "Perfect for holding you right where I want you. Dangerous curves I could ride all night."

She trembled at his description and when he moved to the gentle curve of her belly, she wanted to push him away, but he would have none of it. He burrowed against her, his short hair tickling her until she writhed and giggled.

"So soft and sweet," he praised. "*This* is the embodiment of femininity. You know how I was talking about art? You see hard-bodied men on display, but not women. Women's bodies are meant to be curvy and plush. If I wanted ripped abs, I'd be here with Caleb."

Jack rose above her and filled his hand with her breast. "And dear sweet hell, Betsy. Your breasts have always been the stuff of fantasies. I can't decide if I want to touch them, taste them or just look at them."

He dipped his head and did all three. He took the bud of her nipple into his hot mouth, and every pull of his mouth tugged at something deep inside her.

"I'd keep you naked all the time. Not just for this, but so I could just watch you. The way you move, the fluid grace in every action. It's not practical, but I'd love to watch you bake those cookies naked."

His words caused heat to bloom everywhere. She hadn't known he thought of her so often or in so much detail. Or the things he wanted to do with her cookies.

She found herself agreeing. "I'll do that for you, Jack." She'd do anything for him.

"I've been thinking about how you always smell like vanilla sugar. All through dinner that I couldn't taste, I remembered your mouth, between your thighs, and I wanted it again."

His appraisal had been so intense she'd thought it anger, but that wasn't rage.

It had been need.

CHAPTER SEVEN

ALL THE THINGS Jack had never thought he'd be telling her poured from him in a tidal wave. It was so foreign and wrong to him that Betsy didn't know her own appeal.

It humbled him. All this time he'd believed she knew her own worth and how desirable she was. She'd been as afraid as he was, but she hadn't shown it until now. Even through it all, she forged ahead.

Betsy blossomed under his praise, her stiff body relaxing into his caresses, even arching into his touch.

He never thought in a million years he'd be here with her.

When he left that night, when he said goodbye, he was sure when he saw her again she'd be over whatever it was she thought she felt for him. Then he'd come home broken and yet here she was, as lovely as ever, and she still wanted him.

He'd thought it a sense of duty, or pity, but there was none of that present on her face when he touched her or when she melted against him.

Jack wanted to tell her that she deserved better,

but he realized that questioning her choices was not only high-handed, but an insult.

That didn't mean he was ready for her to see him, or any of the other things he was avoiding, but he'd trust her to make her own choices. If that choice was him, he'd stop fighting it.

He loved how responsive she was to his every touch.

It occurred to him that if he'd had the whiskey he craved so much, he wouldn't be able to do this to her. Wouldn't be able to bury himself in her and be lost in all things good. Maybe, just maybe, her arms would be enough to get him through the dark.

She whispered breathlessly in his ear, "Do you have any condoms?"

He froze. "I might have one in my wallet. I honestly didn't think I'd need one again."

Her laugh was soft. "I might have one in my bag. Otherwise, we're going to Walgreens."

"I'll get it." Jack pulled away from her to go retrieve her tote bag.

She dug into the various pockets and pulled out a small square.

Her legs hooked around his hips and she pulled him down.

He finally tasted something different in her kiss. Something crisp, like an after-dinner mint.

It was an explosion of sensation, of stimulation, and he remembered all the good things that came with mint. Sharing Thin Mints Girl Scout Cookies with his mom on movie night. Gram's butter mints that she kept on the lowest shelf just for his little hands when he was a child. Although it wasn't long before there was a bitter aftertaste of not-so-pleasant memory, too. The smell of mouthwash when his father was trying to hide the liquor on his breath.

Somehow that didn't matter. All of the good overshadowed the bad and made it worth feeling, worth tasting.

Worth remembering.

Now, this moment, it would be twined with sweet mint, too.

"What do you taste?" he asked her as his hands roamed over her body.

"The chocolate chip cookie I had for dessert when Mom wasn't looking, the toothpaste from when I brushed my teeth after dinner, and your lips."

"I didn't know a moment could have a taste," he confessed. "But this one does. My memories do."

"Everything has a taste."

He traced his tongue against the edge of her mouth, over the seam where her lips parted for him and inside. Jack pulled back for a moment just to look at her.

Her black hair falling in waves behind her, the way the twilight fell on the palette of her skin, her mouth swollen and pink from his kisses.

"What are you doing?" she asked.

"Looking at you."

"Why?"

"Because I can." He traced his thumb over the

fullness of her bottom lip, the delicate line of her jaw, down to the fine ridge of her collarbone.

"Turnabout is fair play."

"Hardly."

"No one asked for your opinion. I want to see you. There's more to your body than your leg, and you know it. Why else do you work so hard on that gun show?" She ran her hands over his biceps to accentuate her point.

"Oh you like that, do you?" For the first time in a long while, he felt pride at his form.

"You know I do." She peeled his shirt off. "Jeans, off. Now."

He knew he had to do it if he wanted what was supposed to happen next, if he wanted to be inside her, but he still couldn't stand the idea of her seeing it. It wasn't as if he didn't know it was real, but letting her see, it was wrong somehow.

"Jack, I'm not going to inspect you like some bug under glass. I just want you as naked as I am. I want to know what it's like to be only skin to skin. I'll close my eyes." She dropped her hands and lay perfectly still and closed her eyes as she'd promised.

Jack shed his jeans and covered her body with his, careful to keep the titanium from touching her, but she was oblivious.

It was just as she promised: she didn't care. She didn't suddenly pounce on him and demand to see, or turn on the light and inspect him, she didn't even open her eyes. He took the opportunity to study her again.

Her lips curved in a smile. "If I don't get to stare, neither do you."

He took a deep breath. Inhaled slowly as the word rolled around in his head. Exhaled, decision made. "Okay."

"Okay, what?"

"Open your eyes."

She opened her eyes slowly, sooty lashes fluttering as she focused on him. "There, now. Is that so bad?"

Betsy had allowed him inside her body; the least he could do was let her look at him if she wanted to. "You can look if you want."

"I don't need to. It's just part of you, Jack. If that wasn't okay with me, do you think I'd be here now?" Without looking away from him, she opened the foil packet of the condom with one hand and her teeth; then she reached between them and rolled the latex down his arousal.

It was one of the most erotic experiences he'd ever had, the feel of her hand on him, sheathing him for the act that was to come.

He'd never expected this—any of it. A shadow hovered at the edge of his consciousness, telling him this couldn't last, but that didn't matter. Not with Betsy underneath him, soft and wanting.

He buried himself in her—more than just the simple act of his erection in her sheath, Jack allowed himself to be lost, to feel pleasure without the expectation of pain. The sounds of her soft cries reassured him that he could still do something right, that there was still some use for him, even if it was only to make Betsy Lewis see stars. He could think of worse things.

If that was all he was good for, he was determined to be the best any man had ever been for a woman.

She gasped when he pulled out, dug her nails into his shoulders, demanding he stay. He liked the feel of her little claws curled into his shoulders. Not only did it mark him as hers, but she was demanding her pleasure as was her due.

He fully intended to give it to her.

How many times had he fantasized about being like this with her? How many times had he lain awake imagining what he'd do to her? What it would've been like that night if he'd taken everything she offered?

And how many times had he touched himself in the dark imagining this very moment?

Jack loved the feel of her skin, like satin. So smooth and perfect. He explored at his leisure, taking his time to fit his hands to the curve of her hips, to drag his stubbled cheek along the softness of her belly and finally down to her mound.

He'd been craving this again already, the taste of her on his tongue. He loved the sounds she made, too, breathy little cries of bliss, even as she begged him for more.

This was why sugar tasted like ecstasy, because it was Betsy.

Jack licked and laved, anchored her against his mouth, and in taking what he wanted, he gave Betsy everything she needed. When she'd surrendered herself completely to sensation, to him, that was when he pushed inside her again.

Maybe it was the contrast of being denied sensation, maybe it was because he hadn't done this with a woman in so long or maybe it was just because it was Betsy, but being with her was nothing like anything he'd ever experienced before.

He drove himself forward again and again until she came undone for the second time. A rush of contentment washed over him after he let himself fall off that precipice of ecstasy after her. Betsy curled against him, as if there were nowhere in the world better than being wrapped in his arms.

Jack let his guard down and let himself sleep in the cocoon they'd made.

Only to find himself trapped in a dream he couldn't wake up from—the putrid stench of his own seared flesh in his nose and the pain—the burn so hot it was cold, the shrapnel tearing into him and the thundering explosions overhead reminding him that even though his body was home, his mind never would be.

THE HEAVY BLANKET of warmth was ripped away from Betsy like a thatched roof in a tornado.

A sound of unbearable agony ripped from the body of the man next to her. He thrashed and clawed in his torment.

"Jack?" She sat up in bed and put a cool hand on

his forehead. "Jack?" She said his name again when he howled, caught up in the throes of a nightmare.

"Let me go. It burns," he murmured. "Let me die."

She drew her hand back slowly.

"Don't make me come back, Betsy. Christ, it burns," he moaned, and continued to thrash, clawing at the remains of his leg, trying to put out a blaze on the limb he no longer had.

"Wake up, Jack." She hoped his name would draw him back to consciousness, away from that horrible place. "You're with me now."

"Don't fucking lie to me!" he roared, and she found herself slammed down into the bed, pinned beneath him, his eyes wild and haunted. "You're not here. You can't be here."

His fingers dug half-moons into her skin and she realized he was still asleep, or trapped in the flashback.

"Jack?"

He squeezed harder. "Stop wearing her face, using her voice. I'd rather burn," he snarled.

Her heart cracked in her chest. Even though he held her immobile, his face was only inches from hers, and she lifted her head to press her lips against his.

His mouth was as rigid and unforgiving as marble, until he finally kissed her back. She twined her arms around him and offered him the only comfort she had to give—the only thing she knew could block out the pain.

"This isn't real," he said.

"This part is. I swear."

"You've said that before. And it was just to bring me back, to make me keep my promise."

She remembered what she'd told the nurse. To tell him to remember his promise to come back to her.

He had. He'd heard her and it brought him nothing but torture. "You always keep your promises anyway. It doesn't matter what I said." Except that now she knew that it did. She knew the medics thought he was going to die, but she hadn't realized the only reason he'd fought was her.

Betsy didn't feel any of the warmth that a revelation like that should have brought her. Only guilt for making him live through it, because it would never lie silent and still in his past. It would always and forever be present and solid.

Burning.

She hated that word. She'd never use it again in relation to something good, because it was all sour.

"Wake up," she whispered against his mouth.

The grip on her wrists eased and the mania waned from his eyes. His hands were on her face, smoothing her hair away from her forehead. Although it seemed he was checking to make sure it was really her.

"Betsy?"

"I'm here. I didn't go anywhere."

He buried his face in her neck and she stroked his hair. "I'm sorry."

He was sorry? She was the one who'd made him face his nightmares with no escape hatch. She'd been so sure that he wasn't as broken as he believed.

But she'd been wrong.

Betsy didn't know what to do now, how to make it better. The places where he'd grabbed her throbbed, and she knew she'd be bruised, and he'd beat himself up over that, too.

The alarm on her phone went off, signaling it was time to get up. She had to open Sweet Thing. She didn't want to leave him, and for a moment she didn't think he was going to let her. She wouldn't have minded too much if he hadn't. If she just lay here with him, she could hold him and tell him it would be okay without having a plan to make it okay.

Or without thinking that it was an utter and complete lie.

He rolled from her to his side of the bed.

"Will you bring me that bottle on your way out?" He nodded at the whiskey on the table by the door.

Betsy didn't know what else to do and so instead of giving him some speech about living in the world, or experiencing the good with the bad, she got up slowly and after grabbing her bag to head to the shower, she handed him the bottle.

And when she stepped into the shower to wash away the sins of the day, all she could do was cry.

For the first time, Betsy wondered if she might fail to save him.

It was one thing to hear about PTSD, to watch sad stories on the news and even to see it in the lives of some of the vets she spoke with when she went to the V.A. and handed out day-old donuts. It was quite another to watch Jack experience it—to hear him screaming because in his head, he was on fire.

If the whiskey made that stop, who was she to take that away from him? Who was she to demand that he be more than she could?

Betsy didn't have to relive her drowning every night the way Jack relived what had happened to him, and sometimes she was still afraid of the water. Even there in the shower, with water clinging to her lashes, she remembered what it was like to look up through that heavy wall and see the faces of the people watching her drown. That was only on the bad days. For Jack, it was every day.

You'll see what it's like to be me. He'd said it with such grim finality and Betsy knew he had challenges, but the reality of it hadn't quite struck her. Not until she saw it for herself.

His pain cut her like nothing else.

Not even her own.

She needed the comfort of her shop more than ever, but Betsy didn't know if anything could wring this out of her. She hadn't been able to wash it off with soap and scalding water, so she didn't know if the warmth and happy glow of Sweet Thing could change that. Betsy debated closing for the day, but Monday was V.A. day. She took the product that hadn't sold over the weekend and handed it out to the residents at the dormitory. She knew she was the only visitor some of the guys ever had. She couldn't disappoint them.

Especially since it was possible that someday, it

could be Jack living alone in some dormitory with nothing but the kindness of a stranger to comfort him.

On her way out the door, she peered into the room and saw he'd downed half the bottle.

"Sweetheart?" he drawled in that way that made the endearment seem like an insult. "Don't come back."

She had a whole host of things she wanted to fling at him, but they all disintegrated on her tongue. Instead she closed the door quietly behind her.

CHAPTER EIGHT

WHEN BETSY ARRIVED at Sweet Thing, she saw the lights were already on and India's car was parked in front.

Betsy turned off the engine and swiped the tears from her face. She hadn't even realized she was still crying. She took a few deep, shuddering breaths before pasting on her happy face and going inside the rear entrance.

"I didn't expect to see you this early," Betsy called out before she rounded the corner and saw that a small hurricane had exploded in her kitchen.

Various baked goods were cooling on racks, cookies, cakes, a few things she wasn't quite sure what they were…. The sink was full of pans, mixing bowls and utensils; spills of flour dotted the floor and the stainless steel tables, and there might have been some on the ceiling.

India stood in the middle of it all, her face puffy and red, up to her arms in what looked to be a honey wheat dough while she pounded the ever-loving hell out of it.

"I'll pay for everything," India growled as she continued to wail on the helpless dough.

Betsy blinked. "I'm more concerned about what has you bringing about the dough-ocalypse in my shop. You only bake when you're upset." She glanced around. "And from the look of things, someone ran over your dog."

"Your stupid brother."

"Caleb ran over your dog?" Betsy asked quietly.

She punched the dough this time, not even bothering to pretend she was working it for the purposes of eating it later. "He's a jackass."

"The dead dog is a jackass?"

"Stop trying to make me laugh." India smiled as she spoke. "I don't want to laugh." She stopped punching.

"Do you want to talk about it?" Betsy offered.

"Yes." She flopped down on a stool. "That's the problem. I want to talk about it, but the person I'd talk about it with is the person that's making me crazy." India sighed. "He changed the rules. Don't do that crap. Don't change the rules," she muttered to herself.

"You know, there was many a night that you had great advice for me, so now let me return the favor. Whatever it is that you think you can't tell my brother? That's a bunch of crap. There is nothing he wouldn't do for you."

India cringed. "You don't understand."

"I've been hearing that a lot lately." Betsy began trying to make some sense of the mess of baked goods. She wasn't sure what they were supposed to be, but they were everywhere. "Before you decide that you can't trust him with whatever this is, consider that he never wanted to go into the army."

"Yes, he did," India scoffed.

"No, he didn't. He always wanted to be a cop, but he never wanted to leave Glory. He went for you. If there's one thing I do know, it's my brother. Whatever is eating you up inside, it's devouring him, too." She wondered what exactly this had to do with dinner the night before.

"Everything will change."

"Everything does."

"Aren't I supposed to be the one handing down the sage advice?" India looked at her intently.

"It can be your turn next." Betsy took a bite of something she thought might be a scone. She didn't want to hand out anything she wouldn't eat. It was ugly but surprisingly good.

"So, how did Jack screw up?" India was obviously changing the subject.

"He didn't, I did." She shoved another one in her mouth. If she could figure out what India put in them—

"Walnuts. Coconut sugar. Chocolate chips," India answered her before she could ask.

"I can't stop eating them. They're really good." The dissolved delicately on her tongue when she took the time to savor them. The coconut sugar was made from the sap of coconut flower buds and had a higher nutrient content. It was better processed by the body than beet or cane sugar, and it also gave baked goods a different texture. Betsy loved it.

"Because they're good or because you don't want to answer me about Jack?"

Betsy sagged. "Both."

"You told me in this very kitchen that you knew it was a tough road ahead of you." India poked at the dough ball now as if it were a dead bug.

"I know. But he's hurting now and it's my fault. I may have damaged him more."

"Don't you have more faith in him that that?"

"You didn't see him, India. He was…" Betsy trailed off while she searched for the right words.

"He was haunted," India supplied. "His pain is there whether you dig at it or not. It's like a cancer. He can hide it, for brief periods he can pretend it's not killing him, but all the while it's devouring him from the inside out."

"So you're telling me to what?"

"Don't give up on him. I'm not saying you can dig that out of him. You can't. But you can be there for him while he does it himself." India closed her eyes for a second before continuing. "Or if he can't, and that's possible, even likely…you can hold his hand until it's done with him."

"I feel so helpless." She shoved another scone thing in her mouth, barely tasting it. "You know, I bet that's how Caleb feels, too. If I can see your scars, I know he feels them. He loves you."

"Oh hell, don't say that."

"Why not? He does. Always has. Always will." Betsy didn't bother to say that she thought Caleb more than just loved her, but that he was *in* love with her. India had a hard enough time with the softer emotions without Betsy shoving that in her face.

"I have to hit the head." India used decidedly male slang to say she was going to the bathroom. What she really meant was that she was fleeing the conversation and putting as much distance between herself and anything feminine or soft as possible.

Betsy was ready to change the conversation anyway. "Since you're off today," she called after her, "do you want to go with me to the dorms at the V.A.?"

"And hand out my Frankenscones?" India answered when she came back.

Betsy grinned. "Might as well do something with them, right?"

"Yeah, okay."

She went into the walk-in and pulled out the dough for the glazed donuts.

"Sorry I made a mess of things," India said as she loaded the industrial dishwasher.

"Hey, if you don't make a mess while you're baking, it's not going to taste good," Betsy said, knowing that India meant more than just the kitchen.

When India saw her pull out the ingredients for the fudge she said, "Is it bad enough for the fudge?"

"I think it might be."

"Save some for me," they heard Caleb call.

"It's all for us." Betsy managed a laugh. "We have an hour before Heather gets here and can take over the counter. I'd say that's enough time for the basics. Coffee and fudge."

"Coffee and fudge, huh? If you're going to the V.A., I could be bribed to help," Caleb said as he stepped through the door.

"Don't you people have homes?" Betsy teased.

Caleb's eyes narrowed as they focused on Betsy's wrists. "What exactly is that?"

"Nothing. It's fine." She looked down at the purpling bruises.

"The hell it is." He slammed out the door, but Betsy grabbed his arm just outside in the parking lot.

"It's fine. It was a nightmare."

"I want you to stay away from him, Betsy. He's not the—"

"So help me, if you say he's not the same man who left… Obviously, okay? Obviously." She nodded. "I can make my own choices. He needs his family now more than ever, and we're all he has. Would you really turn your back on him?"

"He's turned his back on himself."

"Oh Caleb. If it were you, do you think there is any chance this side of hell I'd give up on you?"

"That's different. I'd never do that to you."

"You don't know what you'd do. You didn't come back broken. He didn't mean to hurt me. He was having a nightmare. He didn't even *know* it was me." Part of her twinged at the lie. He knew it was her, or at least a nightmare wearing her face.

No wonder he found it so hard to look at her, because every time he did, it reminded him of what had happened to him and why he was living a life he didn't want.

"Betsy, you've convinced yourself you have some guilt here, and you don't."

Betsy wasn't so sure about that.

It was India who finally stayed his hand. She hadn't been able to look at him until this moment, but she reached out and touched his arm. "Let it go, Caleb. If she needs you, she'll ask."

"I do need you, to help me load up the car." Betsy tried to change the subject and hoped the matter was dead.

Caleb didn't say anything else about Jack and did as both Betsy and India asked. Betsy's brother was a gentle giant until it came to her or India. Then he was a cannon and they were gunners.

She knew why the bruises made him so angry, but if India didn't think it was a big deal, then it wasn't. India had lived with abuse, her stepfather hitting her and her mother. After she'd been taken out of their custody, a night that Caleb still wouldn't talk about, she had no way to pay for her education. It was why she'd decided to go into the army.

Betsy sighed. She knew that a small-town veneer could hide a lot of sins. It was tempting to think that no one could be trusted, but then she saw men like Jack and Caleb. Women like India. They each had their own pain, but they were still good people.

Jack. His name echoed in her head, rattling around until even the echo of it clanged like a bell. He'd told her not to come back.

Could she really do it? After he saved her, could she let him drown even if it was what he wanted?

She tried to put it out of her head, but when they arrived at the V.A., all she could think about was how most of these guys in the dorms didn't have anyone.

The dormitory functioned much like a halfway house. There were curfews and check-ins. She donated her day-old donuts and spent the morning talking with them. It wasn't much, but it was what she had to give.

She studied the institutional walls as she made her way to the dayroom and that was when she saw it. A green flyer taped to the wall. PTSD Support Group, it read.

That was so simple, why hadn't she thought of that? A support group. Therapy. Maybe talking to other people who'd seen the same things he had would help him deal with the nightmares.

She wanted to call him, but Betsy knew he was still raw and probably wouldn't answer a call from her anyway. She could be patient and give him some time.

But there was no way she was giving up on him or leaving him to stew in his own misery, even if that's what he wanted.

Betsy snatched the flyer off the wall and folded it into a neat square before tucking it into her purse.

CHAPTER NINE

"PUT ON YOUR sparring gear and meet me outside," Caleb said from outside the screen door, a grim look on his face.

Jack had been expecting a visit from Caleb on Wednesday afternoon. He was surprised it had taken him two days to decide to call him out for what happened with Betsy. When they were kids and they'd argue, rather than let it fester, Caleb's dad had taken them to the backyard, handed them sparring gear and told them to work it out.

There was nothing that a few minutes of sparring couldn't resolve. *Except this.*

"We don't need to spar. I've got it coming." Jack opened the door. "Take your shot."

"Get. The. Gear." Caleb's words were like gristle through a meat grinder. "I'll be in the back."

Jack sighed and knew that whether he wanted to do this or not, it was going to happen. So he might as well go out there and get it over with, but he didn't bother with the gear.

In the days since the incident with Betsy, he'd wondered if he'd be able to taste even his own blood without her. He hadn't wanted to tell her to go, but he'd hurt her. He hadn't known reality from the nightmare. What would happen next time he didn't know where he was? Betsy was too kind and giving for her own good. She didn't know when to give up, and for a moment, he'd started to believe all the castles she'd painted in the sky.

Caleb took off his duty belt, rolled up his sleeves. "Where's the gear?"

"I told you, I don't need it." He deserved whatever contrition Caleb wanted to dole out for his sins.

"Fine. You know what's coming."

Caleb's knuckles connected with his face and sent him reeling. He stumbled and tripped, fell backward and crashed into the ground. Caleb leaped on him like a great cat taking down his prey, his fists continued to bash into his face.

Jack felt nothing after the first bloom of sensation through his nose, shooting up into his forehead, his eyes—then it was simply the absence of any stimulation at all. Good, bad…not even that throbbing numbness that dulls the pain after that initial connection of violence to the face.

Nothing at all.

His friend's face was twisted with all the pain and sorrow Jack wished he could express.

"Fight back, damn it." The punches kept coming. "You did not fucking die over there, Jack." The words were ripped out of him.

He had. He'd died in the sand under a scorching sun, but his body refused to lie down and stay dead.

It seemed that Caleb could read that in his eyes,

he paused, bloody knuckles half-cocked for another round. "You shouldn't have come back. She wanted you, not a ghost, and now you're trying to drag her down to hell with you. Stay away from her." He spat and scrambled away from him, disgust on his face. Jack knew him well enough to know that the disgust wasn't only for Jack, but for Caleb himself and what he'd done. Misguided as it was, he probably thought it would rattle something loose in Jack's brain, fix him.

Everyone wanted to fix him, but he just wasn't fixable.

Sudden pain erupted hot and volcanic in his chest, but it wasn't from the fight. It was the thought of never seeing Betsy again. He knew he couldn't see her, couldn't touch her, but the idea that Caleb could somehow make that choice, take her away from him—

A roar bellowed out from deep in his throat, an inhuman battle cry. Somehow he wasn't simply standing; Jack was flying. He didn't know how he'd done it. It was as if he were outside his body and watching from afar as he launched himself at Caleb.

He charged him like an angry bull, rabbit-punching him in the kidneys as he took him down. Caleb rolled when they hit the ground, still striking at Jack's face.

Luckily for Jack, he was still numb. He was numb everywhere but that secret place deep inside that wouldn't allow anyone else to take Betsy from him, to shut off the light and tell him he could never have it again.

Not even Caleb.

"You won't take her," he snarled.

"If you cared about her at all—" Caleb spat blood "—you'd leave." He wrestled him onto his back. "You'd let her mourn you so she can live her life."

Jack punched him in the kidney again and they rolled. "Guess I'm not part of your family anymore."

"You did it yourself when you laid hands on her, bastard."

"Stop it!" India cried from the narrow alley behind the yard.

"This doesn't concern—" Jack's fist connected with Caleb's face.

Fifty thousand volts of electricity blasted through their bodies and they both stiffened, their muscles convulsing and twitching.

"Actually it does," their tormentor said, each hand wrapped around a Taser. "Mrs. Church called the police. So, when you two are done acting like you're five, we'll take this inside."

"I can't believe you Tased me," Caleb said when he could talk. "I was winning."

"I'll Tase you again. If you can talk, you can walk. Inside, Lewis. Right now."

Jack struggled to get up, and India held out her hand to him. He flashed back to that first night when Betsy had demanded he ask for help. It had felt like begging, but all he had to do was ask. India didn't even want him to ask; she just offered it.

He searched her face, looking for the pity there, but there was only disgust. "It's not going to bite you. Or Tase you. Unless you don't move double time."

Jack took her hand and allowed her to help him up and he wandered into the house behind her.

"Wipe your face." She handed him a dishrag from the drawer by the sink.

Jack accepted it and when he pulled the cloth back, he saw the cloth soaked in blood. His mouth was full of it as well and he spat into the sink. He had an answer to that question. No, he couldn't taste his own blood.

"Now, what exactly is your problem? What had you two fighting like a couple of kids in the backyard? And so help me, the Tasers are out of juice, but I have handcuffs," she threatened.

"I had it coming." Jack was the first to speak.

"I told him to get the gear. Not my fault he didn't."

"No, it's your fault that you charged over here like a rabid bull. Betsy told you it was fine. *I* told you it was fine."

"It's not fine," Jack interrupted.

"I wasn't talking to you yet." She turned her attention back to Caleb. "You could get fired for this. You're on duty. How could you do something so stupid?"

"Because it had to be done," he answered.

"Betsy is an adult capable of making her own decisions. Something that *both* of you have forgotten. No one gets to make her choices for her. Not you. Not Jack. Not me. Not even Lula. You both are so wrapped up in your hero complexes that you forgot Betsy is a person with her own feelings who doesn't need to be saved."

"But she does, India. She doesn't know when to quit, and it's time," Jack managed as his face started to swell.

"If you had this beating coming, why did you fight back?"

Shame washed over him.

"That's what I thought. It's all well and fine to tell her to go, but the thought of someone trying to keep her from you? You wanted to kill him, didn't you? He's your best friend." She smacked Jack on the back of the head, but then her demeanor softened. "Caleb, go in the front room for a minute. I have to talk to Jack alone."

"Like hell." His fists were tight, his body strung like a bow ready to unleash the arrows of hell.

"Caleb!"

"Fine." Caleb, whose face had also started to swell, went toward the front room.

She studied him for a minute before speaking, as if measuring her words. "So, you and me? We're two of a kind. Things happened and they were bad. They were really bad, but you know what? They're not bad here. You're home. This is your family."

"That's why I had to make her go, India. I hurt her."

"That's what happens in families. We hurt each other because no one can see our pain as starkly as someone who loves us. And it's ugly to have that thrown back in our faces. I know." She nodded.

"You only grabbed her wrist a little too hard during a nightmare. When we were thirteen and went on that camping trip to Yosemite, I knocked out Caleb's last milk tooth because of a nightmare about bears."

"You weren't in danger of killing him."

"And neither are you, Jack. If you think you are, why aren't you getting some help?"

"Because I'm sick of help. I'm sick of being told how wonderful it is to be here. It's not. I want it to be over."

"Then stop dragging it out."

His eyes widened.

"I love you. You're one of my closest friends, but rather than rot from the inside out, if you're really done, *be done.* And don't be messy about it, because leaving that for us to clean up is selfish."

Leave it to India to put all the cards on the table.

"But you should think about what it would do to Betsy. I'm not saying you should live for her, because that's a tough thing to put on any one person. She loves you, so don't you think there's got to be something worth loving in you? If it's worth loving, it's worth living."

"Betsy—"

India held up her hand to cut him off. "No, not this again. If you value her, if you love her at all, then you have to trust her. Which means trusting the choices you don't like, too. She's not a child. Think about it, Jack. Think about that really hard. Then make your choice and follow through, whatever it is. Commit yourself to it wholly."

Betsy had said the same thing to him about committing himself wholly.

"Now, I'm going to go in there and deal with man-baby number two. Give me five minutes and then come in and kiss and make up. Or I'm really going to lose my temper."

Jack had a hard time processing what she'd said. He hadn't really given much thought to how his slow rot would affect the people around him. How it would taint them, too. Maybe he shouldn't have come home even for a short time.

He thought about all the men who desperately wished they were in his place, who wished they *could* come home. Those who'd only touched the soil of their country again when they were lowered six feet down into it.

Jack thought about the men he'd met at the Center for the Intrepid in Texas where he'd done his rehab. He'd powered through that because there was nothing else to do. He'd still been in the navy, still following orders.

They ordered him to get the implant, to rehab, to walk again, to get well enough to go home, so he'd done it all without thinking what it meant or what it would mean for him. He'd done it all thinking he still had a home in the navy. A desk job, or teaching at the Naval Academy. But he couldn't teach, he didn't want to be behind a desk. He wanted to be in theater, that was what he'd trained for, what he'd been told all he was good for. Now, he had no idea what he was supposed to do.

A rush of noise and memory swirled in his head. So many sounds clanged in his ears and he couldn't tell what was memory and what was real. He wanted—no, he needed—to block it out. To find some quiet, some peace. No matter what senses he dulled, always there was something blaring in his head. Something he couldn't forget, couldn't process, that bubbled up and boiled over.

Jack tried to focus on the things in the room, something to anchor him to the real. The small sugar bowl that sat in the window above the sink, with the enamel strawberry on the lid. Except it reminded him of Betsy. She'd loved that bright red strawberry against the creamy porcelain, always rubbing her fingers over it. As a little girl, when she'd follow Caleb all over, his mother had given it to her to play with. He always thought someday she'd break it, but she never did.

He focused on the clock on the wall. Jack remembered when his parents brought it back from their anniversary trip to Germany. His father had grudgingly hung it on the wall, complaining about the sound of the cuckoo, but his mother had loved it. She sighed every time she heard it, and just the song would calm her tears, cool her anger and make her forgive whatever it was his father had done. Even when he'd taken out its guts and hidden a bottle of vodka behind the panels. The clock was still and silent, even now. Though its presence spoke of more than its voice ever could.

Which brought him to his friends sitting in his

front room. People who loved him. People it hurt to see him like this. Caleb, who'd bloodied his face.

"I'm sorry," he said as he entered the room.

"You can still fight." Caleb nodded.

"And…" India prompted, overexaggerating her pronunciation.

"And your work here is done. This is between us now."

"No, I'm supposed to take you back to the station. You're in deep, buddy."

"After I talk to Jack. Alone."

"If you think I'm leaving you two alone after you basically assaulted and battered him—"

"He won't be pressing charges, will you?" Caleb gave him a lopsided, swollen grin.

"No, man."

"Caleb, you owe me dinner for this. Something nice. Steak." India sniffed. She looked over her shoulder on the way out the door. "You guys really okay?"

"Yeah." Caleb nodded.

When she was gone, Jack spoke. "I didn't mean to hurt her."

"I know. I shouldn't have… I really thought that you'd…" He couldn't seem to finish a sentence. "I can't say I'm sorry, because I'm not. I don't know what else to do."

"There's nothing you can do. That's what I've been trying to tell you *and* Bets. I told her to stay away, okay?"

"She'll do that as soon as mud pies taste like peanut butter."

"I think she will this time. She was afraid of me." Jack remembered the look on her face. It was just as well she hadn't come back, especially while he was at war with himself. She made him forget how things had to be and made him believe in something else. If only belief in a thing could make it real.

"No, she was afraid *for* you."

"Is that what she said?"

"No, it's what I know. Betsy has absolute faith in you. She always has, she always will."

"I don't deserve it." He didn't mention that he didn't want it. Once upon a time, he would've done anything to keep it. Now it just needed to die a quiet death so all of these memories could, too.

"No one does. I don't know where she learned to have that kind of belief, but the world hasn't ripped it out of her yet. I know it has to happen, but I didn't want it to be you that did it."

"Do you think I want to be?"

"No, but you will be. I wanted to keep her safe just a little while longer."

Jack thought about the things she'd said when they were in bed. When she'd tried to hide her beautiful body from him. "Someone else already broke her heart. I'm not—"

"Whatever Marcel did, he's not you. She didn't believe in him the way she believes in you. Even if she told herself she was in love with him, he was not the great and sainted Jack McConnell."

"What do you want me to do?"

"Honestly?" Caleb cocked his head to the side. "I want you to fix your shit. You don't have to be the kid who left. None of us are. But be a man worthy of the faith and trust that we put in you."

Caleb's words, though quiet, burrowed deep like armor-piercing bullets. Jack wanted nothing more than to be that man. But he finally said, "I don't think I know how."

"That's a step above not wanting to and not caring."

"I've never not cared, Caleb. It would be easier if I didn't."

Jack's gaze met Caleb's, and the rage that was in his eyes was gone. It was just Caleb. His best friend.

He realized that maybe he was so caught up telling people he wasn't the same person not because he thought they didn't know, but because he wished he was the same guy who'd left.

If he had been, his life would be almost picture-perfect.

Maybe that was why he didn't want to come home. This home belonged to that guy. If he'd still been him, it would've been a perfect fit. The sweet small town that thought he was the returning hero, a beautiful woman who loved him...

He didn't need Betsy to tell him that she loved him. He knew that she did.

That she always had.

The old Jack would want to be worthy of that love.

The new Jack knew he never could be.

CHAPTER TEN

By Friday night, Betsy had had enough of waiting.

Mother Nature seemed to be aware of her plan, if the sky was any indication. She was not pleased, to say the least. Dark clouds rolled in from the west. They were like an ocean of burned marshmallows, black and buoyant. She knew they were called mammatus clouds, and their formation meant that the storm was going to be a door-slammer.

Conditions could possibly be favorable for a tornado, which was unusual for October, but not completely unexpected. She'd grown up hearing all of her neighbors and friends say that if you don't like the weather in Kansas, wait five minutes.

Betsy loved the volatility, the energy, of the storm. That was something she'd missed about home when she was in New York. There was nowhere else in the world that had storms like Kansas. Sure, other places could get violent or powerful storms, other places had tornados, monsoons, nor'easters—but there was nothing like watching a clear blue sky change into an electric green, the fine hairs on the back of her neck standing at attention and the clouds rolling in from across the plain like a stampeding army from hell in the span of minutes. She'd seen hail on the clear day, known what it was like to have it rain sideways and she even loved the winter wonderland landscape after an ice storm.

Thunder echoed like a clash of swords and she smiled happily.

Until she remembered Jack's reaction to Johnny Hart's classic T-Bird backfiring. The thunder must be torture for him.

Whether he wanted to see her or not, she wouldn't leave him to face this alone.

Decision made, Betsy grabbed her tote and stuffed some supplies inside. She still hadn't unpacked it from the weekend, but she added clean clothes and her ereader as well as the emergency power source—just in case the weather got really bad.

She didn't know what he had at his house, so she packed a picnic. He probably hadn't eaten. Betsy could always be counted on to feed a situation. She chose some pumpkin cookies, the ones with the anise seed eyes and Red Hots mouths, as well as some bottles of water and homemade white dill loaf for sandwiches. Various and sundry items for said sandwiches and fresh fruit.

Romantic images played out in her mind of spending the storm in front of the roaring fireplace in the front room, of making love on the red-and-white-checkered blanket while the thunder rattled the walls. Then they'd stream movies on her ereader, holding on to each other—all fanciful garbage, she knew.

That was okay, because this wasn't about her. It

was about him and being there for him because he needed her.

She kept repeating that mantra over and over in her head on the drive over. Betsy felt sick, thinking about facing him after he'd told her not to come back.

What she heard in his voice wasn't *I don't want your help;* it was *I don't want you.*

When she arrived, the door was open and the window down on the screen. Betsy knocked, rattling the old metal. "Jack?"

"I thought I told you not to come back," he drawled from the couch.

"Since when do I ever listen?"

"You should start."

She couldn't see him, but something about his tone told her she wouldn't like what she saw when he came into view. He was too relaxed, too flip. She knew it was a facade.

"I brought you something to eat," she offered.

"Then by all means, intrude. What is it with small towns and the people who live there who think that bringing over a casserole entitles you to entry to someone's home? Like it's buying a ticket for a peek at a freak show."

"I didn't stop to think about that." She rather imagined that was what he felt like. It didn't occur to her that the neighborhood would have stocked his freezer for the next year with green bean casserole, broccoli cheese rice casserole, homemade mac 'n' cheese, potato salad, all the things you took to a pig roast or a funeral.

"No, you didn't."

"Jack, I'm not here for a ticket."

"Aren't you?" He sat up and turned to look at her.

"What happened to your face?" she gasped. He looked as if he'd been in a prizefight and lost. His nose was swollen and crooked; one whole side of his face was purple and looked like a split grape.

"The wrath of Caleb."

"I'm going to kill him."

"India Tased me and I'm not feeling any pain." He brought a bottle of that rotgut swill to his lips.

"Are you drunk?"

"Most definitely."

She sighed, at a loss for what to do. She didn't know what had happened, but she couldn't judge him.

Her nose tingled as if she were the one who'd been punched in the face. Tears welled behind her eyes, but if he wasn't crying, she wouldn't do so, either.

Resolve hardened, she sat down next to him and took the bottle out of his hand. Their fingers brushed, electric current shooting straight to her core at the contact. Her first instinct was to put the bottle aside and lace her fingers through his, but she knew he didn't want that. He didn't want to feel a connection. He didn't want to hurt.

So instead she brought the bottle to her lips and swallowed. It burned all the way down and it was a struggle not to splutter and cough at the caustic sensation.

"Feeling strong tonight, Betsy? I know you don't drink this stuff."

"I'm here as your friend, Jack."

"Yeah, so was Caleb." He took the bottle back from her and took another long swallow.

She absolutely would *not* think about his mouth on the bottle. What it was like to kiss it, taste it, to have him move his lips over her flesh and how much she wanted that again.

"So, if you're not here to condemn me or blow sunshine up my ass, what do you want?" He eyed her. "If you're looking to get railed, I can't help you," he said conversationally. "Been drinking all day."

He'd effectively distanced himself from her and everything that had happened between them with that one sentence. He was so casual, so dismissive.

Another bout of thunder rattled the house and she watched his knuckles blanch as they tightened around the bottle.

"You can say whatever nasty thing you want to me, Jack. That doesn't change why I'm here. If you want me to go, I will, but I'll come back."

"Then I suppose you should stay." He guzzled the last of the bottle. "Make yourself useful, then. There's another of these under the sink."

Betsy had a choice to make. She could get up and get him the one thing he needed to get him through the night, or she could refuse because it didn't match up with her beliefs.

Because it killed her hope.

She supposed it wasn't her hope that she had to

worry about, but his. "Okay." Betsy rose carefully and put one foot in front of the other until she was in the kitchen. With wooden motions and regret, she brought him the bottle.

"I didn't think you'd do it."

"We all have our coping mechanisms. This happens to be yours. I told you, I'm here as your friend, not as your lover."

"That's an interesting development."

"Are you hungry?"

"No."

"I am. So I'm going to have a cookie. Pumpkin." She rummaged through her bag and pulled out the package of cookies.

Betsy bit into one carefully, as if she was afraid it was going to bite her back. Jack's eyes focused on her mouth and when he bent in to kiss her, she didn't turn away, but instead of the pumpkin, cinnamon and anise on her tongue from the sweet, all he could taste was ash.

He pulled back, an unfamiliar look on his face. "Can't taste it. I tasted things with you. Sweetness." Jack shook his head. "Now, nothing."

"I know. I can't taste it, either. Like damp paper."

"Good to know." He thrust the bottle against his mouth again and guzzled. The loud report of thunder and a blinding flash of lighting lit up the sky like a strobe light.

She tried to sit by and stoically watch him drown his pain and himself in the whiskey, but she couldn't. No matter what she told herself, she just wasn't wired that way. So she took the bottle again and snagged another drink for fortification before setting it on the far table.

"Thought you weren't going to judge."

He knew her too well. Betsy didn't speak. Instead she pulled on his shoulders and he followed her lead. He reclined down into her lap, the rest of him draped over the couch. She smoothed her fingers through his hair, across his forehead, down his cheek—was careful not to touch him anywhere that hurt.

"You're killing me, Bets." He sighed and even though he tried to put on a good show, this was what he needed. Touch. Comfort. Something more than what could be found in a bottle.

"You're killing *yourself*," she countered softly. "But we're not going to think about that right now. You're going to lie here quiet and still and know that you're safe. You're home. I'm not going to let anyone or anything touch you."

"I don't want to hurt you." He exhaled a heavy shuddering breath.

"You won't. I've had worse than a couple little bruises on my wrists. You probably haven't looked very closely at my hands, but they're so scarred from the ovens and slips of the knife, it's ridiculous. They're not very pretty."

"They're beautiful hands." He grabbed her hand and pulled it down for inspection, as if he hadn't seen the mess of scars and flaws that came with her chosen profession.

At least he was letting her do this. Even though

this was supposed to be about *his* hope, hers blossomed. He'd shed the bitter facade as soon as she made it clear she wasn't demanding anything from him, didn't expect anything from him other than what he'd given her.

She tried not to shiver as the pads of his fingers explored her palms, her knuckles and even her wrists. "I burn myself there all the time," Betsy managed in a voice that was too high-pitched, too tinny.

"I never noticed. Your hands are always so soft. Scars are supposed to be hard. Rough."

"It must be from how many times I wash my hands. I use a lot of shea butter lotion." He didn't care what kind of lotion she used. It was the most inane thing she could say. The man was in her lap because he'd drunk himself nearly into a stupor to deal with something she couldn't begin to understand and she was talking about lotion. Stupid, stupid, stupid.

He inhaled deeply. "Can't smell the sugar. The vanilla. Where did it go?"

His question was almost childlike. A stark contrast to the way he'd spoken earlier. The barely leashed anger and disgust.

"The whiskey took it," she answered. Betsy didn't want to needle him, but she wasn't going to lie to him.

"I should stop, then," he murmured, and turned his face against her stomach, his arm curled around her waist.

Another clap of thunder and strike of lightning rattled the space around them, and he stiffened, but relaxed into her again. She continued stroking the short buzz of his hair tenderly.

The storm seemed to fade in the background compared to the white noise of helplessness that slammed in her ears. She didn't know what else to do for him. Why had she thought she could do this? That she could save him? Her heart ached so much she felt it all the way in her bones.

"I know you love me, Betsy. I wish I was worthy of it." His breathing evened and he passed into sleep with that revelation on his lips.

Alcohol was the universal truth serum.

She'd been struggling for a way to let him know how much she cared about him, and that yes, she did love him. Not with some little girl declaration of happily ever after and bubbles and fairy tales. She wouldn't deny that part of her still hoped for that, but it was more. He had to know he wasn't alone and that she wouldn't turn her back on him no matter which parts had broken.

But that wasn't the problem at all. He *did* know. Now she was at a loss. Betsy continued to watch over him, stroking his hair, his neck, his shoulders with a soothing motion that seemed to calm him. Or maybe he was just too drunk to keep his eyes open. She didn't know. The storm abated until all she could hear was the slight patter of rain on the windows. The soft, repetitive sound lulled her to a state that wasn't quite sleep, but her brain was mercifully silent.

The storm hadn't quite exhausted itself, and when it began to pound and howl, its fury renewed, Jack jerked awake. His eyes were wide, but they weren't haunted. He scrambled away from her—awkward and desperate for something.

He ran to the bathroom, and it seemed that his stomach was rebelling at the inhuman amount of alcohol he'd been swilling.

Betsy sat on the couch for a few minutes, giving him time to comport himself. She smoothed her hands down her skirt, staring absently at the happy cupcake print until she heard the water for the shower running.

She went to the door. "Are you okay?"

"No, Bets. I'm really not."

"I'm coming in." She waited for him to tell her not to, but he didn't, so she cracked the door and slipped inside. "What's wrong?" Betsy laughed nervously. "I guess that's a stupid question."

"You were right. I don't want to spend my time like this. I don't want to be my dad."

"You're not," she said through the shower curtain that hung between them almost like a confessional.

"It's either pain or numbness. Why can't anything feel good?"

"You said *I* felt good," she blurted.

"We've been over that."

"And neither of us likes the answers we found. So we change them."

"How?"

His question caused that little candle flicker of hope to explode, but she didn't have an answer for him. "I don't know yet, but we can figure it out."

It seemed he thought the same thing about the curtain, that it could be used to hide his sins, because he said softly, "I'm afraid."

"Of what?"

"That I can't figure it out. That there aren't any other answers."

"Maybe we should just change the question."

"What would you change it to? Right now if you could change it to anything you want, what would it be?"

There were a hundred things on the tip of her tongue, but only one that was going to get her what she wanted. "Why I'm not in there with you."

A low sound rumbled from his throat. "You can't mean that."

"I do."

"You can have anything you want, Bets. You always could."

She shed her dress with trembling fingers. Both times they'd been together, it had been amazing—until afterward. Then it had all turned to crap. Betsy hoped this time would be different because her heart couldn't stand to break again. She'd heard something somewhere, maybe a bit of prose, and it said that you had to keep breaking your heart until it opened. Her heart was so open it would never fit back together again.

"Can we not do the regret-and-guilt after party, though? If you don't want me to stay, I can go home, but—"

He pulled back the curtain and met her stare.

What she saw in his eyes cut her off. "No more guilt. I'm done with it."

Betsy knew she should've found it comforting, but there was something in the way he said it. Not even his tone, but maybe it was the set to his shoulders... Not that she could pick it to death anyway while she was staring at them. Water sluiced down his hard body and she found her line of sight drawn down every contour, every plane of granite-carved muscle.

She'd thought he was handsome and well made when he left the first time. After BUDs he was leaner, stronger, but now? After the world had had its way with him, it hadn't worn him down like a pebble in a stream. His experience, his pain, had cut straight through him like the glaciers that had formed in the Grand Canyon of the Yellowstone. It was stark, harsh and beautiful.

Most of all she liked this comparison because the canyon was still standing. It had persevered while the the glaciers had inevitably melted away under the sun.

Betsy wanted to be his sun, in every sense of the word.

She stepped into the shower with him, the hot water beading on her skin, causing her hair to cling to her face. Betsy was thankful she'd opted for fresh-faced today, so her makeup wasn't streaking down her face making her look like some kind of demented clown.

Although the intensity on Jack's face made her wonder if it would have mattered. If she could be made up like a circus freak, but he'd still be intent and aroused because it was her, that was a good feeling. Even better than the first time she'd made a successful soufflé.

She stepped close to him, the smell of his body wash strong in her nose. It was comforting and familiar. His hands were hot and slick on her skin. Rough, but still pleasing, like raw velvet.

Just being in his arms like this was an intimacy that bespoke things words and even making love couldn't.

I love you, Jack. It was on the tip of her tongue, welling up like some great fountain, but he already knew. She didn't have to say it. In fact, she knew it was best if she didn't. He wouldn't understand that she was speaking her heart, not asking for a return declaration.

She wanted him to feel it, to be sure. She definitely wanted to hear it, but she knew he wasn't ready. The confession would be hollow and empty because it wouldn't be real. Betsy knew he had to love himself before he was ready to love her. Jack hadn't even asked himself out yet, much less fallen in love. He'd never spent any time in his own head.

While patience was a virtue that she didn't possess, Betsy could be content with this for a time. After all, she had to get to know him all over again, too. She loved him, felt the emotion well in her heart so strong and sure, but she didn't know if she was *in* love with him. Her little girl heart was still in love with the boy who left, but she knew they weren't the same people. She'd changed and so had he. Everyone made sure to drive that point home with a Louisville Slugger. Betsy had been so caught up in her fantasy of him and saving him that she realized she might have forgotten there was a real person beneath that.

And he knew it. It was why he'd fought this so hard, pushed her away. Maybe she hadn't changed so much after all, because it seemed he knew her better than she knew herself.

Of course, the revelation didn't change anything. She still wanted to be here with him, wanted him to touch her. No matter what had transpired or how long they'd been apart, the chemistry still sizzled between them.

She hated it when he was right, though.

For all of his strength, touching him was like holding a baby bird with a broken wing. He clung to her as if his very breath was dependent on hers.

Betsy wanted to make him feel something else good. They both needed it.

She kissed his neck, his sternum, down the hard lines of his pecs, and she journeyed lower still until she was on her knees. Betsy held eye contact as she leaned down toward the place on his thigh that he hadn't wanted her to see. The place where flesh turned to metal. She thought it was amazing that the titanium was part of him.

In fact, she thought it was beautiful. His sacrifice for something larger than himself, his nobility—yes, even tonight when he'd drowned himself in whiskey.

She traced the pads of her fingers over flesh, over

metal, all the time holding his gaze so he could see her reaction and know it didn't matter to her. She pressed her lips to his thigh, and his eyes fluttered closed and he tilted his head back in ecstasy. "I feel."

So she did it again, her hands mapping him, loving him. She wanted him to feel everything, to fill his senses up with all things good, all things right.

His gaze locked on her face and she wrapped her hand around him and took his length into the hot cavern of her mouth. The intensity on his face was as sharp as a knife, disbelief hanging around him like a shroud. As if he thought she couldn't possibly want to do this, want to be here.

Yet she did.

Marcel always wanted her to do this, and it hadn't done anything for her one way or another. It hadn't spurred her arousal and it hadn't even made her happy to bring him pleasure.

But just like everything else with Jack, this was different, too. She felt like a supplicant at the altar of a god. His pleasure was hers. So many feelings roiled through her, and the way he looked at her was as if he thought she was Aphrodite herself.

This was how it was supposed to be.

His fingers threaded through her hair and cupped the back of her skull, but he didn't try to guide her, or set the pace for her caress. This was all as she wanted. He was a blank canvas before her and she could paint her desire with any brush she chose.

Their eyes were still locked when she pushed him over the edge and he found culmination.

But if she thought he was finished, she was mistaken.

After drying them both and wrapping her in a towel, he carried her to the bedroom. She loved it when he picked her up. It wasn't only that it made her feel delicate and feminine; it made her feel cherished.

Betsy loved how his muscles felt while he held her, taut, but it wasn't any great strain on him to carry her.

"You should always be naked," he said against her ear.

"I'll always be naked if you always carry me." In fact, Betsy would swear that a man who could pick her up, especially if his name happened to be Jack McConnell, made all her clothes fall off like magic.

"We'll never get anything done."

"Being productive is overrated."

After easing her down onto the bed, he worshipped her with his tongue, his lips and his hands. In only minutes, he had her screaming and clawing at his back as bliss took her.

When she settled into his arms afterward, she knew something had changed. She hoped it was for the better and that if nothing else, he could sleep through the night.

CHAPTER ELEVEN

JACK AWOKE TO a cold, gray fall morning with a soft bundle of warmth pressed against his side. Betsy burrowed against him like some small, hibernating mammal. Her cloud of hair was a mess over her face, and the sight was endearing. It reminded him of when they were kids and she'd want to come to the backyard campouts with him and Caleb. Many a night after telling ghost stories, she'd climb into the tent with them because she was afraid to sleep in her room alone.

Only they weren't kids anymore. Betsy was very much a grown woman, as evidenced by the night previous.

His eyes fluttered closed as if that could hide him from his actions. He'd been so pathetic, so weak, and Betsy, she just didn't give up. She pushed so hard, no matter the cost to herself. He remembered her lips on that bottle as she tried to drink herself into a stupor with him.

The storm. Christ, what kind of man was afraid of a storm?

Then it occurred to him that it was Saturday.

He had a standing date with fate.

Jack eased out of bed and grabbed his .357. Even though it was gloomy and overcast, he could still see daylight streaking through the windows. He was late. It was usually still dark, still quiet. Yet he could hear the sounds of the world outside. Birds, cars and the neighbor's dog.

He sat on the couch, the metal cool in his hand, a familiar and welcome texture.

He hadn't donned his whites; he couldn't risk waking Betsy.

As if the sound of a gunshot in the living room wouldn't.

Looking at the gun, he thought about what that would do to her. If she had to find his body. She'd be stuck with another one of his messes to clean up. She'd wonder if it was something she'd done. If there was something else she could have done to help him.

The comforting weight of the weapon in his hand was suddenly wrong. Thinking about last night, and the way he felt—the way everything felt—he wanted more of that. Not just the sex, but the feeling.

The living.

He was tired of pain, tired of feeling useless.

Betsy didn't think he was useless; she didn't pity him. She loved him.

He remembered what India had said about love. That if he was worth loving, his life was worth living.

And to do it wholeheartedly.

He didn't want to play roulette with his mistress this morning.

Jack didn't want to die.

He didn't know how to live, but it was quite something for him to realize that he wasn't ready to die.

"Jack? What are you doing?" Betsy whispered.

He looked up to see her standing next to the couch, a look of horror on her face.

She knew. He could see it in her eyes.

"Nothing. Just need to clean my weapon, but I didn't want to wake you up. My kit is still in the bedroom."

"Do you swear?"

"I swear. Do it every Saturday."

"I think that's the first time you've ever lied to me, Jack." She turned and stuffed her feet into her shoes. "I'll put up with a lot of things from you, but lying isn't one of them."

"Betsy," he called out. "Don't go, okay?"

She just shook her head.

"Come here." He stood and held his hand out to her.

"No. Tell me. Say it out loud. What were you doing?"

Jack closed his eyes, trying to shield himself against everything he would see in her eyes. "Deciding to live."

"Is that going to change as soon as I leave?" Her voice was small, quiet, as if she didn't want to ask the question because she was afraid of the answer.

"No."

"You need help, Jack. More than what I can do for you."

He nodded. She was right. He hadn't been ready to see it, not until she showed him that he could still taste, still feel, and most important, that he still wanted to.

"There's a support group at the V.A.—"

"I'll go."

"Really? You don't have to say you will just to appease me. It won't work unless it's really what you want for yourself."

He pulled her against him and she came, hesitantly. "I do. And I know it's going to be hard and I know I don't have any right to ask, but I need you, Bets. I didn't even know I wanted to live until you showed me it can still be good."

Her arms tightened around him. "Let's go try that out."

"How do you propose we do that?" Jack was ready to indulge any whim she had. He never wanted to see that look of pain and disappointment on her face again. He wanted her to forget what she'd seen, because that part was over. It had taken him a long time to come to that decision.

"Let's go to the Corner Pharmacy for breakfast. I want a chocolate Italian soda and you can have a Green River."

"I haven't thought about that place in years. It's still open?" He thought about the soda fountain specialty he hadn't had in years—the carbonated lime drink that had always shocked and pleased his tongue in his youth.

"Of course. It's an institution. Plus, breakfast is cheap. I'll treat."

"You certainly will not." He was offended.

"You're such a caveman."

"And that's bad because…"

Betsy grinned. "I have been stuffing you full of sweets. I guess it's a fair trade."

"Betsy, there will be no trading. I'm a simple man at heart, and while I believe you can do anything you set your mind to do, I still believe the guy should pay on a date."

"Is this a date?"

"Yes."

"Oh." She blushed.

"Sweetheart, I've seen parts of you that your doctor hasn't seen and you're blushing because I asked you out?"

"Sometimes I do things a little backward." She looked down at her feet.

"Unless you don't want it to be a date, then I guess it doesn't have to be. This is what I should have done to start with. I should have asked you to dinner, rather than have you come to my house in the middle of the night like some booty call."

"It wasn't like that, Jack. I know that."

"Caleb was right to call me out. You know that, right?"

"We will not discuss that right now. I'm mad at you both for that display of stupidity."

"Brush your hair, woman. You look like you just tumbled out of my bed."

"I did."

"I know. You're going to be right back in it with no breakfast if you don't hurry up."

A wistful expression crossed her face and she smiled. "Yes, sir."

"Oh I like that." He smirked.

"Don't get used to it." She pulled a brush out of her bag and started yanking it through the mass.

He closed his fingers around the hand that held the brush and guided her to sit on the couch with him, back turned. She'd taken care of him; he could do the same for her.

And he wanted to touch her hair.

With the whiskey out of his system, he wanted to see what it smelled like. Or if he'd lost the vanilla and sugar forever.

He leaned forward, gliding the brush gently through her tresses, and he was mollified to discover she still smelled so very sweet.

"Jack, you don't have to do that," she said, wiggling with a little shiver.

"I want to. I've always loved your hair." Each stroke down through the mass soothed something in him that he didn't know needed soothing.

"Does it smell like your shampoo and soap after last night?"

"No, it still smells like sugar." He leaned against her and inhaled deeply. She shivered again, but settled back into him so that he could continue as he wished.

Jack drew the brush through her hair a few more

times after it lay smooth and neat, just for the pleasure of touching it and being close to her. He liked the way it clung to his fingers, the way she leaned against him.

"You know, we don't have to go out. We could stay in." She shifted against him.

"We could." Part of him wanted to. It would be easier to hide, easier to lose himself inside her, but India was right. He had to do this wholeheartedly. And that meant going out; it meant being seen and not being afraid to be on display.

It meant treating Betsy the way she deserved.

"But you can't get an Italian chocolate soda at Chez Jack, so it's off to the Pharmacy we go."

"Jack, I know I shouldn't look a gift horse—" she began.

"So don't." He used her own reasoning against her. She'd said the very thing when he told her he didn't want to hurt her.

"You're not funny."

"Okay, fine." He caved. "What?"

"You seem a million times different than last night. You can't just flip a switch and fix everything."

"I didn't. Bets, I don't even know if I can stop drinking on my own. I don't know if I'm an alcoholic or if I'm just self-medicating. Especially with what happened to my father. I know I'm going to fall and stumble. I know it's going to be hard, but India said something that really hit home for me, except I didn't realize it until this morning. That's all I'm ready to talk about, and I hope that can be good enough."

She smiled and as always, it was like turning on the sun. "Yes. Of course."

The short drive to the Corner Pharmacy was traveled in a contemplative silence. He found a place to park and really took in the scenery. He hadn't paid attention to the details since he'd come home.

As much as things changed, they stayed the same. Some of the shops he'd grown up with were gone, making way for other things. New restaurants—he saw the bar his father used to go to all the time…part of him had hoped the last time the Missouri flooded its banks the water would have washed it away. He hated the sight of it.

That wasn't the case for all of the quaint downtown. He had so many good memories from the Corner Pharmacy. Green Rivers were an institution. He had no idea what they put in them—they were almost like a mad scientist's experiment—but he remembered many Saturday mornings spent drinking one and wandering around downtown with his friends looking for trouble.

It hadn't been the thing to sit inside, unless you could get a seat at the lunch counter and swing around on the old-fashioned soda fountain stools. Only old people sat in the booths, which was why Betsy headed for the counter.

But Jack couldn't sit with his back to the masses of people. He had to have something solid against him.

"Can we do a booth?" He hated asking.

"Sure." She didn't balk, or tease him. Just accepted it as something that he needed.

They sat down and he looked at the menu.

"Hey, Betsy-boo." One of the waitresses came over. "How are you, sugar? Haven't seen you in here in a while."

"I know, Connie. I've just been busy with the shop and my mom. I've got some help now on the weekends, so it's been a little easier. You remember Jack?"

The old waitress smiled. "I do. Have you been to see Scott?"

Connie Meyer, he remembered her now, and her son, Scott. "No, ma'am. Bets has been keeping me busy."

"As well she should. Let's see if I can remember. Our Betsy will have a chocolate soda, but you used to drink Green Rivers, right?"

Jack found himself smiling. "Yes, ma'am."

"Anything else this morning? Eggs, bacon, toast?"

"All of it times two," Jack said.

"I'll get that started for you." She scribbled on the pad.

"Wait, that was just for me." Jack grinned at her.

"One of everything for me, too. And a couple of coffees. Thanks, Connie."

"You got it, kid." Connie winked at her and went back behind the counter.

"I forgot how much I used to love this place." He glanced up at the decorative tin tiles on the vaulted ceiling.

He'd been worried that the noise would bother

him, but the nostalgia seemed to block it out—the din was part of the atmosphere.

"When I came back from New York, I was in here every morning. Even though it's nothing like the hustle and bustle of the city, it was still comforting. People gathering around food. I've discovered I really enjoy people-watching over coffee. I'd just sit in this booth, actually, so I could watch everyone, and I'd make up stories about their lives. At least for the people I didn't know."

"It could be fun to make them up about those we do know."

"Like who?"

"Connie."

"You better be nice."

"It's not mean. She knows everyone. What if she's actually a spy? What better way to find out what's going on in a community than the local diner?"

"Oh tell me more."

Jack eyed her for a minute and something sparked in his imagination. "Glory is crawling with military and government employees. There's the base and all of the Department of Defense independent contractors. These people are bound to make friends, to frequent local establishments. A kindly, motherly old waitress would be the perfect cover to plant bugs. A pat on the back, a brush of her hand." Jack shrugged. "Haven't you ever wondered about some of these companies? These little storefronts that have some inane, generic name like 'consultants' or 'Branwell

Solutions.' What the hell is that? Acme Security? It doesn't get any more generic than that."

"Assassins." Betsy nodded sagely.

"In some cases, that's true. It has to be. These guys contract out to the CIA, H.S. and all the other little initialed agencies."

Betsy grinned and shifted in her seat as if digging in for something really good. "What if her name is really Katrina and she was a plant here in the Cold War? She had a son and decided to Americanize him so no one would ever know. He was part of her cover."

"Exactly."

Connie brought their coffee to the table with a smile. "You sure are cheerful on this dreary morning. What's so funny?"

"We decided that your name is Katrina."

"Ekatarina, actually." She winked at them. "Cream?" She set the tiny carafe down on the table.

Betsy's eyes widened and they laughed again. "See, that was much more fun than someone you don't know."

"You should write this stuff down, Jack."

"And then what?"

"Get published, of course," Connie said. "You two can write spying cookbooks together. It'll be a big hit."

"Spying cookbooks?" Betsy arched a perfect eyebrow.

"Yeah. She's a chef and he's a spy and…and wait. This is my book."

"You write?" Jack asked.

"Yeah, for VS Books. Really, write that story you were talking about and I'll give you the name of my agent."

"Why are you still waitressing if you're a writer?" Betsy asked her.

"Insurance and people-watching. You learn a lot about people by serving their food. One of these days, Scottie is going to make me a granny, and when he does, I'll probably quit to devote myself to spoiling that baby full-time." She smiled. "Let me go check on your order."

"Jack, you might have been pretty close to the mark."

"You think Connie is a spy for the former Soviet Union?"

"No, but the way you gave her this history and then to find out all of these things we never would've guessed. There is a lot hiding beneath the small-town veneer. You have to write this book."

"I've never written anything longer than a term paper."

"Writing could be for you what baking is for me. With your imagination, you could lose yourself in it, if you had to. Or maybe just whenever you want to."

"So you want to write spying cookbooks?" Jack tried to turn the subject away from him and writing. Betsy was stuck on it and now he knew whether it was something he wanted to do or not, she'd wring a book out of him.

"No. I want more of these stories. Let's do another one."

"Okay, but it's your turn."

"Me?" Betsy looked around and studied the crowd before indicating to a large, balding man who'd just shoveled himself into one of the half booths. "Mr. Boetcher. Dread of gym students everywhere."

"He looks like he ate a class of students. What happened to him?"

"He says it's an adrenal thing, but I think it's because he eats here three meals and three snacks a day and comes to Sweet Thing for coffee and a second dessert."

"Are we playing still or does he really do that?" Jack raised an eyebrow.

She laughed. He loved the sound. It was musical and light, like silver bells. "He really does that. He was a prima ballerina until a car accident shattered his knee and his dreams. All the steroids she was on turned she into a he and he started lifting weights to deal with her anger issues. As a way to make money on the side, he became a gym teacher."

"That would explain why he was so angry all the time and why he told us constantly that football was an angry dance."

Betsy snorted and brought her napkin up to face, eyes watering, as she tried not to cackle and honk like goose. "Oh my God, Jack. He did not."

"I will swear on a stack of Bibles that he did. Ask Caleb."

Coach Boetcher looked their way and nodded. Jack nodded back with a curt wave.

"You're so much better at this than me. One more? Do Mindy Kreskin."

"Who?"

"Over there, I— Damn," Betsy swore.

Suddenly a woman in skintight leggings, leopard heels and a low-cut blouse bent over the table. "Why, Jack McConnell. That is you." She pushed her way into the booth next to them and if Jack hadn't scooted over for her, the woman would've been in his lap.

"So, what are you two darlings talking about?"

It didn't seem right to share this with her, and he couldn't, for the life of him, remember her name.

"Just conversation," Jack answered.

"I could've sworn I heard her say 'do Mindy Kreskin,' so I came over to volunteer." She flashed a syrupy smile.

Realization dawned bright and sharp. He had, in fact, already done Mindy Kreskin. He'd taken her to homecoming and they'd had sex in the back of his car. Not one of his finer moments.

"Kind of you," he acknowledged.

"How long are you back?"

"I don't have any solid plans at the moment. It's been nice to see everyone, but Betsy and I have a lot of catching up to do." He hoped she'd take that as a dismissal, but instead she took it as an invitation. Her hand rested on his thigh.

"So do we. You should come by. It'll be like the old days."

For as much as nostalgia had comforted him, Jack didn't want the old days. They were over and gone. He leaned over and whispered in her ear, "My injury prevents anything from being like it was in the old days."

"Oh you poor baby." She wasn't fazed.

"Mindy, two of your kids are climbing the counter. You better come mind them," Connie called.

Mindy slid out of the seat and stomped, in her platforms, over to the counter.

"So, Mindy Kreskin." Jack nodded. "Head cheerleader, who was not so good at giving head, got knocked up end of senior year. She doesn't have a job, but keeps getting pregnant to get a man to stay. Currently doesn't have one."

"That one was right on the money. She just had baby number four."

Jack shuddered.

"And just think that could have been your life."

"I'd hang myself."

"She told me the night of homecoming—"

"Wait, how did you see her the night of homecoming?"

"I snuck out, of course," Betsy said as if it were the most obvious thing in the world. "Anyway, she came outside and found me seething in the bushes."

"Why were you seething?"

"Why do you think? Will you let me finish my story?"

"Sorry, go on." His mouth turned up into a grin.

"She told me that I should hurry up and get you

out of my system because she was going to marry you." Betsy pursed her lips as if the memory still knotted her panties.

"Whoa. That's crazy." He thought women like that were only caricatures on bad sitcoms and teen movies.

"Jack, for being a smart guy, sometimes you're not so bright. Her mom was the head cheerleader and married the quarterback. That's what she was taught to aspire to."

"That's just sad."

"Why?" Betsy cocked her head to the side.

"What do you mean, why? Weren't we just talking about how sad and pathetic she is?"

"Yes, she is, but not because she had dreams of getting married and having a family."

"That's not what I meant."

"Oh it was. You can't imagine having never left here, never tried to see the world." She said this like an accusation.

"That is foreign to me, but I came back, didn't I?"

"Only for me. You never would've given this place a second thought if I wasn't here."

"Is that so bad?" Didn't she want to be the reason he came back? What else was here for him?

"Maybe not. Do you still want to be out in the big world, Jack?"

"I don't know. I hadn't thought about it."

"You should." She said this decisively, like a primary-school teacher assigning homework.

Their food arrived and when he took the first

sip of his Green River, he was disheartened that he couldn't taste it.

Or the toast, with its real sweet cream butter.

Or the eggs that looked fried to perfection and just a bit peppery.

The bacon, however, was an experience in decadence. He tasted salt.

It was sharp and stark on is tongue, but he liked it. It reminded him of a plethora of salty things that were all tied to memory. Blood, sweat and tears. They were all salt.

But so was sex.

Betsy and bacon. The best flavors in the world. He might have decided he liked the salt better than the sugar.

CHAPTER TWELVE

JACK WASN'T READY to say goodbye to Betsy on Saturday, but she had things she had to do for Sweet Thing, her mother and the life she had that didn't consist of playing nursemaid to him.

So he walked around downtown exploring some more. Revisiting his past.

The stunted half howl of a police siren caught his attention.

Caleb rolled down the window. "You want a ride?"

"Depends on where we're going."

"My house. I'm on my own for lunch. India's stopping by her mother's."

"So you guys do everything together? Does she burp you and change your diaper, as well?" Jack taunted.

"Some days," Caleb agreed good-naturedly.

He opened the door and slid into the car. "Look, man, I'm not going to say I'm sorry for what happened at your house. I'm not."

"Didn't ask you to."

"If you screw up with Bets, it's going to happen again."

"Fair enough."

"You're too cheery and way too accepting. What happened to the guy who was going to kick my ass for telling him to stay away from my sister?"

"He talked to India. And Betsy."

Caleb drove the short distance to Esplanade and to the ragged old Victorian he was restoring in his off time. "I, uh." Caleb stumbled over the words. "I'm still here for you."

Jack knew that, too. "Sometimes there are some things that can only be said with a good sparring. It's my own fault I didn't get the gear."

"Yeah, well, I've got a billon hours of community service to do to keep my job."

"That sucks. Didn't we get community service that time we toilet-papered the Oskaloosa mascot?"

"I think the police chief is that judge's cousin or something." Caleb snorted.

When they pulled up to the house, Jack said, "Looks like the project is coming along."

"Yeah." He tossed him a block of wood that had fine-grained sandpaper wrapped around it. "This is great for thinking. A lot of time in your own head." Caleb handed him a piece of lattice trim. "Sanding off the ugly is meticulous work."

"Don't I know it." Jack didn't balk at the work, not even that Caleb just expected him to do it. That's how things were done. They'd spent many a summer afternoon doing this for neighbors. At fourteen, they'd started a "business" together where they did odd jobs for spending money.

It felt good to have something to do with his hands

again. Something where there was a physical measure of his effort. He felt useful.

"Are you going to sell it when you're done?"

"To India. This was her favorite house on the street."

"I'd forgotten that. She told us her life would be perfect if she could just live in this house." Jack studied his friend. "You didn't tell her you bought it for her, did you?"

"I sure didn't." Caleb grinned. "You know how she is, but I couldn't tell her now if I wanted to. She'd always think it would be some debt she owed me. Hmm. I wonder why that sounds familiar." He eyed Jack.

"Because it would be. You bought her a house. The Badass Barbie dream house. It's not like you loaned her a hundred bucks to get her by until payday. For someone who's never had what you and Betsy have with your family, it's a big deal."

"Shut up with that. You and India are both part of our family."

"Yes, but it's just not the same." Sometimes Caleb was just as wholesomely naive as Betsy. No, *naive* wasn't the right word. Maybe the word he was looking for was *whole*. He'd never had to listen to his parents fighting and wonder if there'd be food on the table. Neither his mother nor his father had ever laid hands on him to hurt him as India's had.

Caleb rolled his eyes. "I'll see you later. Are you coming to dinner tomorrow?"

"No, I've actually got a thing. I promised Betsy I'd go."

"You're going to the support group she was talking about?"

"Yeah. I told her I'd check it out. I don't know if it's going to work for me, but I told her I'd try."

Caleb nodded. "I'm glad."

"The doc from the Center for the Intrepid set up individual therapy sessions, but I haven't gone."

"Maybe you should?"

"Yeah. I guess." They were both noncommittal, but a wealth of things surged and roiled under the surface.

"Good. You'll be missed, though. Mama was glad you came last week."

"It was good to see her. To see India. To see you."

"You're always welcome, brother."

"Even though I'm sleeping with your sister?" Jack teased.

Caleb cringed. "Yeah, if you could *not* mention that ever again, that would be good."

"I'll keep that in mind when your dad comes home."

"He'll be home at Christmas. He would have been back sooner, but something happened and they needed him to stay in Sicily. He'd love to see you, though."

"I'm not stupid. The man is an analyst for the Department of Defense. I know what *that* means." Jack stuffed his hands in his pockets, and silence reigned.

Caleb locked up his tools inside the house. "Do you want a lift home?"

"No, actually. I want to walk." He said his good-bye and headed down the quaint brick sidewalk. He especially liked the places where he could see the brick street underneath the new pavement. It required more concentration to keep his balance, but he liked it anyway. Jack enjoyed the walk across town back to his house. He took joy in the simple fact that he *could* walk home.

He hadn't realized the town he'd tried so hard to get away from would be the balm he needed. A good deal of it was Betsy, but it was the people, too. Like Connie at the Corner Pharmacy. Even Mindy Kreskin. These people, these streets, they reminded him of himself. Not of only his past, but his present, too.

He cast a glance to the sky overhead and found it clear, but that didn't mean much in this part of the country. Even though it had been a good day, better than he could've expected, Jack waited for the storm.

He waited for the black, gritty reminder of the dark. Pretty words, pretty people and kind smiles didn't take away what had happened or the places he'd been. He wondered if the thunder, the lightning, would always put him back in the dark and bring the fear that made him little more than an animal.

If a storm rolled in right at that moment, would he have to run for cover?

He knew he would.

Jack was determined to try to pass the night with no whiskey. Even if the nightmares came, he wanted the things he'd seen that were possible more than he wanted relief.

After all, if it was just relief he wanted, he could have filled every chamber in his .357 with a round.

CHAPTER THIRTEEN

JACK DIDN'T SLEEP.

He closed his eyes, but all he could see behind his lids was fire. His throat had been dry all night, his mouth cottony, and that amber liquid beckoned with a siren's song promising him sleep, tranquility and peace.

Though like a siren's song, he knew it to be a lie, and also like a siren, it would swallow him whole.

Every sound the house made caused him to go on alert, and every possible scenario crept through his head, a stealthy poison. What-if played on a continuous loop until he gave up and turned on Netflix. He clicked on the first movie that popped up and stared blankly at the screen, grateful for the distraction and faux company.

He dreamed, and he knew he was in a dreamscape. He was so thirsty, his throat parched and gritty. There'd been days when he knew what that felt like, to have sand up his nose, down his throat, in his ears, the corners of his eyes...

Jack was on fire, flames all around him, but through it all, he could see Betsy in the distance. He knew if he could just get to her, she could make the pain stop. He ran and ran, but he never got any closer to her. She was still just as far off as she'd been when he started.

When he awoke, fevered and sweating, he knew exactly what the dream meant. He was looking to someone else to put out his fires when he had to do it himself. Jack knew that. He didn't need some dream to tell him.

His stomach roiled and his head pounded. Jack felt as if he'd been run over by a Mack truck. He had a hangover from *not* drinking. The light coming in the windows was bright and hurt his eyes. It made his head pound harder and feel as if his skull were trying to slide out through his nose.

He stumbled from the couch to the kitchen, where he poured himself a glass of water and popped a couple ibuprofens and fish oil caplets.

Part of him wanted to call Betsy, curl up in her and lose himself. The only pain he wanted was to feel her digging her nails into his back while he made her come. He was under no illusions that he'd be in any kind of shape to be in her presence after the group.

He'd tried a support group once before, but all of the emotional vomit followed by backslapping and regurgitated self-help affirmations made him nauseated. He hadn't been ready for it then, but he was ready to try it now. Affirmations and all, if that's what it took.

Around four that afternoon, a knock on the door surprised him.

Betsy stood outside the screen, eyes hopeful and tremulous, with one of those purple boxes. "Hey."

"That for me?"

"Sort of. It's for you to take with you to group. If you're still going."

He accepted the box and peeked under the lid. "What flavor?"

"More of the anise pumpkin with cinnamon smiles. I made way too many of those. I also thought maybe I could give you a ride. You took me to the river all the time, so I'd like to. If that's okay."

"Yeah, Bets." Something in him warmed.

"Do you want me to stay with you?"

"No, I'll be okay. You go on and have dinner with your family. I'll walk home after the meeting."

"That's a long way."

"It is, but you know, I *can* do it." That was important to him, to be able to do those things.

"I'm still advocating the trade thing we have going on." Color stained her cheeks. "I asked you to go and I know it's a big deal, so maybe think about what you want for your turn."

"So this would be the time to ask for something big?" he teased.

"Whatever you want, Jack." She bit her lip.

He couldn't look at her mouth now and not think about the shower, her lush lips wrapped around his shaft, but he'd had that. He wanted a fantasy of her that he hadn't experienced. Something to store up and keep. Something that only felt good, with no bad memories attached. The shower could never be a bad memory, but it had been born out of desperation and panic, rooted in fear.

"The kitchen in Sweet Thing. I want you to bake for me."

"I already bake for you. All the time, I'm thinking about what you'd like, what you can taste."

"No, Betsy." He let his gaze rake over her slowly, memorizing every curve and remembering what it was like to have his hands all over them. "The fantasy we talked about. You. Naked. Cookies."

"Monday after the shop closes. Four," she said shyly.

Jack found it to be a paradox that when she was naked, she'd say or do most anything, but dressed and in the light of day, she blushed so sweetly.

"The things I'm going to do to you, sweet thing."

"You can't get too carried away until whatever you decide you want me to bake for you is done or we'll burn the place down."

"We might anyway." He flashed a naughty half grin. This was when he felt the most confident. Jack knew he brought her pleasure. He knew just how and where to touch her, how to play her body like a finely tuned instrument. This was something he excelled at.

She put the cookies on the table and embraced him. "I want you, Jack. I want you so bad it hurts. Maybe you should come to the bakery tonight."

He wasn't going to turn her down, but he still wanted to wait for his fantasy until it was free and clear from the dark. "I still want my day on Monday."

"Most definitely. Maybe Tuesday, too. Wednesday, if you're not busy…"

"I like how your brain works."

"Maybe then we should have a quickie before you go. Right here up against the wall, if you're feeling spry, soldier." She winked at him.

He was instantly hard and feeling more than spry. He felt as if he could conquer the world.

"I may not be wearing panties," Betsy said, spurring him on.

"You're a bad girl, Betsy. You wear this sweet little face, but deep inside," he said as he pushed his hand up beneath her dress and between her thighs, "deep, deep down—" Jack thrust his fingers into her heat "—you're all kinds of bad, aren't you?"

"Mmm-hmm," she agreed, wriggling to get closer to the sensation.

"This right now is my turn, too. Because I said so. I want to take something good with me, and this is what I'm going to remember," he said as he manipulated her swollen flesh. "Not the pretty image of swollen lips after I kissed you and you said goodbye. Not the past, but now. Here."

She moaned and rubbed herself against him. "Now is so good."

"Yes, it is." Her responsive body, slick and hot for him, was better than anything she could've said to him, anything she could've done.

For the first time, even though Jack was still

waiting for the storm, he wondered if the sunny days like this one would be enough to balance out the darkness.

CHAPTER FOURTEEN

BETSY WAS SO proud of Jack for going to the support group.

She hoped that he meant what he said, about getting his life back.

The look in his eyes that morning as he'd held the .357 in his hands—it had been a grim determination. A sorrow. Even a sense of horrible purpose. She'd felt so many things in that moment. Acute loss, pain for him and how much he suffered to have considered something so awful, and anger. Anger because he was failing her, wanting to abandon her like everyone else.

When the thought resonated, she realized that was truly how she felt. Even though Caleb and India were still in her life and she still had her mother, she felt as if everyone had left her alone and she had no one. It was a revelation because Betsy wasn't *that* girl. She knew she had so much to be thankful for.

Guilt flooded her that during his darkest moment, she'd been worried about herself and how his actions would affect her. For as long as she'd known Jack, he'd always put her first. When he pasted that fake smile on his face, she knew that was for her benefit, too.

Until he told her he could taste the bacon. She smiled thinking of it.

It was a big deal to drop him off for the support-group meeting, both in that he was going and that he let her drive him. He had a hard time asking for or accepting help in any part of his life. But this dinner today was going to be a moment of reckoning. Caleb had had no right to do what he did to Jack. He'd already felt bad enough about something that was an accident. He hadn't actually hurt her. Jack was probably in more pain about having bruised her than the bruises themselves caused her.

Betsy passed her mother in the hall. "Where is my brother? I saw his car."

"He's hiding in his old room."

"If you hear crashes or bangs, don't worry. I'm just beating the stupid out of him."

"He's a Lewis man. There's no beating the stupid out of him," Lula said absently as she continued on into the kitchen to mind what smelled like pot roast.

"Is that roast?"

"Yes, it's what Caleb wanted today. He put in a special request."

"Why do we ever deviate from the fried chicken? I really wanted fried chicken. That's another reason to hit him."

"If you punch him, you won't be able to knead the dough for your bread. You know he's got a jaw like a brick." Lula's nonchalant attitude had been born from years of her children inflicting terror and revenge on each other. This wasn't anything new. "Don't break anything of mine. You know, when you both moved out, I thought I could finally have nice things." She sighed.

"If he wouldn't do stupid things, this wouldn't be a problem." Betsy stomped up the stairs in a fury and flung open the door to his room like the reckoning she planned to deliver.

"Look, Betsy. Be mad. But there are some things that are sacred against all outside influences. Or even inside. You're my sister. He hurt you." Caleb held up his hands either in surrender or maybe to block her blows.

"He *didn't*. Are you going to come beat up my oven every time I burn myself? Think about the logic there."

"The oven is your own fault. You know it's hot. The oven doesn't have a conscious choice about its actions."

"Neither did Jack. He was asleep."

"Betsy, there is nothing you can say or do to defend him that's going to make it okay. But we worked it out. After India Tased us."

"She Tased you, too?"

"Yeah." Caleb looked uncomfortable. "You know, with all of this, he was hurting himself, too. It was a guy thing."

"A guy thing? No, not buying it. Every time you do something I don't agree with, you say it's a guy thing. That's not cutting it. Speaking of India, where is she? I can't wait to hear this story." Discomfort changed to outright pain. "What happened?" Betsy put her hand on his shoulder.

He raked his hand through his hair. "I can't tell her story for her, you know?"

Betsy nodded. "I understand. But when we were talking about Jack, she said she knew how haunted he was and how broken. I think it's not because she sees his pain, but because something happened to her, too. She told me not to give up on him, and it seemed important for her to know that no matter what, I wouldn't." She hugged her brother. "I also told her that she can trust you and that no matter what happened to her, you'd understand and you wouldn't give up on her, either."

"I'd like to think that she knows that." He hung his head. "She's really pissed at me."

"So am I." Betsy sighed and deflated. "But I still love you."

"We're quite the pair, aren't we?"

"Yeah."

"So Jack actually went to the support group?"

Betsy nodded. "I dropped him off and watched him go inside."

"You were checking up on him to see if he was really going to go."

A hot blush stained her cheeks. "Well, yes."

"If he told you he'd go, you know he would. He doesn't lie."

Except that one time that he did.

She'd never get that image of him out of her head.

Jack sitting in the shaft of sunlight, his fingers curled around—

"Hey, Bets?" Caleb cocked his head to the side. "I don't know where you just went in your head, but it was a bad place and you don't need to go there again. Jack's going to be fine. He has you. He has me. No matter what, even if I beat him senseless, he's still family. And he knows it."

"Does he?"

"I shouldn't be doing this, but since you shared some info about India with me, I'll tell you. I saw him yesterday and we talked. He came over to the house and sanded some trim with me over lunch."

"Sanding some trim? Is that what the kids are calling it these days?" Betsy quoted Jack from the last Sunday dinner when he'd been teasing Caleb and India.

"Very funny, Bets. If you weren't such a girl, I'd think you were a man."

"Anyway, back to the important stuff. You. Jack. Trim?"

"He said he was pretty sure you saved his life, and before you pounce and rattle me like a maraca trying to find out what else he said, that was it. He said he wasn't ready to talk about it more than just that."

"Well, he saved mine. So it's only fair."

"I told him that, too. But if your accounts are in the clear, do you still want to be with him?"

"Why? Did he say something?" Betsy realized she sounded as if she were still in high school.

"Didn't I just say he didn't have anything else

to say on the matter? I'm asking because I want to know. I need to know."

"Oh whatever. You can't drop a statement like that on me and not expect to get a reaction."

"Betsy!" Lula called from the door. "There's a call for you."

Her first thought was that something had happened to Jack. She dashed downstairs.

"Hello?" If it wasn't Jack, she hoped it was her dad. She missed him when he was away. She didn't worry, because that would only drive her crazy.

"Betsy?" A voice with a light French accent was on the other end of the line. A voice she hadn't heard in a very long time.

Marcel.

So many things flooded back over her. The elation when she discovered her interest had been returned by the blue-eyed Frenchman. The first time he made her truffles. The look on his face when she told him she was leaving Paris—absolute disdain and disgust. Both at her and her small-town life.

"How are you?" she finally managed to ask.

"Very well, *chérie.* Very well. I am back in New York for the week and I would like to see you."

He'd like to see her? Yes, because she just had that kind of money sitting around and a clear schedule. More important, why did he want to see her? When they'd broken up, he said he couldn't associate with failure. And that she was. Betsy had become the laughingstock. Everyone in the culinary community knew the story of the stupid American ingenue and the death cap bordelaise. "Come to Kansas if you really want to see me," she said.

"If I must. I have something very important to tell you. I want to do it in person." His voice was filled with excitement.

"We could Skype."

"No, no. In person, it must be. When can you come?" He sounded so excited.

Just like him not to listen. "I told you, I can't. I've got responsibilities here. I have my own shop now." Why had she told him that? He'd find a way to belittle her accomplishment, damn her with faint praise. Then the joy she found in her little shop would be tainted. She'd be reminded every day how it wasn't good enough. How *she* wasn't good enough. Betsy hung up the phone before he could say another word.

The phone rang again almost instantly.

With her heard thundering in her chest, she answered it.

"*Chérie,* I think we were disconnected."

Yeah, because I hung up on you. "That must've been what happened."

"Everything is going to change for you. I have such wonderful news."

She was curious, even though she knew whatever he had to say was always painted with the impossible. Like now. *Come to New York,* as if people like her could just do that with no thought for anything or anyone else.

"I mean it, Marcel. If it's so important that you can't do it on the phone or Skype, then you have to come here." Oh what was she saying? She didn't want him to come here. She didn't want to see him again no matter what his news was. He could tell her he'd laid a golden egg and it hatched twin diamond ducks and that still didn't warrant his presence.

"*Oui.* That is just like you. So demanding of your own way." He sighed as if she were a child to be indulged. "I will come."

No! What had she done? She opened her mouth to tell him not to, and he'd hung up. Betsy had enough on her plate without dealing with Marcel's presence. Maybe she could have Caleb arrest him as soon as he crossed the county line?

"Who was that?" Caleb asked from behind her.

"Marcel."

"The stain in the NYC pictures?"

"Yes. That's the one."

"What did he want?"

"For me to go to New York because he's in town."

"I hope you told him to take a flying fu—"

"Language!" their mother yelled from the kitchen. Sometimes it was as if she had supersonic hearing.

For a brief moment, Betsy wondered if her mother had heard her encounter with Jack. That was too horrible a possibility to even consider. "I said no, but then he said he had some news that he wanted to tell me in person. And stupid me, I told him if he wanted to tell me in person he'd just have to come here. So he is."

"I really hope that even if he offers you the Holy Grail you say no."

"Why is that?" She cocked her head to the side.

"Because when you came back from Paris, you weren't the same. It was more than the mushrooms."

"Well, yeah. I drop-kicked all my dreams into a steaming pile of buffalo crap. Of course I'm not the same. Whatever Marcel has to say, it's too late."

"It's never too late. Isn't that what you've been trying to tell Jack? Kind of hard to convince someone else of something that you don't believe yourself, isn't it?"

"The internship was a onetime thing."

"There are other chefs to study under. Other people with gifts as wonderful and other people who've made mistakes. What if he's found some way for you to have your dream?"

"I thought you just said even if he offered me the Holy Grail—"

"I changed my mind. If you can live your dream, you should. Glory was never what you wanted."

What about Jack? She wasn't thinking about her dreams of a career, of living in Paris, of going back to NYC or seeing and experiencing the world. She just wanted to hide herself and Jack away from all of it in the safe cocoon of his bed. "I doubt he's done anything for me. Although I can't think why he would come here to tell me anything. There's nothing that could be that important. *I* was never that important to him."

"Stop with the woe is me. So what if you weren't? He can be a means to an end, and as long as you remember that's all he is, what does it matter what he thought of you or said to you?"

"I don't know what my dreams are now," she confessed.

"You should always be dreaming, Betsy. Mom told us that every night of our lives, that we should always dream awake."

"What about the shop?" she offered weakly. "Say he did have some amazing opportunity. I can't just leave my business."

"What about it? We can cover that—India, Mom and I. If you want it, we can make it happen. You've been so busy trying to take care of everyone else, you've forgotten to take care of you. I thought maybe this thing with Jack was you taking care of you, but he's another crusade."

"He's not!"

"Maybe you don't know it yet, but he is."

"I was in love with him long before he lost his leg."

"Are you in love with him still? Or the idea of him?"

Betsy didn't like how the question made her feel. Unsure and awkward, itchy like bugs on her skin. "We're getting to know each other again. So I can't answer that the way you want me to. I love him, of course. He is family. But…" She couldn't put it into words and she wasn't quite ready to do so, either.

Caleb put his hands on her shoulders. "Betsy, you're one of the kindest, most loving people I know. That said, you're also used to getting what you want.

Make sure that what you're doing isn't just finally getting that toy that never showed up under the tree. That you're not replacing Paris with Jack."

"How do you go from punching him in the face to protecting him from me?"

"I don't know. Talent?"

She rolled her eyes. "Can you please just stay out of it?"

"No."

It seemed the storm had passed, and Betsy knew it would. She knew what Caleb had done had been because he cared about her, but he wasn't helping. She wished she and Jack could escape it all and just be Jack and Betsy without all the entanglement and meddling from other people.

Even if they were people she loved.

CHAPTER FIFTEEN

JACK DIDN'T LIKE the smell of the place.

It was sterile and smelled...*institutional.* That had a flavor, too. It was like bleach and mold—a strange and unnatural combination.

Jack inhaled the scent of Betsy's cookies. They wiped away everything bad. There was a table at the far corner of the wall with coffee, some store-bought cookies and a pitcher of water. Nothing looked very appetizing. He didn't want to put the cookies on the table; he wanted to hold them close like a security blanket.

They reminded him of why he wanted to be here.

Jack took a cookie out of the box and bit into it. He couldn't taste the pumpkin, but the little Red Hots smile on the face burned his tongue. It was spicy.

He took another bite.

It seemed right somehow that this moment would taste like cinnamon—sharp but still palatable. He didn't know if he could say it was pleasant yet. Threaded through with the rest of the cookie, and dulled by the texture, it was something that met two needs. Jack could do this.

He snatched two more cookies from the box before sacrificing the rest on the table.

"You're going to be popular," a voice said from behind him.

He turned to see a kid who couldn't be any older than a minute. He looked impossibly young, but lean and hungry as if he knew what it was like to starve. As if he could glut himself on the world and still, he'd never be sated. Even with his youth, there was something haunted in his eyes. Jack recognized it because he'd seen it in the mirror.

"Why is that?" Jack asked.

"All of the guys love to see those boxes from Sweet Thing."

Jack's first instinct was to put his fist through the kid's face. He took a deep breath and reminded himself that the kid meant Betsy's shop, not Betsy herself. He couldn't know that was his nickname for Betsy. God, but he had to get a handle on this rage thing.

He wasn't normally a jealous man. He wasn't wired that way. Betsy had become something holy to him, and he knew she wasn't. She was a flesh-and-blood woman the same as he was simply a man.

"I almost ate them all myself," he managed to say.

"I would have." The kid grabbed one. "I'm O'Neil."

"McConnell." He shook the kid's hand that wasn't full of cookie.

"You're the guy they gave the medal to."

"Yeah, that's me." What else was he supposed

to say to that? All of that made him uncomfortable. He'd done his duty and his job; it was nothing special.

"Miss Sweet Thing herself was there that day, wasn't she?"

"Look, O'Neil. If you want to keep your face, don't talk about my girl."

He held up his hands. "Whoa, I didn't know. None of us did. All the guys are going to be heartbroken to hear it. Good for you, man."

Dick-broken was more like it, his brain growled. He realized that he might have spoken out of line. Betsy had never agreed to be his. Jack was in a support group for PTSD, for fuck's sake. He wasn't fit for a relationship.

Nevertheless, she's mine. He'd deal with that later.

He stuffed another cookie in his mouth and wandered over to the circle of chairs. That sensation where his skin was too tight and itchy was back, like a swarm of bugs crawling all over him.

Jack tried to find a seat where he wouldn't have his back to a door, or exposed. There was no such luck. He just knew he was going to have some freak-out before this was over.

"Looking for somewhere to sit so you're not exposed? Yeah. Not so much. We just have to trust each other to watch everyone's back. I think that's part of it," O'Neil said. "Sometimes the new guys sit on the floor against the far wall."

No, he wasn't going to do this. He knew where he

was. He was home. He could sit down like a regular person and have a conversation.

Couldn't he?

Everyone took their seats and nodded to each other in silent acknowledgment. Jack searched all of their faces and in each one, he saw a brother. No matter how age had marked them, or youth still smiled on them, no matter anything else about them, what bonded them all together was in their eyes. A soul-deep wound that festered.

Jack was immediately comforted by the fact that he wasn't alone, but he ached for his brothers, too. He didn't wish his pain, or terror, on anyone. Not even to know he wasn't alone in the dark.

An older man wearing jeans and a polo shirt sat down in a chair that seemed to have been left open for him. He wore a tag on his shirt that read Volunteer.

"I see we have a new face tonight." He held out his hand for Jack to shake. He had a firm grip, solid. "I'm Andrew."

"Jack."

"Glad you're here, Jack. Wait for me after group and we'll talk, if you like."

Jack nodded.

Andrew addressed the rest of the group. "So, last time we were listening to O'Neil's story. Is everyone okay with picking up where we left off?"

O'Neil swallowed hard, but he lifted his shoulders and straightened his spine. "It wasn't a good week.

Sharma took the baby and left. I can't blame her. If I could leave me, too, I would."

They waited, quiet and still, for him to continue. A heavy weight settled over the room, like a blanket, a shroud…the lid of a coffin.

"The storm. Lightning struck the house and it was a trigger. I took her and Caty downstairs and I wouldn't let them leave. It wasn't the storm outside, it was insurgents. They were trying to kill us and no matter what she said to me, I wouldn't believe we were home, safe. She got a restraining order and because of the gun, I can't see my daughter. I'm going to lose my job. I'm an M.P. I wanted to go into civilian law enforcement when I get out in June, and that's not going to happen."

"I thought we agreed you were going to store your personal weapons for now?" Andrew asked him gently.

"I couldn't. I just couldn't leave them unprotected."

Andrew nodded. "But didn't we decide together, as a group, that Sharma and Caty would be safer?"

"I couldn't."

Jack could see his own pain, his own fear reflected in the boy's eyes.

Andrew seemed to sense that O'Neil needed a breather. "What about everyone else? How did you come through the storm?"

It wasn't just Jack. These men around him were all strong men, all brave men, and they'd feared the storm, as well. That knowledge was both a blade and a balm.

Another man spoke. "I did okay. My wife and I spent the night in the basement watching eighties movies with a bottle of rum."

"That's really good, Bobby."

A bottle of rum is really good?

Jack's incredulity must've shown on his face, because the guy spoke again. "I know, right? That is good. A year ago, I would've been sloppy drunk by myself with my weapon in hand and I might not have made it through the night."

"What about you, Jack? You're here. You might as well jump in with both feet," Andrew said.

"It never gets any easier to share. You just have to do it," O'Neil added.

Jack took a deep breath, filling his lungs and concentrating on that sensation of feeling full, of feeling alive. He didn't want to share those intimate moments with Betsy. Those were his—only his. Especially because these guys knew who she was and had talked about her. "That's me every Saturday morning," he confessed.

No one said anything and there was no judgment on the faces that watched him, no pity. Just empathy and understanding.

"I, uh, I'm supposed to be dead. I lost my leg to an IED. When the device was launched into our camp, I was prepared to die to save my brothers. Only I didn't die. After a bright flash and pain like I've never felt before, a burn so hot it was cold, I woke up in Ramstein with a limb I don't have still burning and a nurse whispering in my ear to remember my promise." Jack breathed again, focused on the act of inhaling, exhaling. Normal functions of life. "I was sure fate had screwed up. It's okay for me to be a name on a wall somewhere. It's okay to have given my life for something bigger than me, but I'm still alive with no life to live. I'm on medical discharge, my career taken from me. I'm no use to anyone. So every Saturday morning, my .357 and I give fate a chance to fix its mistake."

"So then why are you here? If you think fate made a mistake?" Andrew asked.

"The girl I made a promise to? I told her I'd come home. I was pretty pissed at her for demanding that promise from me. When the nurse asked her if there was anything she should tell me because they were sure I was dying, she said to remind me of my promise. And I never break my promises. So I came back."

"And she saw you on a Saturday morning, didn't she?" Andrew asked.

He nodded. Glad that the man had filled that part in for him. He didn't want to share their intimacies. Didn't want to expose what was between them to others just as broken as he was. "She did, and even though she asked me to come, she's not why I'm here."

"No?" Andrew asked.

"I decided that maybe I shouldn't be arguing with fate. I want to live. And what I've got right now isn't living." Warmth unfurled in his chest. It felt good to say these things. To put the words out in the world.

"You were in Mosul," Bobby said, something like wonder in his voice.

Jack nodded. "A lot of us were."

"No, it was you. You're the reason I came home. What are the chances, man?" Bobby got up out of the chair and came over and clapped him on the back. "I...used to blame you for saving us. Kind of like you blaming fate. Then I met my wife and I knew why I'd been saved. To be with her."

The itchy feeling was back. Jack didn't like being praised for killing, even though it was something else he was good at. "Glad you made it home."

Bile rose in his throat. This was what he'd saved him for? Nights spent drowning in rum because he thought he'd end up back in that hell? Death might've been kinder.

Andrew keyed to his distress instantly. "Do you want to tell us about Mosul, Jack?"

"I was captured and then I wasn't." He didn't want to talk about it.

"Okay, Jack. That's a good start. Maybe another time, when you're ready."

He'd thought his trauma was from losing his leg, but in that moment, he knew he'd been using it as a crutch. *Ah, the fucking irony, there.* Killing was his job, but he'd lost himself in Mosul—after the torture.

Jack chewed on that for the rest of the meeting. He didn't hear much else that was said, but at his last cookie, slowly chewing it until it disintegrated in his mouth, it reminded him that he'd made it home from Mosul.

That all the guys in this room had come home, even if they'd left pieces of their soul over in the desert.

He reminded himself that didn't matter, that whatever he'd left over there could stay. They could keep it. They'd paid for it in blood, too. There was more than ash, more than this. There was Betsy, there was bacon...

"Jack?" Andrew's voice came from somewhere far away.

He looked up and was snapped back into the present. All the chairs were empty and the purple Sweet Thing box was gone. "Sorry. I was lost for a minute."

"Yes, you were." Andrew nodded. "You did a brave thing today, coming, sharing. I hope you come back."

"It's worse than I thought it would be, but it's better, too."

"A lot of guys say that. If you're interested in supplementing with private therapy, I have a practice." Andrew handed him a card. "I give this card to everyone. It has my cell number on it and I answer it 24/7. You can always call me. Even if you're not my patient."

"Thanks." Jack stuffed the card in his pocket.

"I really do hope you decide to talk about what happened. We've all heard what it was like from Bobby's point of view. I think it would be good for him and the rest of the group to see how it affected you."

"What do you mean?" Jack's skin got tighter, if

that was possible. He felt as if one more word would be the thing that sliced him open and spilled his guts all over the floor.

"He's made you superhuman in his memory and why he thought of himself as a failure for so long. He was sure that the man who'd done those things couldn't possibly have to deal with any fear, or pain."

"That day I didn't. I turned it off. That wasn't something to be admired," Jack confessed.

"Many of my patients say that, too. Now you just have to learn there is no shame in surviving."

Jack nodded. "Maybe I can try next week."

"You know we meet tomorrow, too?"

"I have plans tomorrow."

"With the girl you made your promise to?"

"That's the one."

"Will she be sending any more cookies? I didn't get one." Andrew grinned.

"I'm sure she will. She hands out what doesn't sell over the weekend here on Monday mornings."

"She sounds like an angel."

"She is." Jack was uncomfortable talking about her now. He didn't know how things stood between them, what he wanted and what was just a pie-in-the-sky dream that got him through the night.

"Okay, then. Until next week." Andrew walked him to the door. "Don't forget, if you need me, call. Day or night."

"Thanks." Jack walked out into the evening, the air just a bit chilly and the stars just beginning to peek out from their cloudy nests.

He was so conflicted, his wounds raw again, but he didn't feel as if he'd been picking at a scab. It felt purposeful. Like resurfacing a wound so it could heal. If that was really what would happen here, he was ready to put in the work.

Jack tried to avoid Fourth Street while he walked. It was a main drag that was dangerously busy. One of the old-timers who worked out at the state prison rode his bicycle to work every day and had been hit four times. Stubborn bastard said it kept him young. He was in his nineties, so maybe there was some truth to that.

Jack disliked walking in this area because it was so congested and more modern, but once the businesses gave way to the old Victorian houses and the places in the road where he could still see the brick, he enjoyed the journey. He found that for as much as he'd longed to be out in the world, for a big life, he liked the quaint downtown area and the small-town charm.

Even if it meant putting up with the town busybody dropping off a casserole he refused to eat every Thursday.

He'd thought that after the meeting, he wouldn't feel like talking to anyone, that everything would be raw and painful. It was raw, but it was okay. He was glad Betsy had asked him over tonight, because he needed something normal, something good.

The back of Sweet Thing came into view and he realized Betsy had been living above the shop when she wasn't helping her mother. A small, flowered deck cradled the back entrance and sported a table and chairs with overstuffed pink cushions. He could picture her there in the early mornings with a cup of coffee, her hair in a bun, wearing a crisp white apron as she watched the sun come up.

He made his way up the stairs and knocked.

When she opened the door, her eyes were red-rimmed and puffy. All thoughts of his own needs fled.

"What's wrong?"

"It's stupid."

"Whatever it is, it's not stupid." He wrapped her in his arms and suddenly, for all of her ferocity and strength, she was small and breakable. Whatever it was, he wanted to fix it for her, take away whatever hurt her and crush it out of existence.

"Would it be cliché of me to ask you to take me to bed?"

"Some things are cliché for a reason. It was a long day for me, too. Do you want to talk about it?"

"I'm sorry, I didn't even ask about group."

"You don't have to. I'd rather you didn't. It's already touched you enough. You don't need any more of this."

"But I want it, Jack. I want to help you, support you. If you can live through it, I'll survive hearing about it."

"No, Bets." It was just like her to deflect whatever was going on with her and bring the focus back to him. That was just the kind of woman she was.

"Fine." She sighed. "Is it really okay that we're

just going to bed early like old people? That you walked all the way over here and you're not even getting sex out of the deal?"

"Betsy, it will be my honor and privilege to listen to you growl like a baby bear all night."

"Are you suggesting I snore?" She looked indignant.

"I'm not suggesting it. It's a statement. A fact. An absolute."

"Oh my God. I'm such a tool. You're not going to be able to sleep, are you?"

"Probably not, but I'll try." He didn't care about sleep. Jack was right where he wanted to be.

"I understand. Would you rather go back to your house?"

"No, I want to see where you live. What the space is like that's only yours."

"Jack, you're kind of perfect. Do you know that?"

"I should argue with you, but I'm not going to. You'll figure it out on your own." He cradled her close again. Jack wasn't going to even try to sleep. He didn't want to take the chance that he'd screw this up. This felt too good. The nightmares could take hold of him when he slept, could stamp out everything he'd accomplished. He wanted to hold on to this for a little while longer. Jack knew he couldn't hold back the tide of dark forever, but just a bit longer would be okay.

CHAPTER SIXTEEN

BETSY DIDN'T REALIZE how much pink she used in her decor until she saw Jack McConnell sprawled in her bed among the hot pink sheets, the pink-and-black rockabilly duvet... He was all hard, delicious man.

What she liked best was that he didn't care everything was pink. It could be puce, for all it mattered to him. He just wanted to be beside her.

She wasn't ready to get up; she wanted to stay in his arms where it was warm and safe. Her bed could be a haven for both of them. Betsy knew he'd planned to stay awake, but at some point during the night, he'd felt safe enough to sleep.

Before they went to bed, she'd taken him on a tour of the loftlike apartment. Shown him where the two keypads were for the alarm systems, given him the numbers and explained in detail, with visual aids, how it worked. She wanted him to feel at home in her space. She still felt like a horrible troll for demanding he come spend the night at her place without even thinking about how trying to sleep in a new place might affect him.

Her alarm went off again after she snoozed it, and she turned it off. If she wanted to open the shop, she'd have to rouse herself from her little hideaway. Jack, too. She didn't want him to wake up without her and be disoriented.

She stole a few moments to study his sleeping form. She was overwhelmed by emotion, so much so that it choked her and she had to blink away unshed tears. She chided herself for being overwrought and mentally ticked off the days.

Oh yeah, she was in serious PMS-ville.

"Jack?" She brushed her cheek against his and she suddenly found herself flat on her back beneath him.

Only there was no terror or rage in his eyes, just lust. "You wake the sleeping dragon…"

She laughed. "I didn't want you to wake up alone. I'm headed down to the shop."

"What if I just keep you in bed with me?"

"I guess I can't fight it." She gave an ultra-put-upon sigh, as if this wasn't exactly where she wanted to be. "I'll just have to deny the masses their doughnuts." For the first time, she'd rather be doing something else than opening her shop. She could stay like this with Jack and not think about the world outside, or the phone call from Marcel and what it meant.

"Hmm. I'm not sure which I want more. Sugar from your shop or sugar from you."

"You better think very carefully about that answer."

He laughed and rolled to the side to let her up. "You're going to give me both later, so I don't have to choose. I'm spoiled."

"You are. You have an assignment while I'm gone."

"Oh really?"

"Yeah. I want to hear more about the spying wait-ress. I expect words on the page when I return."

"Bossy much?"

"Since when is that new?" She flashed him a grin. "Please? I really want to know what happens to her."

"Why don't you write it, then?"

"Because it's your story. You came up with it. Just write it down."

"I don't know how to write."

"Fine, then be prepared for an oral report."

Jack smirked. "Now, that I can do."

"That's not what I meant." Heat suffused her cheeks as she thought about him doing just that.

"You remember how you always used to say that your feelings were mixed into your food? I think you should imagine oral-reporting all day and see how it affects your customers."

"Why would I do that?"

"Because I'll write you that story if you do the recon."

"You think you're smart." Betsy couldn't fight the smile that curved her lips. She was definitely in-trigued and wanted to read this one now, too.

"Cagey, maybe."

"Fine. I will." She licked her lips. "And while you're up here all by yourself all day, I'm going to be downstairs. Rubbing and kneading dough, stroking it and working it until it's just right, and thinking about you doing the same thing to me."

"I need to know what that tastes like."

"Come down for a treat, then. You can see how it affects the customers, too. Nothing better than first-hand information, right?"

"That's a deal."

Betsy kissed him one last time, her lips lingering over his. "See you soon." She grabbed her apron and went downstairs and into the shop.

It was still dark outside and Betsy was glad for the solitude. She wanted to replay what had happened with Jack over in her head until she was sure she'd committed each nuance and sensation to the forever stone of her memory.

She didn't know where any of this would take them, but wherever they ended up, she wanted to have the good times outlined in her head more thoroughly than the bad.

Betsy considered Jack's proposition, to think about all the delicious things she knew he could do to her while she worked the dough. She wondered if it was something as simple as working her phero-mones into the dough.

Emotions were chemical reactions, so it made sense that whatever the chef or baker was feeling was transfused into the end product. Another chemical reaction, just like baking.

Donuts were first on the list. She decided to do something a little different today. Instead of the usual batch of glazed, she was going to do glazed, maple-glazed and vanilla-glazed. The vanilla were for Jack, and she was going to call them Better Than Sex donuts.

Her mother had a recipe from an old PTA cookbook called Better Than Sex cake, but Betsy decided she was just going to borrow the name for now.

Of course, she'd only let that slip to a few select patrons. She didn't dare paste that out on the display case. Someone would have a stroke, she was sure.

Betsy considered Jack while she worked.

His tongue. Most definitely his tongue. He was good with all of his body parts, but if ever there were to be some culinary ode to any body part, it would be that particular thing. He could wound with it, heal with it, tease with it and make her come so hard she saw comets and nebulas. It could be soft, it could be hard, it could be sharp—but it was always what she needed it to be.

His hands were next on the list. There were so strong and broad, but elegant somehow, too. She knew those hands had brought others pain, sorrow and even death. There was no doubt Jack McConnell had blood on his hands, but they were gentle tools, too. He used them for building, for protecting, for wringing pleasure from her as he would water from a sponge.

Jack's eyes could strip her as effectively as his hands, laying her bare and vulnerable with only a glance. His arms were amazing, too. She loved the feel of them wrapped around her....

Betsy meant to catalogue him from his head to

his toes, but there was one particular bit of him that demanded her focus. Part of her wanted to take a picture of it and mail it to Marcel to show him that even a woman like her could catch a man like Jack.

No, no. She couldn't think of Marcel. She was only thinking about good things. Things that made her hot and wet. She focused on Jack, what it was like to cling to his shoulders while he drilled into her.

Betsy didn't know it was possible for her mouth to go dry and water at the same time. She breathed deep, imagining him there with her, taking her from behind while she worked on the dough.

He was right; she was naughty. She wondered what he'd say if she told him that was what she'd been thinking about. If he wanted to follow through on her fantasy, too. The table was just the right height for him to bend her over it like the most wanton of women.

She remembered the shower with him. Betsy loved the way his corded muscles bulged as he fought for control of himself while she pushed him higher, harder and faster. Betsy shivered thinking of it.

Finally she thought about the first time there in her bedroom when she'd ridden his mouth to completion. His face had looked very much like a glazed donut.

Her thighs clenched and her core contracted and she wondered if she was ever going to be able to look at donuts in the same light again.

She ached for him, more than just in her panties. Betsy wanted to go spend the morning lounging in his arms. She wanted to drink coffee with him over the morning paper, go for another round in the shower and curl around him like a cat to be petted and indulged.

Betsy stayed lost in her dream world until all the donuts were finished and the shop was ready to open. She wondered if her desire had transferred itself to the product. If she opened late and went upstairs to have Jack sate her every need instead, she might never know.

She went to the tiny bathroom and changed her apron, freshened her makeup and snapped two clip-on earrings into her hair net. She made a food safety and fashion statement.

Betsy opened the shop and she had a line out the door. She didn't have time to see any of her customers' reactions while she handled the rush. Around nine it started to slow down and India walked through the door, in uniform.

"Something new?" she asked, looking at the counter.

"Yeah. Vanilla-glazed and maple-glazed." She motioned for India to come closer. "The vanilla-glazed ones? They're experimental. Better Than Sex donuts."

India eyed her. "Oh you think so?"

"I don't know. I need another opinion."

"Hit me with two. And two maple, just in case."

"You know Caleb doesn't like the maple."

"None of these are for him. If he stays in the car,

he misses out. I'm not fetching his beer, his sandwiches and most definitely not his donuts."

"You know he just doesn't like that whole cop/donut stereotype."

"That's because he would eat ten if we'd let him. He's going to get so fat when we're old."

"And you'll love him anyway," Betsy teased.

"Probably." India snorted. "But I won't have pity on him when his knees go."

"Should we start planning the wedding? Wasn't it by thirty you two decided that if you hadn't met anyone else, you'd marry each other?"

"You can drop that like a hot potato."

Betsy laughed and handed her the vanilla-glazed Better Than Sex donut.

India accepted the wax-paper-wrapped treat and sniffed it delicately before taking a small bite. Her eyes widened and she looked at Betsy as she chewed. She took another, bigger bite, and a small sound that was almost like a moan issued forth. "Sweet baby Jesus, Betsy."

"Good?" Betsy bit her lip.

"Better than good. Better than sex."

The shop had gone quiet and the people eating stopped what they were doing to look at India and Betsy. "Yes, people. Better than sex. This donut." She crammed the rest of it in her mouth, and her eyes rolled in the back of her head. "It's like... I don't know. I can't even say." She finished the donut and said, "I need a box. Give me six. I would order a dozen, but Caleb won't have any pity on me or my knees, either."

Betsy boxed them up in her signature purple box. When India tried to pay, Betsy shook her head. "Nope. My payment will be you eating them in the car with my brother."

"I don't even want to know. You may have the face of an angel, but you're evil."

Once India left, Betsy quickly sold out of the sex donuts—and all of her other pastries. She even got a commission for a cake for a secret wedding.

She was sure that today was the kind of day that dreams were made of—even if they weren't in Paris.

JACK SPENT THE MORNING trying to do as Betsy requested with the story they'd talked about, but he couldn't see the story without the people in front of him. When he tried, all he could see was death and blood.

He hadn't thought about Mosul since he'd wandered out of the encampment covered in the blood of his enemies. When he dreamed, the night terrors—they were always when he was burning—it was the IED.

Only now that he'd spoken of it, remembered what he'd done, it seemed that wasn't what he was remembering at all. It was the torture. The leg he'd lost—he'd been injured. Something—his memory wasn't quite right. Instead of the place he tried to dig at in his mind, when he ripped back the curtain, there was only Betsy and the place where he'd hidden away from the pain until he could get free and make them pay.

For a moment, he'd allowed himself to forget there was a price to be paid for surviving. He'd allowed Betsy to convince him that he could have a normal life. He could write his stories and she could bake her pies, and they'd buy a charming Victorian to restore that looked over the river.

Stop it. If only he could get out of his own head. He could have those things. He'd started tasting again. He could smell things.

Most important, he could feel them. He wasn't going to let anything stop him. Least of all the tragic voices in his head.

Jack wandered down the stairs and into the shop. Betsy was cleaning up the tables and Jack went back into the kitchen to get the broom and the mop.

"You don't have to do that," she said when he started sweeping.

"Sure I do. You'll be done faster." It wasn't only that he wanted her to be done faster; it was that he had to do something to feel useful.

She laughed. "I saved you one of my donuts. Like the one we talked about."

He arched an eyebrow and cocked his head. "Oh really?"

Betsy nodded. "I sold out of them. I'll definitely have to make them again, although next time, I think you should help."

"I'm more than happy to help." He swept her

against him and nipped at her neck. "Maybe a little of this while you're working?"

"When I was kneading the dough, I thought about you being there, maybe bending me over the table."

"Your wish is my command."

"Here, eat your donut or we'll never get done."

Jack was stuck with a sudden moment of clarity so bright it was like shining a searchlight in his eyes. This could be his life—this routine they'd fallen into. It wasn't big, or important, but he was happy. As long as he blocked out the voices, the sounds...

Until he took a bite of the now-famous donut.

It was all vanilla sugar on his tongue, just like Betsy. The sweet tasted not only like what he associated with her, but like her desire. Like the taste of her skin, her heat, her slick—

"You sold these?" he growled.

"Yes, what's wrong with them?"

"They taste like you."

"You did say I taste like vanilla."

"No, Bets. Like *you*." He savored the way it melted on his tongue. "They taste like your sweetness after I made you scream my name."

He was torn between wanting to lick his fingers, and finding every single one of the people who bought one and finding some way to erase it from their memory, from all of their senses. This was a flavor to be experienced, savored with sight, scent, touch and taste.

Jack didn't want to share.

Betsy blushed. "It does not."

"Oh but it does. Remember when I kissed you after?"

She blushed harder.

"Kiss me now."

"Jack, you're… Fine." She leaned in for a chaste peck, but he wouldn't allow it. Instead his tongue pressed against the seam of her lips and she opened for him.

He willed her to taste the vanilla, the sugar, the sweet that was more than physical, but almost something on a metaphysical level.

She moaned softly into his mouth.

"Do you taste it?" His words were a ragged whisper.

"All I taste is you."

"Never make those again for anyone but me."

"But they were such a hit," she teased.

"I'll make it worth your while." He crashed his mouth into hers. "I'll do everything you wanted on that table, under it, over it…"

"You'd do it anyway."

"You're right. I would." Because touching her was the only thing that silenced the noise in his head. The whiskey had dulled it, but Betsy could make it go quiet and still.

"Let me lock the door." Betsy broke away from him, but only long enough to secure the door and draw the blinds before she was back in his arms. "I thought you wanted me to bake naked."

"It tastes like you already did."

"What are you favorite tastes now?" She ran her palms over his biceps.

"You. And bacon."

She laughed, a musical sound. "Then I'll make these tomorrow again, but with bacon. All your favorite things together."

"I don't think your clientele will appreciate bacon donuts."

"Whoever doesn't appreciate bacon donuts doesn't belong in my shop anyway." She tightened her arms around his neck.

"I've noticed as tastes have started to come back to me that memories have a taste. Feelings have a taste. The group last night was cinnamon. It was sharp and spicy. It burned a little, but it was sweet, too."

"I can show you what *today* tastes like." She took his hand and led him toward the kitchen.

He wanted that. He wanted to know what today and all the tomorrows could taste like. He wanted to know what he was fighting so hard for.

"Today tastes like pink," she said as she worked the button on his jeans. "It tastes like cotton candy. It's all spun sugar and beautiful things. Pink is the color of happiness."

She was right. Betsy's dress was pink, with white hearts on it. Her lips were pink, and as he tugged down her panties, he knew pink was the color of all good things.

She bent over the prep table. "Take me hard and

fast. Then I'll bake for you and you'll know exactly what pink tastes like."

Jack tangled a fist in her hair and sank into her softness.

He lost himself in her, but not in the pink. Not in the sugar. Not in the good things. He was just lost. Her body clenching around him and pulling him deeper caused him to bite down on his lip so hard his own blood was on his tongue.

And he tasted it. The copper tang burned through cinnamon memory and knocked down the wall he'd built in his head with a wrecking ball.

He continued to thrust inside her, and she cried out, arched against him, but he wasn't present. He was in Mosul. He drilled into her, looking for that release, that pleasure—but there was no escape from the hell in his own head.

BETSY SENSED THE CHANGE in Jack, in the way his body moved against hers. There was an underlying ferocity and desperation in his actions, and it wasn't because he was close to his pinnacle.

His fingers dug into her hips and he drove forward almost mechanically. For as much as she wanted to offer him comfort, though, what he was doing felt too good. Her heart told her to stop, to turn and look into his eyes, but her body wanted just one more moment of bliss. Then another, and still another.

She was so full of him, consumed by him, and if she was honest, she'd been using her body as well as the baked goods to save him. If he couldn't find solace in pleasure with her, Betsy didn't know what else to do.

And she wasn't ready to fail, wasn't ready for this to be over, and more important, she wasn't ready to let go and allow the darkness to have him.

So instead she met his intensity and the power of his thrusts. She closed her fingers over the edge of the table and anchored herself to accept whatever he wanted to give her. No matter how hard, how deep, how fast. She wanted more of him, needed it more than her next breath.

"More," she demanded.

And he obliged her.

This was exactly what she wanted from him. He was unrestrained—wild. He wasn't treating her like some holy, breakable thing. He took her as if she belonged to him, and as if he belonged to her.

She loved the weight of him against her, the contrast of his brute strength against her softness, the absolute and utter bliss he brought her with every stroke. He hit the core of her again and again, sensation radiating out all the way to her fingertips and the soles of her feet.

His culmination took him quickly, but he didn't stop. His hips kept moving and grinding against her like some kind of automaton. His grip slackened and she turned, to face him.

Jack's eyes were glazed over and it was obvious to Betsy that he wasn't there.

But rather than being afraid, she felt her heart splintering, thinking of the pain he must be in.

"Jack?" They sank to the floor and she wrappend her legs around his hips to lock him against her.

A tormented sound was ripped from him and she watched as the shadows receded and Jack came back to himself.

Horror followed awareness and he tore himself away from her.

"Jack?" she asked again.

"I'm so sorry."

"For what?"

"I could've... I have to go." He got up and started to right his clothing.

"Hey, it's fine. It's more than fine, actually." Betsy offered him a shy smile.

"You don't understand, Betsy. I wasn't there. I wasn't with you."

"I know," she whispered. "But you came back to me."

"I could hurt you."

"The only thing that hurts right now is that you're trying to leave again." She vaulted to her feet and put her hand on his shoulder to comfort him.

He tightened his hands into fists, then splayed them, only to curl his fingers against his palms again.

Betsy could see the evidence of his frustration. "Look, you say I don't understand, so help me. Explain it to me, because I want to understand."

"Do you?" he snarled suddenly, and she found herself pressed up against the wall, his face only inches from hers. "Do you want to know that even while I'm looking at your face I know the exact placement of at least ten different items, not including your knives, that I could use to kill? That even with as strong as you are, as tough, I could snap your bones like twigs."

"But you wouldn't." She knew Jack would never hurt her. Betsy freed her hand and cupped his cheek.

His eyes fluttered closed for a moment. "Yes, I would." He nodded emphatically and exhaled heavily. "If I thought you were someone else. Or maybe not. Maybe it's worse because it's you. Do you know what I would do to someone I thought was trying to hurt you?"

Betsy supposed that was meant to frighten her, but it didn't. She felt safer, dangerously cherished. Maybe even loved. "Jack." She stroked her thumb over his cheek.

"I'm broken, Bets, and I'm trying like hell to put myself back together, but there are still pieces missing."

"Maybe you can't see it, but you're still the same hero you were when you left. Even more now because you know what it means to sacrifice. There is nothing wrong with you."

"I can't—*we* can't do this. Whatever this was, it was good. But it's over. It has to be. You're going to get hurt and I just couldn't live with that."

He slammed out the door and Betsy was sure he'd ripped her heart out of her chest as he went.

CHAPTER SEVENTEEN

JACK KNEW WALKING away from her now was the right thing. It was the only thing.

He kept thinking about O'Neil's story, how he'd held his weapon on his wife and baby girl. He'd thought he was protecting them, but he could've hurt them. Maybe even killed them.

It was a fucked-up thing to take a man and make him a predator, to paint him in honor and glory for his horrible deeds and then expect him to slip back into his place with the expectation that he'd forget what he'd been taught.

Jack knew Betsy still didn't understand, that she thought maybe he just didn't want to get better. He did. Betsy had done exactly what she set out to do. She wanted him to remember who he was, wanted him to choose to live his life. He wanted that more than anything, except keeping her safe.

Jack walked the few blocks to his house and all he could think about was her. The way she felt beneath him, the way she wanted him and the way she looked into his eyes with absolute trust.

That's what had done it.

If she'd shown some fear, or any other reaction

besides her unwavering faith, he might have convinced himself everything would be fine. But because she trusted him implicitly, he was determined not to fail her.

He had to keep her safe from all threats. Even herself.

With every step he took away from her, the chasm in his chest split further apart, the wound torn wider until finally, when he stepped onto his porch, it was as if a black hole spawned inside him.

But he wouldn't let himself drown in it. Not like before.

As he trudged up the steps, he noticed three more covered dishes sitting by his door. Rather than finding them irritating, he was able to see the meaning behind the gesture. These people weren't just trying to get their look at him. They were trying to show their support in the only way they knew how.

Betsy had taught him that. When other aspects of the needs pyramid weren't being met, nourishment was the easiest to provide and it was the one most commonly used to fill the gaps.

Jack didn't want to learn a lesson; he didn't want this clarity. It was like deconstructing himself and he wasn't ready for that, because he didn't know how to reconstruct himself.

He needed to get out of his own head for a while.

"Jack," a voice called from behind him.

He turned to see Connie. She was holding yet another covered dish.

"Are you here to kill me for blowing your cover?"

She smiled softly. "I brought you homemade mac 'n' cheese. With bacon. I couldn't help overhearing part of your conversation with Betsy about the bacon. Oddly enough, it's what seemed to help Scott after the fire at the Fifth Street Warehouse. It was one of his first real calls and a beam fell on him. We thought we were going to lose him. For the longest time, he couldn't smell or taste anything but smoke."

Jack was immediately at war with himself. He knew Scott had always had a thing for Bets. It made Jack think about her, them together, about her feeding another man, bringing him back to life the way she'd helped him. He wanted to lash out. To find a place to spill all the pain that welled inside him.

He wished things could go back to being black-and-white. Good and bad. Right and wrong. Only maybe things had never been so simple.

"Thanks, Connie." He accepted the dish from her hands.

"Have you started writing that book?"

"No. I don't have anything to say that people want to read."

"Betsy would read it. I would read it." She paused for a moment. "This might be a stupid question, but are you okay, kiddo?"

Leave it to Connie to mother him when he needed it most, but wanted it least. "Yeah."

He wasn't, of course, but he didn't need to spill his venom at her. She was a nice woman who'd brought him bacon.

"Let's get you inside, then, and settled with a nice

plate." Connie didn't wait for him to invite her in; she just took charge and shuffled him along.

He'd thought for so long that Glory didn't have anything to offer him, that the only thing that was here was Betsy and memories of a life he couldn't have. Part of that was still true, but Connie made him see how much more there really was.

These were the people he'd fought for, killed for and almost died for. How could he ever have thought there was nothing for him here?

It was too much. He didn't know how to process being so full of darkness, but so full of all of these other emotions, as well.

"It's kismet that you came home when you did. It's still warm." Connie set the dish on the stove and bustled around his kitchen as if it were her own as she made him a plate and handed it to him. Then she frowned. "Jack McConnell, there's a layer of dust an inch thick in here." She started flinging windows open and then foraged for cleaning supplies under the sink.

When she opened the cabinet, she was greeted with a stash of empty bottles of Old North Bend. He steeled himself for her recriminations, for her gasp of horror, for anything besides what she did.

"If you get me a box, I can take these to the re-cycling center on Second Street." There was no pity on her face, or judgment.

"There's one on the back porch."

"Good. Now sit down and eat before it gets cold."

Jack didn't see any other option than to do as he

was told. So he sat down on the couch while Connie hummed as she dusted. It was with great anticipation that he took the first bite. As he chewed, it was like chewing gum after all the flavor was gone. There was no taste, maybe a hint of salt from the bacon.

It wasn't what he'd hoped, but it was better than ash.

He realized that's what his life had become. It wasn't what he wanted, but it was better than what he'd had before.

"You don't have to do that," Jack said after he'd finished his bite.

"Of course I do. You don't have your mother here to look after you, and the look on your face tells me that Betsy won't be over to do it. If I was gone, I'd hope that some dear soul would take it on herself to give Scott a little TLC every now and again. We all need it once in a while."

He wasn't hungry, but he made himself take another bite of the mac 'n' cheese anyway.

After she dusted, she swept and then tackled the kitchen. Opening his freezer and seeing all of the covered dishes, she raised an eyebrow. "Is that Francine Kirk's green bean casserole of doom? Oh my Lord, there's two. What's she trying to do, kill you?" Connie clucked and pulled the casserole dishes out and stacked them on the counter. "I'll dispose of these for you and no one ever has to be the wiser."

She continued to poke through his freezer. "Alma Bloom's potato salad. That's a keeper. Brenda's broccoli cheese rice casserole, no. If you put that in your microwave, you'll think there's a dirty diaper in your kitchen." She added a container to her stack. "Jemima Flynn's pineapple upside-down cake, you should definitely eat that."

He didn't want any baked goods that weren't Betsy's. "I won't eat it. You can take that, if you like."

"Are you sure?" Connie's eyes narrowed in a predatory fashion. She reminded Jack of a cat who'd just caught a particularly plump mouse.

"If it doesn't come from Sweet Thing..." he confessed with a shrug.

"Do you want to tell me what happened?"

"No."

"That girl loves you, you know."

"I know."

"You love her, too, in case you hadn't figured that out yet."

Yeah, he'd figured it out. That was the problem.

She sighed. "Youth is most definitely wasted on the young."

Connie went back to digging through his freezer. When she was finished, she stacked the dishes, and put the bottles in the box she'd found on the back porch.

"Let me carry that for you," Jack offered.

"No, I'm stronger than I look. You sit there and enjoy your warm, full tummy and have a nap. Things will look better later. I promise." She carried the box outside. "If you need anything, I left my number on your fridge."

Connie closed the door behind her.

Jack thought about the two unopened jugs of Old North Bend he had sitting in the garage. Things would definitely look better when he was too drunk to see them.

He went to the garage and pulled out one of the jugs. He unscrewed the cap, anticipating the burn that took his breath and his pain away.

He stopped halfway to his lips.

And then poured the contents of the jug down the sink in the kitchen.

He didn't want the whiskey.

He didn't want to be numb.

But he didn't want to be in pain, either.

What he did want was to feel normal. That seemed like an easy thing, to acknowledge that in his own head, but after everything, it was much easier to focus on what he didn't want than what he did. Because that meant dreaming, wanting and hoping.

Jack wasn't sure he knew how to do those things anymore.

CHAPTER EIGHTEEN

BETSY FINALLY SURRENDERED. She realized she couldn't keep chasing a man who didn't want her.

That didn't change the fact that it cut her. It cut her so deeply that it broke something inside her. Something more vital than her heart.

She couldn't even find solace in her kitchen anymore, as evidenced by the rather foul lump of dough that lurked like a blob from a horror movie on the prep table in front of her.

The same prep table where Jack had last touched her.

She wanted to scrub it again, as if that would scrub away all memory of him, of every time he touched her, and every time he said goodbye.

Betsy shoved the misshapen dough ball off the table and into the trash with a furious swipe of her hand. It was the third one.

She cursed.

"Whoa, I think you need a Concealed Carry to be packing that kind of heat."

Betsy looked up to see India standing in the doorway. She managed to a small smile. "Shouldn't you be harassing my brother?"

"I came by for my usual but saw the closed sign out front. You okay?"

Betsy wanted to say that she was fine, but she wasn't. The words just wouldn't come. "I don't think so."

"It's Jack, isn't it? I'm sure that you did more than you know for him. I think he's closer to the man he wants to be now than when he first came home."

"Sometimes I think this is my punishment."

"Why would you ever think that?"

Betsy looked up into India's eyes. "Because I wanted him. Because I thought that now that he's broken, I could finally have him."

"Betsy—"

"No, it's true. When I started this, I convinced myself that I was doing this for him. That I was settling a debt, but I wasn't. It was utterly and completely selfish. This is what I deserve."

"I don't think Jack would agree with you."

"Of course he wouldn't, but that doesn't make it any less true." She sagged against the table. "What am I supposed to do?"

India picked up one of the cookies that was still on the cookie sheet. Betsy hadn't gotten around to dumping the batch yet. It was why she'd closed the store. Everything she tried came out tasting like dirt.

"I wouldn't eat that."

"Whatever." India inspected it, turned it this way and that in the light before popping it into her mouth. Suddenly her nosed wrinkled and she gesticulated wildly, looking much like a bird trying to take flight.

Betsy pointed at the trash can and India spat out the mangled, partially chewed cookie. "What the hell was in that, raw sewage?"

Betsy shrugged. "Angst, I guess. Heartbreak, with a side of self-recrimination."

"It tastes like crap and is completely unacceptable. This is your career. You can't bomb it over some guy. Even if it is the sainted Jack McConnell."

"I bombed my chance in France. I should at least do the same for Jack."

India narrowed her eyes. "Now you're being stupid. You weren't stupid before, but that, that was stupid. You didn't really want Paris. If you did, you would've found a way to make it happen, Betsy. Nothing ever stops you from getting what you want."

"How can you say that to me?" Betsy erupted. She knew India was just trying to help her and be supportive, but she didn't want support. She wanted someone to fix this, because she didn't know how. Not just Jack, but everything. "You don't know what it was like. Everyone knew what happened in Paris. Before I came home, I had three interviews set up. London, New York and even Kansas City. Do you know what each one said to me? They wanted to meet the *bouchon de mort* girl. The death cap girl."

"And I say again, you didn't really want it. Only three interviews? How many chefs are in the world? How many restaurants? You chose three. Let them speak to you. Let them be curious. The Betsy I know would've used her notoriety to make eating her food a sport for adrenaline junkies."

"Cooking is different. There are few doors and they rarely open. When they close, they stay closed."

"This pity party is grosser than that cookie."

Betsy sagged further. "You're right. That was an invite to the pity party." She sighed. "I don't know what to do with all of these feelings."

"Well, whatever you do, stop putting them in the pastry."

"Where else should I put them? Jack doesn't want them and neither do I."

"I thought we decided this was gross and we weren't going to do it anymore. How about what are you going to do to get your man?"

"He. Does. Not. Want. Me."

"Uh, I beg to differ, Miss Better Than Sex Donut. You can't say he wasn't the inspiration for those."

"He's pushed me away so many times."

"And he's going to keep pushing." India pursed her lips. "Believe me, I know. People like you and Caleb are utterly terrifying to people like Jack and me. You've got this surety about you the world will always come through, and for us, it hasn't."

"Not if you don't let it."

"Exactly." India gave her the big sister glower. "Now get out of this funk. I need my donuts. You know aside from Sunday dinner with your family, that's the only food I get that doesn't come in a box."

"You lie like a rug. Caleb cooks for you."

"Since he bought that house, *my* house, it's been pizza and takeout. Every spare minute goes to that house."

Betsy was convinced that Caleb had bought that house for India. She couldn't believe that India hadn't figured it out yet. It was as obvious to Betsy as a cat would be at a dog show.

Maybe she had figured it out, maybe that was why she was so scared? It was so much easier to think about India and Caleb than it was her own mess with Jack, even though he was never very far from her mind.

JACK WASN'T SURE how he felt about doing a private session with Andrew, but at nine o'clock on a Tuesday morning, he found himself standing outside his office ready for his appointment.

After what had happened with Betsy, he'd accepted that the support group wasn't going to be enough.

"Good to see you, McConnell. I'm glad you made it." Andrew opened the door and ushered him inside.

"I almost didn't."

"Many don't. Sometimes it take two or three appointments before people actually come inside." He motioned to a chair to indicate where Jack should sit.

"So, how do we start?"

Andrew sat in the seat opposite him. "We just talk. Maybe start out with what caused you to seek a private appointment and what you want out of our sessions."

"I want to be healthy." His answer was automatic.

"What does healthy mean to you?"

"It means that thunderstorms are just weather phenomena and my brain and body occupy the same space at the same time."

"Can you expound on that?"

"I don't know. It was coming back to me slowly, but that's stopped."

"Do you know why?" he prodded gently.

"I stopped seeing her." Jack sighed and knew he'd have to tell Andrew what had happened if he expected this to do him any good. "I had another incident where I almost hurt her."

"What was her name?"

Jack didn't want to say it. Saying it made everything more real, but he supposed that was what he was there for. "Betsy."

"Did Betsy break it off with you after this incident?"

"No."

"Then are you sure that she was in danger?"

"We were having sex, or our bodies were. I bit my lip and it bled, and then I couldn't tell the difference between the past and present." He tried to block out all the things that those words made him feel. Shame, anger, pain...

"Jack, blood is a very powerful trigger. It may happen again the next time you see blood. It might trigger your memories, if not a more visceral reaction, for the rest of your life. That's not uncommon."

"I don't want to be common. I want to be well."

"Part of being well is accepting that you're not perfect and that you don't have to be."

"No, maybe I don't need to be perfect. But even as

damaged as I am, I'm still a weapon. I need a safety, just like a gun."

Andrew nodded. "You're on the right track. Can you see the difference in your thinking between now and when you first came home? Between now and when you first came to group?"

Jack looked at him blankly.

"When you came to group, you said you were useless. Now you acknowledge that you're a weapon. Weapons have purpose, Jack."

"To kill."

"And to protect," Andrew corrected gently.

Only, he couldn't help bringing the comparison back to a gun. "A broken weapon is the most dangerous. Guns misfire, hang-fire, squib-load…and they don't do the job and can result in the death of the wielder."

"This is true, but you're not a gun. You're a human being, and you're not broken. You'd be broken if you could experience everything that's happened to you, everything that you've had to do, without requiring some kind of coping mechanism. Many people experience only one of the major traumas you've endured and need help to work through it. You've lost a limb, your family, your career, your worldview and the foundations you've been building your life upon. Needing a little help to rebuild isn't unreasonable."

"It feels like it is. It feels like I could do it if I was stronger. If I was harder. If I was more."

"That's because you were spec ops. You're all taught that if you're stronger, harder and more, that you can tear down the world brick by brick with your bare hands. Some of you do. And when you're deployed, you need to believe that. You're real-life superheroes, but it's different when you come home. The cape comes off and the world you thought you knew is gone. It will never be the same, because you're looking at it through eyes that have seen hell, not to put too fine a point on it. How can anything ever be real again?" Andrew nodded. "It's a process."

"You sound as if you know from personal experience."

"I was in the first Desert Storm and the army paid for my education. It's why it's so important for me to work with veterans. But we're not here to talk about me. This isn't my time, it's your time. We've talked about what you want out of our sessions. Let's talk about the bigger picture. What do you want out of life? What are your plans?"

Betsy. She was all he wanted. The day he spent with her, the way she felt in his arms. He wanted that forever, and he knew that she'd give it to him. No matter what it cost her.

"I hadn't gotten past roulette," he admitted.

"Oh I think you have. I think when I asked that question you thought about your Betsy. That's okay to want to be with her, but I have to advise against basing your happiness on the actions of another person."

Jack knew that. In any event, he'd already said his goodbye. He knew this was the right thing. He knew it down in his soul because it hurt.

"I want you to think about that before our next session. Think about where you are, where you want to be and how to get there."

"Where I want to be? I want to be a SEAL." *And I want to be with Betsy.* He left that unsaid.

"You'll always be a SEAL. No matter where you go in life or what you do, nothing can ever change that."

But Jack felt that it had changed. As soon as he'd found out the navy didn't want him anymore, he felt like a compass with no north. Being a SEAL wasn't just his job; it was who he was.

"I want you to start keeping two journals. One about your everyday life. Think of it like a logbook. The other about whatever comes into your head, okay?"

"Whatever comes into my head? Like fiction?" Jack seriously doubted that this man or anyone else wanted to know the things that were swirling around in his head like some giant crap stew.

"Anything. Everything. Freewriting." Andrew must've seen the doubt because he added, "Can you do that?"

"I can, but I don't know if I want to."

"You think about it. Maybe try it for a week and then if you don't like it, if you don't think it could be a useful tool, we'll try something else."

Jack wouldn't say it couldn't hurt to try it, because it seemed the most innocuous things were the most painful. But he wanted to feel some semblance of normalcy again. If this would help him find his stop so he could get off the crazy train, he'd try it.

"Okay," he agreed.

"Good." Andrew nodded. "By the way, this Friday is the Halloween dance down at Haymarket Square. Some of the guys are going to have a booth to raise money for the group. We do fund-raisers all year and then we choose a veteran's family to adopt at Christmas. If you think you can tolerate the crowd, you should come. The hometown hero would bring in a lot of donations."

"Guilt-trip much?" Jack asked without rancor.

"Hey, whatever it takes, right?"

Whatever it takes, Jack agreed silently.

CHAPTER NINETEEN

BETSY HAD ZERO interest in Halloween this year.

Usually, it was one of her favorite holidays. She loved dressing up, she loved the excitement in the air, the way the weather changed and pumpkin flavored everything. She especially loved the apple fests in nearby Missouri, the orchards and farms that had their wares for sale. The tiny country stores that the city people flocked to so they could stock their cabinets with homemade jellies, jams, local honey and fresh cider.

The Red Barn Farm was one of her favorite suppliers. Only this year, she hadn't bought anything. There were no treats brightening up her front window, and Betsy feared she'd lost the ability to bake.

She didn't want to go to the dance. There was no one there she wanted to see. Betsy had even had a couple offers for dates, but she wasn't interested in that, either.

Jack hadn't called or written, sent smoke signals or runes, so he obviously didn't want to have any contact with her.

Betsy looked at the costume she'd laid out on the bed.

The poodle skirt she'd made herself, but instead of

a poodle embroidered on the hem, it was a large, glittery spider. The fitted sweater set looked as if it had been spun from iridescent cobwebs, and she'd appliqued bats on the toes of the vintage saddle shoes.

She'd go, if only to show her face and assure everyone that Sweet Thing would be back open soon. She'd give herself some time to grieve losing Jack McConnell. Then after that, it was business as usual.

It had to be. She had too many responsibilities to curl up and die just because Prince Charming had lost his saddle.

Betsy shimmied into her Spanx, not minding the extra layers. The nights were already turning chilly. She pulled on the rest of her costume, tucked her house key into the small pocket she'd sewn inside her bra and walked down to Haymarket.

It was only a few blocks and the street had been blocked off for the dance anyway. The square was lit up with hundreds of little orange lights. They twinkled like happy little fairies, and fat orange pumpkin faces grinned at her from every surface. Most of the local restaurants had booths on the far side of the square and there were vendors of all kinds. An upbeat tune blared from the speakers, and some of the townspeople were already dancing.

India was suddenly beside her. "Not one word," she warned.

Betsy paused to take in her costume. She was dressed like some comic book character in an outfit that put everything on display.

Betsy snorted. "You know, in those boots, you're almost as tall as Caleb."

"Too bad I'm not taller. It would serve him right. It's his fault I'm in this stupid getup."

"Oh really?"

"Dare gone wrong." She shifted, obviously uncomfortable. "One would think he'd at least have gotten my size."

"I think he did. You look really—"

"If you say I look really hot, I'm going to strangle you. I'm never going to live this down at the station." She huffed and blew her bangs out of her face.

Betsy had actually been about to say that India did indeed look very hot. She never did much to play up her feminine side, and dressed as a superhero, she was smoking hot. "Well, you do. You're gorgeous, India."

She was thankful for their exchange. It was normal. It was expected.

And seeing her brother dressed as a superhero was not.

The tights, dear Lord, the tights. What had been seen couldn't be unseen.

He strutted toward them, and India's face turned the same shade of red as her boots.

"Where is the brain bleach?" Betsy teased.

"Right over there, and you know, you can kill me for it later, but right now I'm going to go dance with Jack."

Betsy followed India's route of retreat and saw it ended in the circle of Jack's arms. She knew there was nothing between India and Jack, but that didn't stop her from wishing it was her instead of India dancing with him.

She'd worried over him for no reason. He was doing fine without her. He looked better than he had the last time she saw him. Betsy was glad he was doing well, but it flayed open her wounds to see that being away from her hadn't affected him at all.

He was dressed as a pirate, peg leg and all. The knee breeches he wore clung to his hard thighs, the silk shirt open at the chest… She was torn between despair and arousal. She continued to drink him in— the silk bandanna he'd tied around his head, and even the gold clip-on earring added to the aura of his look. It was Halloween, it was a costume, but damn if she didn't want to be pirated by a reprobate such as him.

His eyes scanned the crowd and suddenly fixed on her. His face was unreadable, and Betsy just wanted to flee. She wanted to hide from the sight of him, from the weight of his presence, and the sharp edges of all the dreams that had shattered like glass.

The song ended and she watched as Jack maneuvered India toward Caleb. When they met on the floor, he handed her off, almost like a father giving away the bride. India's face was still red, and Caleb looked like an angry bear.

Jack was suddenly next to her. "Do you want to dance?"

No. She didn't even want to look at him, let alone dance with him, but she found herself caught up in the circle of his embrace anyway. It was so good to touch him, to feel his warmth wrap around her, the scent of him. A familiar ache thrummed inside her to touch him more, to be touched more, but she restrained herself.

"A pirate?" She struggled for something to say.

"I figured I already had part of the costume." He flashed her a grin.

She would've laughed if she hadn't been on the verge of crying. Betsy had to fill the space between them with words; otherwise she'd fill it with her need of him. "So, how are you?"

"Trying."

"That's good." She didn't know what else to say. Betsy never wanted to leave his arms, but because she felt that way and knew he didn't, she also wanted the song to be over so she could run and hide from these feelings she'd been avoiding.

"I've been thinking about that night," he said.

"Me, too." Hope flared, dangerous and sharp.

"We didn't use a condom."

That burgeoning hope was snuffed like an errant candle. "No, I guess we didn't."

"I wanted you to know that if there are consequences, you can come to me."

Whereas the hope had been a tiny flicker, her anger was like a rocket. "I can come to you?" she hissed. "Are you kidding me? Why would I do that?"

"Because that's what adults do."

"Oh really? Well, if you're too dangerous, too broken to be with me, you're sure as hell not stable enough to have anything to do with a child."

Her dagger struck home and drove deep. She saw it hit its mark when his smile froze and his eyes emptied like a bottle that had been turned on its side.

"I'm sorry, Jack. I didn't mean that."

"No, you're right. You're absolutely right. If something happens, I'll meet my financial obligations."

Her dagger had been a double-edged sword because it sliced her just as deeply.

"You'd tell me, wouldn't you?"

She swallowed hard, unable to dislodge the lump in her throat. "Of course."

"Take care of yourself, Bets." He released her and disappeared into the growing crowd.

In that moment, all that could've been hit her hard and fast. The house, and the yard, the dog…a flaxen-haired baby in her arms. Jack's son. All of the things she'd been afraid to want outside of a teen fantasy.

She didn't want the fantasy. She wanted the reality. She wanted Jack and she wanted forever and she couldn't have it.

Betsy was standing there among a crowd of people, shattering. And no one could see it—the fine cracks that dug deep through the whole of her, as if she were some figurine who was just waiting to fall apart.

"Betsy?" A familiar voice rang in her ears. He said her name like *Beht-see*. As if it were two separate words.

She spun to see Marcel.

Marcel Babineaux, soon to be master chef, and deflowerer of virgins, was in Glory, Kansas.

The place he'd once referred to as the innermost circle of small-town hell. What was he doing? What was even more insane was that after the way they'd left things, he thought she'd be happy to see him.

Happy to see him after he'd been the one who started calling her *bouchon de mort* girl. The chef had just thought it apt and it had stuck.

"I have the most exciting news, *chérie.*"

"I didn't think you'd actually show up here. I thought you despised small towns." She couldn't believe he was here or what he could possibly want from her.

"Oh I do, but this was worth it." He grinned.

She waited, having no idea what he'd possibly think was worth flying to Kansas.

"Truth be told, *petite,* I really thought you'd find a way to come to New York."

"Why would you think that?" Betsy fixed him with a hard appraisal.

"You wound me. My, how life has changed you." He cocked his head to the side. "I thought it would be New York that stripped you of your innocence. But it wasn't. It was living here without passion."

"Without passion?" She almost choked on her incredulity. "Are you stoned, Marcel?"

"Ah, no. You are so different. Once, you would've been waiting with bated breath to see what marvelous thing I had to share with you. Now it's as if you don't care."

It wasn't *as if.* It was a fact. There was nothing he could say that held any interest for her.

"I've convinced Chef Abelard to accept you back."

Except that.

"You what?" She was sure she hadn't heard him correctly.

"I wronged you, Betsy. A slip of my tongue meant in jest shouldn't follow you for the whole of your career. I told him about your shop, I made for him your lavender apricot soufflé and I told him I will eat the food you prepare. I believe in you and your talents. You're in. You must pack immediately. Especially since he made this offer weeks ago. I have assured him you want this."

His words hit her in the face, one right after the other, like snowballs with a hard-packed ice center. "Marcel, I can't leave. I have a business to run." Her excuse sounded hollow even to her own ears. "And there's this wedding cake commission—" Only it was Chef Abelard. He could launch her career. The career she'd dreamed about with big-city life and worldwide acclaim.

Everything she thought she wanted was within reach.

Everything but Jack.

It was funny how dreams did that, the fluid nature of them, the ebb and flow. She dreamed of Jack, she dreamed of France, but never together. Now she'd had Jack and it was over. Was France the consolation prize?

"This is not the reaction I expected." He shook his

head. "I was startled when you didn't come when I first called. You are not the same girl I met in New York."

Yeah, because it was still all about him. She sighed. "You already said that, but I guess people are like dreams. They change. Thank you for everything you've done, but this is so sudden and unexpected."

Betsy was reminded of her mother's old-school romances where the hero swept the heroine off her feet and after the hero's passionate confession, the heroine would demure and say it was all so very sudden.

But Marcel was no romance novel hero.

"I hadn't realized how—" he looked around "—well you'd taken to coming back here." His nose crinkled in dismay. "Perhaps there is somewhere we can go talk? Maybe we can catch up?"

Betsy looked around for Jack; she didn't know why. He'd made it clear that he didn't want to be with her, but just the sight of him made her feel stronger, more capable, as if she could conquer the world.

And Marcel, he made her feel as if the world could conquer her if she wasn't careful.

"We could do that. Where are you staying? We can get my car."

"I was hoping to stay with you, but your *maman* told me that you're seeing someone."

"I am."

"And this someone, he would mind greatly if an old friend slept on your couch?" There was a certain twinkle in his blue eyes, the fun-loving charm that had attracted her to him in the first place.

"If you were just an old friend, there wouldn't be any question. But we were more than that and I certainly wouldn't lie about it."

"He is jealous, then? Passionate?"

"No, he's not jealous. Because he trusts me." More like he didn't want to be with her anymore, but Marcel didn't need to know that. In her heart, she was still with Jack. Part of her always had been.

She didn't know what she was thinking when she tried to convince herself that she wasn't in love with him. Betsy lived and breathed for Jack McConnell.

"Perhaps I shall stay with Lula, then? I went to see her before I came to find you. I saw the picture of us still on your mirror."

Jack was right. She should've taken the stupid thing down.

"Those were good times." That wasn't a lie.

"They could be again, *petite*."

"We can talk, we can catch up, but I'm not ready to give you an answer today, and if you push, my answer will be no."

"Even though your family thinks that's a mistake?" he asked gently.

"Yes. I have to live in my skin. They don't."

"You're so much stronger than you were in Paris. You've always been beautiful, but now this power from you, you're stunning."

Betsy turned to look at him as they walked and stopped. "That's a different story than the one you were singing in Paris, too."

Marcel looked genuinely confused. "What do you mean?"

"You're pretty, but you'd be so much more beautiful if..." She let the sentence hang.

"If what?"

Betsy had always wanted to confront him about the way he'd treated her, the way she heard his voice in her head every time she thought something bad about herself. While she'd wanted it, she didn't know if she'd have the gumption, but she did. As she looked at him now she realized he wasn't perfect, either. A newfound sense of self filled her and she answered him. "If I lost thirty pounds, if I did my hair a certain way, if I did a million things to change myself. If I did things that weren't me."

"Then I was a jackass. I don't remember behaving so horridly, but if I did, you have my utmost and sincerest apologies. You've always been beautiful, Betsy."

She eyed him. She was faced with a choice here. She could accept his apology graciously or she could be petulant and hold on to the past. Betsy wanted to be petulant, but she also knew that forgiving him wasn't about what it did for him. It was about what it would do for her. Maybe his voice in her head telling her that she wasn't enough would finally be silenced.

"Thank you." She turned her attention back to the sidewalk and the path toward her shop and her car.

"No wonder you didn't want to come to New York again."

"It's really not that I don't want to go to New

York, but what kind of life do you think I have that I can just drop everything to go to New York on a whim? Or France?"

"One that you'd find any reason to escape. That's how you made it sound before." His tone wasn't unkind and it made her pause to wonder: Had she?

She realized she had. His worldliness made her humble small-town roots feel like something to be ashamed of, something to be scrubbed off in the bustle of the city and to be hidden under art, culture and her talent for lavender apricot soufflé.

"I guess it's interesting how time can provide a little clarity."

"You're right. I think that I expected you to be waiting for me, Betsy. I guess because it always seemed like you were waiting for something. I just assumed you'd wait for me, too."

She had been, she realized. Whether she was conscious of it or not, she'd always been waiting for Jack. She still was, if she was being totally honest with herself.

Maybe France was what she needed? This kind of opportunity presented itself rarely. Now here it was again, knocking at her door and daring her to reach for it. Caleb said they'd find a way to manage the shop for her. Her father had paid her rent on the place for five years with a bonus he earned on his last trip for the DOD. She didn't have to worry about the money.

Betsy studied Marcel again for a long moment. She remembered what it was like for him to touch her, how he made her feel. She remembered why she thought she'd loved him. The way he made her laugh, what it was like sharing a kitchen with him. That was something she'd never shared with anyone else—that was why she'd thought she was in love with him. The way their culinary arts meshed together.

His honesty now endeared him to her more than any memories they shared.

"You've changed, too."

"Not so much, I don't think. A bit more humble, maybe. I thought as soon as I opened my own restaurant, I'd be the toast of the city. I'm struggling to keep the doors open. But I know that once you complete your training, we'd be unbeatable."

They'd shared a dream of opening a café together once, but now it just seemed hollow.

"That was a long time ago."

"Not so long, Betsy."

It seemed like another lifetime to her.

She wanted desperately to change the subject. "Are your bags at Mom's?"

"Yes."

After that, they rode in awkward silence to her mother's house. It was difficult to navigate the maze of one-way streets of downtown with so many sections blocked off for the dance at Haymarket, so she focused on the street, the traffic and everything but the man sitting next to her.

She unlocked the door and asked, "I guess Mom put you in my room?"

"She did, but I was hoping we could talk for a while yet."

"Betsy, is that you and your young man?" Her mother called.

Her young man? No, her young man was back at the dance. Without her.

This was so surreal, seeing him standing in her mother's foyer. She'd never imagined what it would be like to bring him home to meet her family.

"I appreciate what you've done for me, Marcel, but I should warn you, I'm probably going to say no."

"Give me some time to try and convince you."

"I think it would be easier to convince her if you were already in Paris. Can you imagine Paris at Christmas? All the little cafés, and the lights?" her mother said helpfully.

"You told my mother why you've come?" she blurted.

He nodded. "I did."

"I wish you hadn't."

"Why? So she won't tell you to go?"

She sighed and wanted to look anywhere but at the man, and the choice in front of her. Her eyes rested on a bottle of blackberry cordial on the sideboard.

"Mother."

"What?"

"Not now." Because blackberry cordial was all about Jack.

"What's this?" Marcel asked.

"Besides a long story?" Betsy asked. She didn't

want to explain to him. It seemed wrong sharing anything about her and Jack with him.

He laughed. "Okay, then, do you have any short stories?"

Betsy knew he thought he was being funny, but it made her think of Jack. Of the stories they'd made up together that morning at the Corner Pharmacy. *Everything* made her think of Jack.

It hadn't been like that when she and Marcel broke up. She'd been hurt, but she hadn't really thought about him very often—unless he was voicing that nasty narrative in her head.

But it seemed she'd made him into the bogeyman. He was nothing like the caricature she'd built of him in her head. Either he'd changed, her perception had or both.

"I'll get the Rosa Regale instead." Her mother offered her a smile. "It pairs better with the chocolate torte anyway."

"Is this Betsy's chocolate torte?"

"Yes. She keeps my freezer well stocked with goodies." Lula smiled.

This was so strange to be standing here playing the polite game with Marcel. Maybe the struggle to keep his restaurant open had humbled him.

"Why don't I go cut the torte?" She used it as an excuse to flee, leaving her mother to carry the burden of the conversation. It was pointless anyway; she wasn't going back to Paris and that was the end of it.

CHAPTER TWENTY

JACK HATED BURPEES more than poison ivy, and after the scorching case he'd developed on his last camp-out as an Eagle Scout, that was saying quite a bit. He especially hated them now that he had his prosthesis to deal with. It was much more work.

Squat, palms flat on the floor.

Kick his feet out into push-up position.

Two-count push-up.

Return to squat position.

Jump up.

Rinse, repeat.

His drill instructor told him that burpees had been designed by the devil himself in the deepest pit of hell.

So why was he doing them? To get his body back in optimum shape in hopes that his brain would follow. When it did, then maybe he could start using logic again instead of his heart.

His phone rang, but he ignored it. Jack kept moving through the motions, working his body and pushing it to the brink. Sweat dripped down his forehead, but he didn't swipe at it. He simply repeated the motions, doing five more burpees today than he'd done the day before.

His phone rang again and didn't stop ringing. He thought it might be Betsy, that she might be in some kind of trouble. It was Caleb.

"She's still waiting for you."

"Will you please mind your own business? I can't help what she does."

"My friend and my sister are my business. And I think you can. You need to tell her that she has to go."

"I did."

"Not just away from you, but away from Glory, too."

"What do you mean?" A hard knot of dread twisted in his gut.

"Marcel is here. I know you saw him."

He'd seen him all right. Jack had despised him on sight.

His teeth were too white, his mustache too thin and his eyes too narrowly set. He reminded Jack of a rodent. His first instinct was to charge over to where they stood and stake his claim.

But he had no claim. Betsy wasn't his and she never could be. Even so, she sure as hell wasn't going to be Marcel's. "Look, if you think I'm going to push her toward that jacka—"

"She has another chance at Paris, Jack."

The words slammed into him, each one a bullet of larger caliber than the last. Betsy's dream. *Paris.*

Tutelage that could launch her career and give her the way out of Glory that she had always wanted.

"I already broke it off with her. I don't know what else I can say that would do more than just picking at the wound." Yes, he did. He knew exactly what he could say to her.

What he didn't know was if he was strong enough to do it. To watch the light in her eyes dim and finally strip him of that hero's mantle she'd pinned to his shoulders. Jack thought he didn't want it, didn't deserve it, but he didn't know if he could bear to give it up. It was the only thing he let himself keep—the memory of the way she looked at him. The man he could be, the man she believed he was.

There was the conundrum.

If he did this, if he made her leave, he'd really be all those things she'd painted him as. Only she wouldn't believe anymore. He'd have finally crushed it out of her. If he didn't have Betsy as his guide-post— He knew before he finished the thought what his choice would be.

The irony of the whole situation wasn't lost on him. For his shot at redemption, he had to give up the one thing he cared about.

"I understand." He'd make her go if he had to haul her kicking and screaming on the plane himself. His whole body ached, but it wasn't from the burpees.

"I knew you would. If it's any consolation, I know you're the right man for her."

Caleb's words were worse than bullets. Now they were more like dumping gasoline on a hundred open wounds. They cut, they hurt, but they were like some strange disinfectant, too. He knew it was the right thing.

But he wasn't doing it because it was the right thing. He was doing it because it was the right thing *for her.*

He disconnected the call with Caleb and dialed her number. She answered on the first ring.

"Can we talk?"

"We are talking," she said, her voice shaky.

"Can I see you?"

Betsy was silent for so long he thought she'd hung up. He'd understand if she did. He kept waiting for her to say that he couldn't keep doing this to her, dragging her close and then pushing her away. He couldn't have her but keep her at a distance, too. He knew that. He waited for all of those things, but she said none of them.

Instead, when she finally answered, she said, "When?"

"Twenty minutes. The place by the river."

"I'll be there."

The call disconnected and his hands curled into fists, his nails digging into his palms. Yes, he'd already told her she had to go, but now he had to make her.

Jack thought about the scent of her hair, the feel of her in his arms and the certainty that after today, he'd never know those things again. Even though he'd broken off things between them, he guessed he realized that part of him always expected Betsy to be there.

All along, it hadn't been her who needed him.

He needed her.

And for her to be happy, he had to stand on his own.

Jack wouldn't be a coward. He showered and dressed, focusing on the simple act of moving forward, and it got him where he needed to be.

Their special place by the river where they'd said goodbye what seemed a lifetime ago. Jack hated it. He hated that it was special, that it was where they took their pain. The land itself seemed to draw it from them like a sponge, a sin eater's loaf of bread and salt.

She arrived shortly after he did. When she stepped out of the car, he saw Betsy had brought their blanket, the red-checkered one, and a picnic basket.

"It sounded like you had something important to say, so I thought I'd bring the blanket." She held it up like some kind of peace offering.

"That's good, Bets." He nodded.

"I'm not going to like this, am I?" She clutched the blanket against her chest.

"I talked to Caleb."

"Ah. He told you about Marcel and Paris, didn't he?" She spread the blanket out and they sat down.

"He did. The question remains, why didn't you?"

"You said you didn't want to see me."

"No, you had to know about it before he came. He wouldn't just show up. It was that day you said you had a crappy day, wasn't it? Where you just wanted to hide in bed. Why would you want to hide from that? You always wanted to escape Glory, and this is your opportunity."

He studied her face, the range of emotion that waxed and waned over her features.

"Because I already failed once, Jack. I almost killed people with my mistake and I lost everything. Why would I deserve another chance?" She flopped on her back and stared up at the sky.

He'd learned her cloud watching was a tool she used to hide from things. If she could see different things in the clouds, she didn't have to face what was in front of her. She'd done it when she told him she loved him the first time.

"Why do any of us? Why did I? I didn't almost kill people. I did. I failed, too. Can you really look at me and say you lost more than I did?"

"I didn't choose to be a SEAL. I didn't choose to go to war."

"No one chooses to go to war. We choose to stand up and fight for what's right, for what we believe in, for the people we love. Sometimes that takes us to war, but no one ever chooses war."

"Maybe I didn't lose a leg, but I did lose a piece of myself, Jack."

"And now you have to go find it. Marcel has given it to you on a platter. Don't you think if I had the chance to be whole again, I'd take it?"

She didn't say anything. She put the back of her

hand over her mouth and closed her eyes, breathing in deeply as if she was trying to steady herself.

"Don't piss this away because you're afraid."

"I'm not like you, Jack. I *am* afraid. Would you reach for what you wanted if you thought it was just going to be jerked out of your reach at the last second? Or worse, if you thought you'd get close to the gold ring only to throw it away yourself?"

He knew exactly what she meant. He was feeling that very thing. He swallowed hard. "You think I'm not afraid? How convenient for you, and that painted-up image you have of me. Don't you remember the thunder and lightning, the whiskey so I could bear to sleep? That was rooted in fear and you wouldn't let me do it, would you? So how can you let yourself? Hiding from what you want is just as destructive. If you don't go, you'll always wonder what it would've been like if you had." He held up a hand when she would have spoken. "No, maybe not tomorrow, maybe not even the day after that. But there would come a time when you would be rotten with it."

"I just can't, Jack. I can't go. I don't want to go. Why can't anyone accept that? Dreams change. You forget, I've been once. It didn't work out. I was laughed out of Paris. Why would I sign up to endure that again?"

"Because it's what you want. You'll never be happy with a small life."

"My life isn't small!" she snapped.

"I know that, but do you?"

"Save this Zen finding-yourself crap for your support group."

He might've believed she was angry if her voice hadn't cracked on the last word. She was hurting. She needed him to do this, needed him to give her a hard push out of the nest.

"You came home, baby bird." He couldn't resist brushing his knuckles against her cheek in a forbidden caress—her skin was so very soft. "But now it's time to spread your wings again."

"And crash to the ground and be eaten by wild coyote puppies." She sniffed.

"Why do you think you're going to crash? Look at everything you've done with the shop. Do you know fifty percent of new businesses fail in the first year? You have your own shop. Your own business. You're making enough money to support yourself and you still give away a lot of your product. The guys at the V.A., even if you never speak to half of them, you've made an impact on their lives for the better. And me? You saved my life. You're magic, Betsy. It's time to use that power for yourself."

"Some cultures believe that once you save someone's life, it belongs to you."

"If that was true, I'd already have your ass on a plane."

"Really?"

She looked so wounded. As if she hadn't heard anything he'd just said except for the part about how he'd get rid of her.

"Yeah, really. Go to Paris."

"Will you at least let me say goodbye?"

"What do you mean?"

"The last time you touched me, you just walked away from me. I didn't get to say anything, do anything. You didn't listen to me at all. Then you were just gone."

He knew where she was going. She wanted to have some goodbye fu— No. He couldn't call it that. Not now. There was nothing he'd ever done with her that could be anything so crude as fucking. He made love to her. Even that wasn't enough to describe what touching her meant to him.

"Betsy—" he began, intending to warn her.

"Let me have this and I'll go to Paris. I'll do whatever you want. Just, please. Let me have this one last thing."

He could see the effort it took for her to speak the words.

"It's your turn to send me off, but this time I won't keep your tags, and I won't demand you come back."

CHAPTER TWENTY-ONE

BETSY KNEW THIS was goodbye for real this time. He thought he was saving her and she'd had no luck convincing him that she wasn't some breakable damsel in a tower.

She needed it, though, so she could have some closure with him, touch him and be touched, something to replace the memory of their last time together so it was something beautiful instead of all that pain.

She had no doubt this would be painful as well, but it would be of her choosing. Betsy wouldn't replay everything over in her head wondering if she should've done something differently. When she replayed tonight in her head, it would be because she wanted to remember Jack.

"Bets, what you're asking isn't fair to either of us."

"No, it's not. And it wasn't fair of you to leave me that night, either, without talking it through. But both are done and you can't change it. All you can do is trudge forward. I get that you don't want to be with me, but would it hurt to say goodbye?"

"It would hurt a lot." Jack cupped her face. "Both of us."

She thought of the first time she'd sent him away

and she wished for a bottle of blackberry cordial. "If you really want me to go, Jack, this is my price."

"You're the devil, Betsy."

"If I am, you're an angel who's begging to fall."

His laugh was bitter. Jack's jaw clenched as if he endured some physical pain, but he dipped his head and brushed his lips over hers. "You want me to take you right here, right now out in the open where anyone could see us?"

"No one can see us here except for cops looking for teenagers who are doing exactly what I intend us to be doing, and they won't bother us, either. I told India I was coming here to talk and I didn't want to be bothered."

He looked out over the muddy swirling water as it rushed by them. "Why?"

"I told you," she said stubbornly.

Betsy stopped thinking about goodbye. She pushed tomorrow out of her head. All she wanted to think about was this moment. She wanted it to be sweet and pure, with no taint of sorrow and regret.

"You saved me, Bets. You did what you set out to do. Knowing that, do you still want this?"

She looked up at him. "What do you mean?"

"I'm getting counseling, I'm going to group, I'm not drinking. I didn't drink tonight. I'm trying, just like you wanted. I'm barely treading water, but I'm not drowning. So you can go to France and you don't need to worry about me."

She opened her mouth to speak, but he kissed her,

and all thought of speech died with the hot press of his lips on hers.

Betsy's fingers did a quick dance over the buttons on his shirt. She needed to feel his skin. She memorized every intake of breath, every flex of his muscles, the play of the light on his body.

She knew she wasn't supposed to think of him as beautiful. He was a man, so he was supposed to be handsome, rugged, purposeful—but he was beautiful.

All of him.

Betsy wanted to show him how he looked to her, and maybe if he didn't know it, that she never saw him as broken. Maybe lost, but not broken.

She had to tell him that she didn't want France, but Betsy couldn't find the words, not with the way he kissed her—it stole her breath away. It was just as well, because it was still goodbye.

Jack had made that clear. She couldn't keep doing this. She couldn't keep hoping and dreaming about something he didn't want, or wasn't ready for.

This would hurt less if she could just go without touching him again, without another memory of what it was like to lie in his arms.

But she couldn't. Betsy would devour every moment, every touch, every shared breath. She meant what she said when she'd agreed to make a good memory to replace the bad. It was different somehow if they said goodbye together, rather than him leaving her standing alone in the dark—yet again.

She pushed the shirt off over his shoulders and

splayed her palms on his broad chest. She loved touching him, the way her hands slid over his skin. He was so hot and hard all over. This was better than any fantasy of him she'd had—and she'd had so many.

The thought kept coming back to her, and it was like a new discovery each time.

He suddenly broke the kiss. "Bets, I don't have anything."

She knew he meant protection, but he hadn't used any that night in her shop. "I don't care."

And she didn't. She wanted this part of him, this memory; she wanted for just this moment for there to be no barriers between them.

She waited for him to protest, to say it wasn't a good idea, to list all the reasons why it shouldn't happen this way, but he didn't.

Instead he kept kissing her, kept touching her.

"I remember the taste of blackberry cordial," he mumbled against her mouth.

The first night they'd said goodbye.

"Can you taste it on my lips now?" *Along with the same sorrow that shadowed me then?*

"Make me taste it, Bets."

She pressed her mouth to his with all that intensity that stormed inside her. Her lips were swollen with their passion, tender and raw, just like her heart.

"I need you, Jack. I need you now."

This wasn't about the orgasm for her; it was about the connection. Her heart ached, and the impetuous part of her personality that Jack had always indulged demanded that she tell him everything in her heart.

It was sure that he just didn't understand what she wanted, and once he did, he'd give it to her, as he always did.

Only it wouldn't be like that this time.

Being joined with him, being skin to skin, feeling his heartbeat against her palm and his hips grinding against hers, it was so right and made her feel something she'd never had with Marcel.

She felt whole.

She felt home.

No, Betsy didn't want to go to Paris. She wanted to stay. She wanted to be with him.

Betsy tried to tell him with every caress, every cry of pleasure and every time his mouth crashed into hers.

When her body and soul couldn't take any more, she told him with her voice.

Betsy orgasmed beneath him, crying out, "I love you."

He froze and pulled away from her. "No, Betsy. You don't. Right now you want to hide and you want to use me as an excuse. I won't let you do that." Jack started pulling on his clothes.

"You don't know what I feel. You're not inside my head."

"I'm more inside your head than you know. Someday when you have everything you ever wanted, you'll thank me for this. For not letting you settle."

"I'm not settling. I'm in love with you!" she cried.

"I've loved you forever." Her voice was softer now. "I've loved you as a little girl loves, that's true. But I've also loved you as a woman."

His mouth straightened into a hard line. "Don't say that."

"Why not?" She put her hand on his shoulder.

He turned to face her. "Because I don't love you. Not like that. I care about you, you're sexy as hell, but I'm not in love with you and I never will be."

And just like that, he'd cut out her heart.

You don't mean that, she mouthed, unsure if sound actually passed her lips.

"But I do. That's what I had to tell you. There is nothing for you in Glory." He straightened his clothes.

"I know you don't mean that," she said again. After what they'd just shared, the way he touched her, as if she were made of spun gold. Jack loved her. He'd always loved her. He…

"I don't want to hurt you, Betsy, but if you won't listen, I'll have to be cruel."

"You're just doing this to make me go."

"That check is still on your mom's sideboard. Cash it. Be on that plane." He walked to his car and he didn't look back.

He didn't argue with her. He didn't disagree that he was just trying to make her leave. But he'd said he didn't love her, not like that, and he never would.

When he knew her fear was of failure and humiliation, why would he say those things unless he meant them? There were other ways to get her to go to Paris. If he wanted her to go so badly, he could've offered to go with her.

Something hot streaked down her face and splashed on the backs of her hands. Tears, hot and rancid.

She dashed at them with her balled fists.

Betsy wasn't going to leave Glory and go to Paris just because he said so. Just because he said there was nothing for her here.

It was because *everyone* wanted her to leave. No one wanted her to stay. They all thought they could make better decisions for herself than she could. None of them believed in her enough to think she knew what she wanted.

Yes, she was afraid, but rightfully so. And her dreams had changed. She wished she could go back and not fail, but she didn't want to go try again. Not with the humiliation of what she'd done hanging over her head. Maybe she would go to Paris, and she wouldn't even go see Chef Abelard. Maybe she'd spend that check on cafés, museums and expensive shoes. Or maybe she'd go to the Bahamas and spend it on swimming suits, Mai Tais and cabana boys.

She'd had enough of it. Her brother's meddling, her mother's, even India's. Everyone kept telling her what she wanted, what she should know, as if their lives were perfect and they were qualified to hand down advice like sages from up on high. Screw them all if they thought it was okay to plan her future without her say-so.

And Screw Jack McConnell in particular.

She flopped back on the blanket and stared up at the sky, but she wasn't looking for shapes; she wasn't looking for anything. Betsy was waiting for the flood of tears to pass, to sink back down inside her where no one could see them.

It seemed she'd spent her whole life waiting.

Well, she was done with that now.

She scrambled to her feet and scooped up the blanket that had been home to so many hours of hoping, dreaming—*waiting*. She flung it over the ledge. Betsy didn't watch to see it swallowed in the churning, muddy waters.

And she didn't look back. If Jack could walk away without a backward glance, then so could she.

At least that was what she told herself.

Shame flooded her hotter and even more acidic than the tears. What a fool she'd made of herself over him.

Part of her kept protesting that it had to be a lie— he was doing what he thought was best for her because he really did love her. He was that kind of man. That was the little girl whose voice got quieter and quieter as the days passed, replaced by one more logical and stern. The one who favored reason over hope.

The one who said if a man wanted her, he'd say so. If he wanted to be with her, he would. That he could offer to go to Paris with her because that was also the kind of man Jack was. He'd planned invasions of small countries. He could certainly figure out how to stay with a woman if he loved her.

He'd made himself clear.

He didn't want her.

And even though she knew it was overwrought and patently untrue, it felt as if Glory didn't want her, either.

She left the picnic basket where it lay, walked toward her car and drove straight over to her parents' house, where Marcel was staying.

Everyone was gathered in the family room drinking coffee, eating another of her desserts. Caleb looked up at her expectantly and she flashed him a glare filled with as much venom as she could muster.

"Everyone is getting what they want. I'm going to Paris." Then she focused on Marcel. "How soon can we leave?"

"Don't you want to spend the holiday with your family?"

"That wasn't important to you when you told me I had to come to New York."

"I may have been a bit overexcited. Abelard will wait until January. I'm just thrilled you've decided to take him up on it."

"No, it's now or never. I don't want to wait until January. If the chef is otherwise occupied until then, I can finally see Paris and do all the touristy things I missed the first time." She walked to the sideboard, where the check from Jack was still stuffed haphazardly in the torn envelope. "I have a generous benefactor, after all." She knew she sounded petulant and childish, and above all, angry, but she couldn't help it.

"Whatever you wish, *chérie*. I will check flights." Marcel pulled out his phone and began swiping at the screen.

"Just wait a minute, Betsy," her mother said.

"No. You all practically shoved this down my throat because you all know what's best for me. So now you don't get to say anything else."

Lula turned to look at Caleb. "What did you do?"

"I didn't do anything."

Betsy glared at him again. "You know exactly what you did."

"There's a flight to New York tonight. We can fly out from there tomorrow afternoon."

"Fine. Get your things, and we can get a car service to the airport from my place."

"Betsy, honey," her mother began again.

She relented the merest fraction of an inch and hugged her. "I love you. I'll call you from Paris."

"Are you sure this is what you want to do?" her mother asked softly.

"No. But no one will stop meddling until I go. So I'm going. Caleb said he'd take care of the shop, so I expect him to do it. Marcel, I'll be waiting in the car."

She fled the warmth of her parents' house, her childhood, to pursue a dream that was no longer hers.

Betsy remembered what Jack had told her about living the life everyone had carved out for him here—how it was like living in someone else's skin. She wondered if maybe now she knew what that felt like.

IT WAS QUITE the climb down the embankment to retrieve the checkered blanket, but Jack managed. It had gotten hung up on some exposed roots and it swayed in the slight breeze like a banner of surrender— a white flag splattered with the blood of what might have been.

His desires.

What she thought she wanted, and the magnificent future that almost wasn't because she was afraid. He wouldn't let her do that to herself. Jack knew that as long as she thought he needed her, she'd stay.

And he did need her. He needed her more than the breath in his body, but he wouldn't take away her dreams to have her. Jack knew he still had too far to go before he was even a facsimile of whole—he was barely functional.

No, that wasn't true. He was a little more than barely. A month ago, he wouldn't have considered trying to scale down the ledge, and neither would he have laughed at himself when he got a root tangled around the titanium limb and he almost had to remove it to get free. No, he wouldn't have laughed. He wouldn't even have been outside, much less down by the river with Betsy.

He held the blanket close, and the familiar scents wafted around him. He gripped the blanket so tightly his knuckles were white with the effort.

She said he'd been drowning before—drowning in the whiskey and the dark. But he hadn't felt as if he was drowning; he didn't know he couldn't breathe.

This…this absence of her, this was drowning, this was suffocating.

Betsy took all the air with her, all the light.

And suddenly he was so very thirsty, so very empty. There was a hollow space inside him that needed to be filled.

He told her that he was all right, but he wasn't.

Jack didn't want to die. He wasn't going to go home and eat his gun. But he couldn't feel all of this now. He needed something to give him some silence. A reprieve to that blessed numb nothing he could only find in the bottom of a bottle.

He knew it was wrong, he knew it wasn't the answer, but he drove to the liquor store anyway. He sat outside in his car for a full fifteen minutes before he went inside. Jack kept telling himself to start the car, to drive home, because he didn't have to do this. Jack knew he could choose.

And he made the wrong choice.

He went inside and bought a nice bottle of aged scotch. As if it weren't sordid because it was expensive. Jack wasn't fooling himself. He knew exactly what he was doing and why it was bad.

But he was so unbearably empty.

"Need someone to share that with, handsome?" He looked up to see Mindy Kreskin behind the counter. "I get off in an hour."

Part of him wanted to say yes. The act would be as empty and meaningless as what he was feeling now.

She wasn't Betsy, though, but neither was the scotch.

He closed his eyes and breathed.

"Maybe some other time." He pulled out his cash for the scotch.

"You sure about that? I hear Betsy is leaving for Paris again."

News traveled like wildfire in a small town. "Yes, she is. I'm so happy for her."

"So happy for her you're going to drink yourself into a stupor all by your lonesome, McConnell?" She gave him half a smile.

"What's best for the people we love isn't always what's best for us, now, is it?"

The haunted look in her eyes told him that she knew exactly what he meant. "No, it's not." She sighed. "Does that woman know how lucky she is?"

"I don't think she feels very lucky at the moment."

"You, Paris, the career of her dreams? What more could she want?"

"Everything, I hope."

"What about you, Jack? What do you want for you?"

"That is for me." Suddenly the pain wasn't so empty, his insides not so hollow. For Betsy to be happy, it really was enough. He exhaled heavily and smiled. "Buy yourself something pretty, Mindy. I changed my mind about the scotch," he said as he handed over some money.

He walked back outside before she could say anything else, or he could change his mind.

Jack drove home. He was still hurting. There was that giant black hole inside him, but there was that flickering hope, too. The candle in the dark that burned because of Betsy.

CHAPTER TWENTY-TWO

BETSY HAD A lot of time in her own head on the flight to New York, and she knew she'd have even more on the flight to Paris. She didn't mind so much; she was glad that Marcel didn't expect her to entertain him. She didn't have anything to discuss anyway. The scene with the mushroom bordelaise kept replaying itself over and over in her head on a loop.

It was like watching a horror movie where she'd scream at the heroine not to run in heels, or not to go check the inhuman noise coming from the dark woods, but she did it anyway and the audience kept watching even though they knew what was going to happen.

She watched herself prepare: picking the mushrooms, talking to Marcel, tossing them merrily in her basket as if she hadn't a care. Betsy had been so sure of herself, utterly absorbed in the experience of the moment rather than paying attention and keeping herself grounded in the present.

Stupid, naive Betsy, always with her head in the clouds.

Not anymore. She decided she was going to keep both feet firmly anchored to the earth. It was the only way to get by. Her stomach twisted in on itself and nausea climbed the back of her throat.

She wasn't ready to face the man who'd laughed her out of Paris.

Maybe they were all right. Maybe she'd run away from this, just as she was running away from Glory.

Betsy sighed. She supposed she should've thought about that before she went off like a rocket and cashed a check she didn't want, boarded a plane to a place she didn't really want to go and basically threw a tantrum.

Her emotions had been all over the map lately, and it seemed the slightest things upset her. Not that Jack telling her that he didn't want to be with her was a slight thing, but she knew that going in. She'd told him it was okay, and if it wasn't, she shouldn't have said it.

She'd get him a cashier's check and have Caleb drop it off to give him back the money. Betsy couldn't spend it. It felt like blood money.

Although Caleb, she was still angry with him and she didn't see that changing any time soon. He was sorry that she was pissed, but he had no remorse for what he'd done. He had to learn that it wasn't okay for him to meddle in her life.

She really wished her dad had been home, or he'd at least been somewhere where she could talk to him. He was always the voice of reason.

Even without talking to him, she knew what he'd say. He'd tell her to go to Paris. He'd tell her that even if her dreams changed, she had to finish what she started.

That didn't make it easier to be *bouchon de mort* girl.

She looked over at Marcel and studied his profile. His dark hair, his perfect cheekbones and the way he drummed his fingers in time to the beat rocking through his headphones on his thigh. He was so familiar, yet foreign to her all at once.

Her stomach rolled again and she tried to turn off the loop in her head as she settled deeper back into the seat and thought yet again how much she despised mushrooms.

Paris was just as beautiful as Betsy remembered. The city of lights and lovers. There was a different scent to the air, something like wine and pastry, but she was sure that was more memory association than anything.

"Are you ready?" Marcel asked her kindly.

"Ready? For what?"

"The chef has sent a car for you. We will go directly to his flat. You will cook for him." He motioned to the sleek black car that waited for them.

"What? No. I thought I was rejoining the group." Panic seized her by the throat.

"You will, but you must cook for him. For us. I'll be there with you, Betsy."

So many different emotions bloomed and alternately wilted inside her as she thought about what it meant to cook for Chef Abelard. This really was an amazing opportunity. Her stomach rolled again, doing dips and turns like a roller coaster.

"I think I'm going to throw up."

Marcel gave her an indulgent smile. Jack would have told her that she was going to be fine. He would have held her hand. He wouldn't have just given her that stupid smile, as if to say he was so much worldlier than she was. He would have told her that she had her own bakeshop and she was a successful businesswoman. He would have told her that she didn't have to prove anything to anyone but herself.

And he'd be right.

But when would she ever be able to stop comparing everything and everyone to Jack and what he would do?

"Fine. I'm fine. Let's go." Betsy straightened her spine and steeled herself for what was to come.

She watched the scenery go by and before long, she was taking it all in with the joy and excitement of a tourist. There were lights everywhere, the Christmas markets were open and Betsy found herself in love with Paris all over again.

The car finally stopped in front of a swanky-looking white-marbled building. Of course Chef Abelard lived here. Just standing in front of it made her feel small and insignificant.

But Betsy wasn't either of those things. She thought about her Better Than Sex donuts. She thought about the flavors she'd slowly brought back to Jack's life. She thought about everything she'd accomplished.

And finally she thought about Marcel. She'd practically demonized him in her head for the way he'd made her feel about her skills, about her body and about herself as a person. He wasn't the bogeyman, and neither was Chef Abelard. No one could make her feel anything she didn't allow them to.

Even if she bombed this, it didn't matter.

She realized this moment right here was what everyone wanted her to know. This was why they'd all pushed so hard to get her to come back.

Her nose burned with that prickle that made her eyes water. Damn, but she was so emotional. She couldn't believe she was ready to cry standing there on the street. She hadn't even cried (where anyone could see her anyway) when they'd laughed her out of the group and out of Paris.

A doorman held the way open for them, and Marcel led her inside.

She followed him and they were shown to an elevator that required a special key, where they were taken up to what Betsy could only call a penthouse. It was good to be an internationally celebrated chef.

The elevator doors opened directly into the flat and Chef Abelard greeted them.

"I'm pleased to see you returned," he began in a heavy French accent. "When I spoke with Marcel, he seemed to think that you wouldn't. That your small Midwestern life with Crock-Pots and hoedowns had swallowed you whole. I'd hate to see your talent so wasted."

She thought again about India working in her

kitchen. Her stupid brother stopping in for his daily donut. Jack. The guys at the V.A. That was wasting her talent?

Her first thought wasn't that she should be glad that he wanted her to return. Or that at one time she'd agreed with him about Glory. It was that he was a pompous ass. She met his appraisal head-on and didn't look down at her hands, or try to shy away from his inspection. She inspected him back and found him decidedly lacking.

Abelard was amused. "You're going to need that fire if you're going make it in this business. Come, cook for me, *Bouchon de Mort*." He motioned to a counter in the most beautiful kitchen she'd ever seen. Everything was stainless steel and glass—an array of tools, machines, knives, they were all on display like some kind of museum exhibit. Betsy knew what each thing was for, and how to use it to deliver the best culinary experience.

Sweet Thing was smaller, and though she had stainless workstations, it was nothing like the sleek lines of the chef's kitchen. It was intimidating, but Betsy knew she could do this.

She ignored his barb, even though it still wounded her deeply. Instead she turned her attention to the lovely, gleaming kitchen. She was more impressed with that than she had been with the glittering streets of Paris. For Betsy, that shine of stainless steel and appliances was more beautiful than the stars. It was a blank canvas and the foods her paints.

"What shall I make for you?" Betsy asked quietly.

"Your supplies are there." He motioned to a prep table. "There is one catch. You must choose the proper mushrooms. There are three bowls. Two are edible. One is the death cap. You should be very sure about your choice because we will all dine together."

Betsy was sure she was going to vomit this time. She hated mushrooms. She hated them so much. If she could obliterate them from the face of the planet, she would.

Her mother always said in for a penny, in for a pound. She knew that what she said next was exactly what the chef wanted to hear.

"I will prepare mushrooms bordelaise." Her voice didn't waver.

"Wise choice." Abelard nodded.

With shaking hands, she inspected the mushrooms. She could do this. She could. They all looked alike to her, one blending into another like a swirl of velvety color. Since the incident, she'd avoided cooking—staying strictly within her comfort zone of pastries. She'd especially avoided mushrooms; she couldn't stand the sight of them. She tried to remember what he'd said in the class before he set them loose to gather the mushrooms.

She looked for white gills, but they all looked white to her. She looked at the coloring on the caps, the shape of the caps. Again, they all looked the same to her.

Panic seized her again. If she made the wrong choice here, it wasn't about her career, or her trip to Paris or even Marcel. This could kill someone.

She picked up a sample from each bowl in turn and inspected them very closely.

Betsy had thought it was stupid that he made the students gather them themselves, especially when one could order almost any ingredient needed. But she understood now. Preparing food was a privilege—it was intimate. Something she'd chosen, touched, it was entering a person's body to nourish it.

Or alternatively, damage it.

Betsy had always known that, but it had never been driven home in such stark relief. That's what the chef had been trying to teach her.

She needed to own her mistake. Betsy hadn't accepted the gravity of what she'd done or the trust placed in her. She'd run home to her family and they'd given her Sweet Thing. She hadn't done anything to earn it.

"I see you understand. This is good."

Marcel looked at her askance. "I don't. What's he talking about?"

Betsy exhaled and inhaled.

Abelard spoke again, completely ignoring Marcel. "Do you remember your lessons?"

Betsy wanted to say that she did. It was on the tip of her tongue, but she didn't. Not all of them. Panic clutched at her throat again with bony fingers and choked her.

The moment with Jack when he was thrashing on the floor, so wounded and in so much pain, came back to her in waves. She'd demanded that he ask for help. Demanded that he swallow his pride and just ask for help.

Maybe she wasn't as broken as he was, but all the lessons she'd been trying to teach him, Betsy had the epiphany that she should've been trying to teach them to herself, as well.

She lifted her chin. "No, Chef. I don't remember. I'm sorry. Can you please help me?"

Betsy waited on tenterhooks to see what he would do. If he would laugh at her again, call her stupid, send her from his house with the command that she never come back. And she realized that she could handle any of those things.

"Smell them," he directed.

She picked up a mushroom from each bowl yet again and smelled each one in turn. They had a faint, generic earthy scent. Except for the one in the last bowl. The faint scent of roses clung to it.

Betsy remembered his instructions in class that day. He'd said if they had trouble, to remember that flowers were for the dead. She smiled and took the bowl and dumped it in the trash.

He and Marcel both gave her a nod of approval and she began preparing the other two kinds of mushrooms for the bordelaise.

"Are you sure you want to do that?" Marcel asked when she mixed them.

"Yes." Confidence surged. "Now get out of my kitchen." She knew from the way her baked goods turned out that the food would capture her emotion, and she wanted this to taste like victory with no taint of doubt.

Betsy continued to cut and slice, adding parsley to the mushrooms. She turned on the stove and set cloves of garlic to brown in olive oil. It took her fewer than twenty minutes to finish and when she was done, she served the dish.

She had to take the first bite, but she did so with confidence. It had a nutty, earthy flavor and when she smiled, everyone else took their bite.

But it didn't sit well on her stomach. In fewer than five minutes, she made a mad dash for Abelard's bathroom and she was reminded just how much she hated mushrooms.

EVEN THOUGH BETSY couldn't keep it down, it was still a success and Abelard offered her his tutelage, which she accepted.

She discovered Marcel had been less than truthful about barely keeping his restaurant in New York open. He had moved back to France and was now working for Chef Abelard. He'd apologized for the lie but said it was hard to admit his failure to her.

Betsy found joy in cooking again. Not just baking, but everything Abelard was teaching her. November quickly merged into December, and while Paris was certainly beautiful, as was the apartment Abelard had secured for her with her unused tuition, Betsy longed for home.

She still longed for Jack.

And her mother's cooking.

She found that more and more foods upset her stomach and that tepid tea and dry biscuits were more often than not the best choice. She wondered if she had some kind of intestinal bug. It wasn't until she was sitting in the upscale café on the corner across from Abelard's sipping that tepid tea that Marcel offered her another answer to the mysterious illness.

"Betsy, I'm not sure how to ask this politely."

She looked up at him, curious. "I suppose you should just ask, then."

"Could you be pregnant?"

Her hand flew to her stomach, as if somehow the answer would be there in braille under her palm. She thought about all the times she'd been intimate with Jack, and there had been two times that he hadn't used a condom.

She hadn't had her cycle since.

Her mouth fell open and dangled there like an old hinge.

"My mother was sick like this with my sisters," Marcel added. "I remember for so long she could only eat dry biscuits and tea with a spoonful of honey."

Jack's baby.

Tear pricked her eyes and before she could stop them, they streaked down her face. She didn't know how to feel. She remembered thinking about what it would be like to be here in this moment, only she thought they'd be together.

She tried to take deep, soothing breaths. After all,

she might not be pregnant. There was no reason to get amped up over nothing.

Only, it wasn't nothing. Part of her knew without a doubt that she was carrying Jack's child. It resonated inside her with all the clarity of silver bells.

You'd tell me, wouldn't you? he'd asked.

Of course she'd tell him.

But she'd said something hurtful, sown doubts about his abilities to parent. So that he'd said he'd be prepared to meet his financial responsibilities. Jack would be a wonderful father. He'd do whatever he had to do to make sure his child had a good life. Why had she said that to him?

More important, how would she tell him?

Would he even believe her or would he think it was just some ploy to keep him in her life after he was ready to be gone?

Marcel stood. "It seems that you have a lot to think about."

"I'm sorry," she said when she realized she hadn't answered him. "It really is a lot to think about," Betsy repeated dumbly.

"I'm sure it is. If you need me, you know where I am." He studied her for a long moment. "I was waiting for the right time, Betsy. But it doesn't seem there will be one. I didn't want to add to your burden, but you should know that Jack isn't your only option."

"What do you mean?"

"I'd hoped that when you came to Paris we could start again, but your heart is too full of someone else. If he is not the man you thought he was, don't discount me."

She didn't know what to say to that, so she just nodded and he seemed to understand that she needed time and room to breathe. He squeezed her shoulder and left her alone with her thoughts.

If she were home in Glory, she'd just call him and tell him that they needed to talk in person. It made things a bit harder when she was all the way in Paris, but this wasn't something she could tell him over the phone.

What would she do about studying with Abelard?

So many questions with no answers.

She took a deep breath and reminded herself that she needed to confirm her suspicions before losing her mind. It could be anything from a stomach virus to a spoke in her cycle.

Worrying was a waste of imagination, but her brain couldn't stop playing the what-if game.

CHAPTER TWENTY-THREE

AFTER THE WAY they'd left things, the last thing in the world that Jack expected was to see a call from Betsy on his cell.

The same feeling he'd had at her parents' house before he went inside for Sunday dinner for the first time after he came back bubbled up inside him—that sense that after this phone call nothing would ever be the same for him.

He wondered if he had to go to France and put the fear of hell into someone, because that's what he'd do if someone had hurt her.

"Are you okay?" He didn't bother with the niceties.

"I think so." Her voice fed something starving inside him and he waited to hear the sound of it again. He supposed that was stupid, to say he could taste a sound, but he could. Everything with Betsy was about taste.

But she didn't speak.

Which ignited a dark and terrible thing. "Is Marcel a dead man? I can be on a plane tonight."

"You'd do that for me?"

"Of course I would." *I love you. I'd do anything*

for you. "What happened doesn't mean I don't care about you." That was the bitterest lie he'd ever uttered and it was sour and rotten on his tongue.

"Yeah, you said that." Her voice was so soft he almost couldn't hear her.

"I did." He waited through another long bout of silence. International minutes weren't cheap. It must be something serious if she was watching the seconds tick by just breathing at him. "Do you need me to come?" He was just as quiet. Jack was afraid to offer, afraid of what it meant if she said yes. Afraid of what it meant if she said no. But her silence was even worse.

She made a sound that could have been anything from a laugh to a sigh. "Is it strange that I don't know?"

"No." He didn't think it was strange at all, because he didn't know if he wanted her to need him or not. If she did, he would go. Part of him wanted her to still need him. He wanted to be her knight in shining armor, her hero, her everything. That was the selfish part. But in his heart, he knew that it would be best for her if she didn't need him and for her to see that. To be confident and strong, to understand how amazing and powerful she really was.

Then there'd be no stopping her, and Jack McConnell would be a pit stop and a memory on her road to glory.

Jack had never known something could hurt like this without a physical wound.

"I'm coming, Bets. I'll text you with arrival times."

"Okay." She sighed. "Thank you, Jack."

"Anytime." Christ, why had he said that? *Anytime? Dumb ass. You're flying to Paris and she didn't even ask you to come.*

Anytime.

Stupid.

"I'll see you soon." He disconnected and dialed Connie.

"Hey, Connie. You said I could call you if I needed anything and I think I need something." *Shit, I'm as bad as Betsy.*

"What do you need?"

"Can you watch my house for a few days? Set the faucets to drip if the temperature freezes, that sort of thing?"

"How long are you going to be in France?" She laughed.

"I don't know."

"Oh so it's that kind of trip. I'll take care of it, kiddo. I can't promise no wild parties, though."

"Connie, you do whatever you want."

She laughed again. "Bring our girl home."

That was the last thing he wanted to do. He wasn't going to do anything to jeopardize this for her.

If she was homesick, he'd bring her a little bit of home. If she was lonely, he'd spend time with her. If she needed someone to tell her it was okay, he'd do that, too. But he would not tell her to come home.

"I'll see what I can do. Thanks. I'll leave the key under the mat."

As he was booking his flight, he wondered what it had been like for her to fly to Paris with Marcel. He wondered if she thought about him at all. She was so angry when she left, and rightfully so. He knew what he said hurt her. It hurt him to say it.

When he started packing, he looked at the two journals on his desk, the ones Andrew had asked him to keep, and he debated whether or not to bring them. In the end, he decided that he should probably take them. Even though they were his words, it was easier to write some things than to speak them.

He shoved them into his duffel and grabbed his passport.

He was going to Paris.

The crowds, the strange sounds—they were all things he would've had a problem with not too long ago. But if he stayed focused on what he had to do, he found that, while it was uncomfortable, he could do it. Like retrieving the blanket.

Like making Betsy go. It was uncomfortable, but he could do it.

JACK HAD NEVER been to France before, but the only sight he was interested in was Betsy. And seeing her again, even stepping off a plane in the airport in Paris, it was like coming home. Glory wasn't home; Betsy was.

Her eyes were wide, tremulous. She looked both hopeful and afraid. Seeing her was like aloe on a burn, and he drank her in. She'd changed, yet she was the same. She still had a sweetness about her, but there was a grit, too. He couldn't put his finger on it. Maybe it was simply because they were in Paris and rather than the rockabilly fatale, she'd adopted an Audrey Hepburn kind of understated elegance.

"I can't believe you're here." She flung herself into his arms and he caught her easily.

She smelled like vanilla and lavender, no trace of sugar. "You haven't been baking."

"No. Abelard says I love it, so it comes easily to me and I must work on other disciplines."

"So obviously, you passed whatever test he had for you."

"I did." She pulled away from him and looked up into his eyes. "The only reason I passed is you."

"What did I do? You were the one who was here. You did it." And he was so proud of her.

"Only because I asked for help. I didn't realize how hard it was, or what I put you through."

He was suddenly uncomfortable and that feeling of his skin being too tight was back in full force. Was this why she'd brought him here, to tell him this? "Again, that was all you, sweet thing." The endearment escaped before he could stop it.

She smiled softly then. "There's the Jack I know." Betsy fidgeted with her hands, smoothed invisible wrinkles from her red blouse the way she did when she was nervous.

"What's wrong, Bets?"

She still wouldn't look at him. "I made you come all this way and now I don't know what to say."

"You don't have to say anything."

"Damn it." She sniffed. "Why couldn't you have been this way before I left?"

"What do you mean?"

"Nothing." She shook her head and plastered a smile on her face. "I'm just so glad to see you."

"You, too, Bets."

"You know, and I probably shouldn't say this, but when I first applied for the internship here, I imagined you'd be here with me. I was such a little girl then."

Jack didn't say anything. He couldn't, because he was at war with himself. He missed her so much, needed her because she was the sun. But she needed to do this by herself more.

"I'm scared." She looked at her hands again.

This, this he could handle. This he could do. He understood fear and if she needed him to slay dragons, that's what warriors were for.

He tilted her chin up gently to force her to look at him. He wanted her to see the sincerity in his eyes and know she was safe. "Whatever you're afraid of, I'll take care of it."

She laughed, a high-pitched titter. "I didn't want to tell you here."

"Would you rather we find a place where we can look at the clouds and talk about their shapes until you're ready?" he teased, reminding her of when she'd first told him she loved him. She'd been afraid then, too, but had forged ahead. Jack was trying to remind her that she was fearless.

But instead she said, "And that turned out so well."

"Betsy, you've made it all sound so dire. It's not like you're the head cheerleader trying to tell the quarterback she's pregnant."

Only she didn't think it was funny. She paled. "No, I was never the head cheerleader. But you were the quarterback, so yeah, it's kind of like that."

Jack might as well have been hit in the face with a shovel. A starburst started from the bridge of his nose and radiated outward until his fingers and toes were numb. His face was numb, his body was numb—everything was just frozen.

Pregnant.

Betsy. Was. Pregnant.

He'd be a father. He couldn't be a father. He was too much like his own dad right down to the drinking—only he'd never hidden his bottles in a cuckoo clock. No, no—he'd stopped. He was in control of himself. He'd do whatever Betsy wanted him to do.

And for a second, he let himself think about what it would be like to have this fairy tale with her. To have a family, a life together. He wanted it so badly he could taste it.

Unless she was settling.

"God, Jack. Say something," she pleaded.

"What do you want to do?" he asked quietly.

"I kind of thought you'd have an opinion. You

said if it happened, to tell you. So I am. If you want to see the doctor's confirmation—"

"You thought I wouldn't believe you?" How could she think he'd—

"I didn't know what to think. Everything has been so screwed up between us that it's like we're not even Betsy and Jack anymore."

"We'll always be Betsy and Jack." He pulled her close again and she came willing, pliant in his arms. "Until the wheels fall off." He rested his chin on the top of her head. "There's a lot to talk about, but we don't have to do it at the airport."

"Are you hungry? I could cook for you."

"You're already baking a new human. I don't think you should have to do anything else." He gave her a small grin.

"We could go back to my apartment," she offered. "It's quiet. I don't know if you'd rather stay at a hotel."

"Do you want me to stay with you?" He didn't know if he could keep his hands off her. He missed everything about her. The memories of her were already faded from overuse, and just being with her was enough to bring them to vivid life all over again.

"Yes."

IT WAS BOTH strange and wonderful having Jack in her apartment.

But it made Betsy realize that Paris wasn't what she wanted at all. She'd been torn about wanting to go home, but seeing him and thinking about her future and about the child they'd made together, she'd never been surer.

Even if he didn't want to be with her, they couldn't both be good parents if they were living in different countries.

She still couldn't believe he'd come. She called, and he came, no questions asked.

He dropped his duffel bag by the door and looked around. She gave him the tour as she had done with the place above Sweet Thing. She showed him every lock, every safety precaution and every escape route. He'd taught her to think that way, and she liked that she knew those things. It made her feel just a little bit worldly and wise.

Jack seemed to approve of most of her safety precautions, except the balcony. It made him frown. The first glimpse of the glass doors and the corners of his mouth drooped until it was full-on disapproval.

"Are you happy here?" he asked.

Betsy looked at him in surprise. She'd expected him to berate her about the doors. He seemed so stern standing there, his jaw set and his eyes watching her every movement. She took the time to really think about his question.

"Happy enough, I suppose. This has been an amazing opportunity. I mean, I'm living in Paris. I've learned so much from Chef Abelard, and I've confronted my fears. You were right about that, but I can't help thinking how the decorations are coming for the Winter Ball at the historical society. If they've put up those lighted wreaths on all the street lamps downtown. I wonder who is going to stuff India into a dress. I wonder who is going to feed my guys at the V.A. on Christmas Day. And my dad. He's going to be home for Christmas for the first time in years. Those are all things that appeal to me much more than Paris."

"Because they're safe and what you know?"

There was no accusation there as there had been when he told her she had to come, she had to do this. "No, I don't think so."

"It would be perfectly normal, you know. Especially considering that you're pregnant. You're all alone here."

"I'm not alone. I have friends. But it certainly isn't Glory. All those things that make people ridicule small towns I find charming and homey. I love the city, but I love Glory more."

"To finish your internship, you'd have to stay a year. Longer, to take time out for the baby."

She couldn't tell if it was a statement or a question. "Yes."

"I could move here to help you."

Her heart leaped in her throat. Joy flared, but then the light dimmed. She couldn't take him away from the support system she'd fought so hard to get him to build and accept. This wasn't just about her and what she needed.

"Don't make that face. I know what you're thinking." He flashed her a look and for a second, he was the golden boy again.

"You keep asking about me, what I want. What I need. What about you? This isn't just about me."

"No, it's not. It's about the baby, and what I want is what's best for her."

"What is that?" She cocked her head to the side.

"For you to marry me."

Her throat constricted and she was sure her heart stopped. "Why would you say that?" It was everything she hoped for and everything she feared all at once. She wanted to marry him, but she wanted it to be because he loved her, not because she was pregnant. Betsy realized she should've expected something like this. Of course in his mind that would be the answer.

"Because it's true, and before you start telling me how draconian it is that I asked you to marry me because you're pregnant, think about it logically. Ramstein is four hours from here. You can deliver on U.S. soil and still finish your internship. If we're married and something happens to me, you'll automatically be entitled to all my benefits so you and the baby will always be taken care of. It just makes sense."

"Even if I don't want to stay here? I don't need to finish my internship. I've learned everything I can from Chef Abelard because I don't need international acclaim. I don't want it. I want Sweet Thing." And all the dreams that were tied up with it.

"I don't want you to give this up because you're afraid I can't hack it here."

"I know you can."

"Or did I read you wrong and you don't want me involved?" He looked out the window as he spoke.

Her words came back to haunt her, as she knew they would. What she'd said about him not being fit to be a father. "No, Jack." She put her hand on his arm and he looked at her.

She wanted this man. She wanted him so badly, she'd take him any way she could get him. He was offering her everything. Home, family and most important, himself.

But she wanted him to love her.

No, she wanted him to be *in* love with her. She wanted to be the first thing he thought about in the morning and the last thing he thought about before bed. She wanted to be his everything.

She wanted to be to him what he was to her.

When she imagined him proposing, it had always been something desperately romantic, worthy of novels and bards. But Betsy thought about the first time they'd made love in her old room. It hadn't been as she'd imagined it, but it was even better because it was real.

This was real. It wasn't perfect, but life rarely was. She could say no, waiting for something that would never happen, or she could accept Jack's proposal—and him—the way they were. Imperfect.

"Ask me," she whispered, her voice shaking.

"Will you marry me, Betsy?"

She'd said once that they'd drink blackberry cordial at their wedding, and now he'd asked her, but instead of filling her with joy, it made her heart feel cracked and fissured.

His eyes searched hers as he waited for her answer. As if he didn't know what it would be, as if he didn't know that she'd been waiting for this day since she was a little girl and told her mother that she'd decided she was going to marry Jack McConnell.

"Yes. Of course, yes."

He pulled her against him. "I swear, I'll make you happy, Bets."

She inhaled the scent of him and let his warmth wrap around her. He was so strong, so hard everywhere and so familiar.

And he was hers.

"Will you take me home? I want to spend Christmas with my family—our family."

"Anything you want, little mama."

The way he said that caused shivers to dance down her spine and her body to heat and ache everywhere he touched her.

"Anything at all?" She scored her nails down his back in a light tease. Betsy didn't mind being the aggressor when it came to their bed sport, because she knew he wanted her. He couldn't hide that visceral reaction. Even now his body's response was immediate.

"Anything."

He picked her up and she wrapped her legs around his waist and she remembered the last time they'd touched like this, remembered how she'd cried out that she loved him, and how he said he didn't love her.

She pushed it out of her mind. Betsy refused to think about it. That was then and she wouldn't let the past define her. He'd committed his life to her; so what if he wasn't in love with her?

"Jack." She said his name as much to ground herself in the moment as she did to plead with him for more. More skin on skin, more friction, more everything.

"I've missed you so damn much." His hands moved over her body languorously.

The times before, they'd been so intense, so hurried, as if the moment would be snatched away from them. This was different. He seemed almost reverent and maybe even a little in awe as he touched her.

Or perhaps that was just her imagination.

It was on the tip of her tongue to tell him that she loved him, but he knew. He didn't need to hear it, especially since he wasn't going to say it back. Betsy knew she shouldn't say she loved anyone, not just Jack, with any expectation of reciprocation. She'd read somewhere that, when love speaks, it should be because it can't remain silent, not because it expects something in return.

She brushed her lips against his and he quickly took command of the kiss. Again, it was different. Perhaps he was more confident of his own appeal? There was definitely something different about him, and it was utterly delicious. Jack McConnell wore his damage very well, but he wore his power even better.

Betsy tilted her head to the side to give him more access as he trailed languid kisses down her throat. He lingered at her collarbone, his hot mouth giving way to the light scrape of his teeth against her skin, making her shiver with anticipation.

"Do you need some heat, sweet thing?"

No, she was already so hot she was dizzy. Betsy clung to him, her arms tight around his neck and her legs still locked around his waist.

"I thought about this, about you, the whole flight."

"Tell me."

"Taking you against the wall, holding you up just like this and hearing you scream my name." Both hands were on her hips now as he held her up and ground against her simultaneously. "The vanilla sugar taste between your thighs on my tongue. I don't know how you're so damn sweet, but I crave it."

She shivered again.

"Yeah, you definitely need more heat," he growled against her ear.

Then his mouth crashed into hers, all strength and domination, but she melted under the barrage. It was almost as if her body didn't belong to her, shifting and arching against him with an agenda of its own.

"Please, don't make me wait. It's already been so long."

"I've been writing, Bets. Just like you wanted me to."

Oh God, why was he telling her about this now when she was ready to explode in his arms?

"And it's all about you, just like this."

She clenched her thighs as she imagined him making up his stories about her, about them together. As she imagined him pleasuring himself to those same stories.

"I brought my journals, if you want to read them." His hands were traveling her body again, pushing up beneath the soft material of her blouse. "Or I could read them to you."

Betsy made an unintelligible sound and rolled her hips against him.

"Yeah, I'll read them to you tonight. The first one is about a beautiful girl who sends her man off to war with the best gift ever on a red-checkered blanket with a bottle of blackberry cordial."

"Does he say no?"

"He's more a bastard than I was, because he wants her to remember him, too."

"What does he do to make her remember him?" she asked, breathless.

"This." He laid her down gently on the sofa and peeled her slacks and panties down her legs before dipping his head between them.

She loved that he always wanted to taste her, and that it seemed to bring him almost as much pleasure as it did her. The first touch of his tongue was always ecstasy. It was if her pleasure was his prime directive.

"And the girl," she gasped, as he laved at her. "What did she— Oh."

"She stopped talking and surrendered to his every dark desire," he teased before continuing his work.

The light abrasion of his stubble against her thighs spurred her hotter and his tongue moved faster, taking her ever higher. She was so close to the brink, and it was a full-on campaign to push her over the edge.

Her world contracted to a pinpoint so tiny she thought it would crush her; then it exploded outward like a burning star.

Betsy was still quaking with the aftershocks when he stripped bare and pulled her onto his lap. "Take what you want from me."

She braced her shaking hands on the back of the sofa and shifted until he was inside her, her full breasts and tight nipples brushing against his lips. He put his tongue back to good use licking the puckered rose-tipped flesh just as he had done between her legs. Her channel was still spasming with pleasure and gripped him hard and pulled him deep. She rode him as he demanded, and it made her feel powerful to see him so vulnerable and needing her.

Betsy suddenly understood why he liked to please her. It must make him feel the same.

He tightened his arms around her and she increased her pace. Betsy found her own ecstasy spiraling again and she moved faster, harder—all for that heat and delicious friction.

"That's right, sweet thing. Take it deep."

She'd always thought dirty talk was something to laugh at, but his commands were anything but funny. They stirred something primal and hungry, and she wanted to drive him past the point of bliss, just as he did her.

Sweat-slicked and straining, their bodies moved together toward the pinnacle of release.

Suddenly his palm was on the back of her neck and her eyes flashed open as he drew her down close, but he didn't kiss her. Instead he was looking into her eyes as he found completion.

Betsy didn't know if she'd ever seen anything as beautiful as Jack McConnell with all his muscles strained, the cords in his neck visible with exertion and his erection thrusting up into her as she brought him the ultimate pleasure.

She bit her lip to keep from confessing once again that she loved him. She sagged against his shoulder as they were both spent, and he ran his fingers absently up and down her spine.

And for a moment, she was glad they didn't need any words between them, glad for the shared and easy silence. She wanted to bask in this.

After a while, he asked quietly, "How soon do you want to leave?"

"I already resigned from the internship. I'm ready to leave on the next flight. I want to go home. Take me home, Jack."

CHAPTER TWENTY-FOUR

BETSY HAD ALWAYS thought coming home to Glory was a punishment. The first time she'd come back from Paris, it had been like a death sentence. Now she couldn't imagine wanting to spend her life anywhere else.

Or raising a child anywhere else.

It had taken them all of a week to book their flight home, and she was ready to be in Glory.

She watched the familiar scenery speed by the windows like an animated flip book. "I know you've done a lot of flying in the last few days and you're probably jet-lagged like crazy, but could we drive through downtown when we get to Glory?" she asked Jack. "I want to see the mayor's tree and the lights."

"You got it. Being a SEAL trained me for no sleep. Anything else you were missing in particular?"

"Besides everything?" Betsy laughed. The car slowed and they turned down Broadway. "Oh look, the Harvey Girls house is lit up so beautifully. The doctor next door has a candle in every window." She sighed. "I wonder if it's on the candlelight homes tour this year. I'd love to see inside again. There's so much history here."

"And there isn't in Paris?" Jack teased.

"You know what I mean. Paris is worldly. She's very beautiful, but she's like a model. Beautiful art, but not very livable. At least not for someone like me. Glory is like my fat and sassy grandmother with her lace-trimmed Sunday dress, but serviceable shoes and apple pie."

"Speaking of grandmothers, you know we didn't actually get much talking done. When do you want to tell your family? More important, where are you sleeping tonight?"

For some reason, his question made everything more real. She was going to spend the rest of her life with him. That meant they would live in the same house, sleep in the same bed. They'd share the same struggles. There would be victories and losses. She understood that now in a way she never had before. This wasn't playing house, or pretend. This wasn't castles in the clouds. This was real.

Suddenly she was terrified.

Was she really strong enough to do this? Could she love him enough for both of them? It was strange, but before she'd gone to Paris, she thought she could. But after she'd conquered her demons, now she wasn't so sure. She kind of thought it was supposed to be the other way around, but Betsy never did anything the way she was supposed to.

"Bets? You okay?"

She searched his face and found concern sharp in his eyes. "No, I'm really not. We're getting married. Do you know what that means?"

"Well, yes. Generally, it involves the joining of bank accounts, Christmas card lists, cohabitation, et cetera. To my understanding anyway." His hard mouth curved into a gentle smile.

Betsy held up her hands, as if what she was trying to say could somehow be held in her palms.

"Look, if you changed your mind and you want to think about it, that's okay. I understand you're scared. I won't lie and say I'm not scared as hell, too. But I'll stand by you, Betsy."

In that moment, Jack proved yet again that he was her hero.

"Why don't we save the family reunion and all the questions for another night? Tonight, we'll just hide at my place with some takeout and movies," he said.

"Can we make a pillow fort? I'm not going unless there's a pillow fort." This was safer territory. It was familiar and silly, and it was something that was theirs from a simpler time.

"Yeah, there can be a pillow fort." Jack grinned and turned down the road toward his house.

Even though she tried to put it from her head, she couldn't help wondering if this was what their lives together would be like. If they could still be the best of friends, it would be almost perfect. Pillow forts, playing the cloud game, laughing together and making love—it was an ideal life.

And that was how Betsy knew that he was never going to be in love with her the way she loved him. Because nothing could be perfect. Life just didn't work out that way.

But that didn't mean she wouldn't enjoy the good moments as they came.

Like stealing Jack's T-shirts for sleepwear. "I'm going to raid your closet," she said after they were inside.

She went upstairs to his old room and saw that he'd moved his things back from the den. Betsy pulled an old No Fear shirt out of the closet. She also stole a pair of his socks. The shirt was well worn, the cotton soft against her body. Wrapping herself in his shirts always felt like wrapping herself in him, or so she used to think. Now that she'd had the real experience, it wasn't even close, but she still liked the sensation.

When she came downstairs, the requested pillow fort had been constructed from the cushions on the couch and she smiled.

"Knock-knock."

The corner of the blanket was pulled away and Jack said, "'Come into my parlor,' said the spider to the fly."

"That makes it sound like you have something nefarious planned."

"I do, I do. I'm going to make you watch old reruns of *The A-Team*. Unless you plan on subjecting me to some horrible chick flick. Then I might have to hang myself."

"It's only fair. If you make me watch *The A-Team,* I'll subject you to a *My So-Called Life* marathon."

"But you love the *The A-Team*. What did I do to deserve all of that Jordangela angst?" Jack propped his laptop open on his thighs, and the familiar music started when he hit Play.

Betsy laughed as she settled in against his chest, his arm around her, and for a moment, everything was fine. She exhaled a heavy breath she didn't know she was holding. All the tension fled her body and she just listened to the steady beat of his heart beneath her ear. He pushed his fingers through her hair absently and for a moment, it was as if nothing had changed.

"You were right, you know."

"What do you mean?" he asked.

"Right now we're just Betsy and Jack."

"Who else would we be?"

She could feel his smile. "I don't know. It's just, it seemed like nothing would ever happen to me and now everything is happening all at once." Betsy steadied herself for what she said next. She was afraid of his answer, but she had to say it. "I don't want to be the girl who got pregnant to keep the hometown hero. And I don't want you to be the man who resents his wife and children because his glory days are behind him."

"They're all Glory days when you live here," he teased.

She was silent. That was all the answer she needed.

"Betsy, it was supposed to be funny. Look, if I didn't want to marry you, I wouldn't have asked. We're still us."

"Do you swear?"

"To the sun, the moon and the stars, sweet thing."

"I don't need you to take care of me, you know," she said quietly, informing him, in case he really didn't know.

"Maybe it's the other way around, Bets."

She didn't think so. Not now. Back when he was still broken, maybe. He was still wounded, still fighting, but he'd dragged himself out of hell all on his own. She couldn't have done it for him, as much as she wished she could have. He'd been through so much.

"What did you want to be when you grew up?"

"What kind of question is that?"

She shrugged. "When you were a kid and anything and everything was possible."

"A SEAL."

"No, before you decided you were going to save the world. There had to be something." She scooted closer against him.

"I guess I went through a phase that all kids go through. I wanted to be an astronaut, a paleontologist, a Formula One racer."

"You're much too tall to be a race car driver." Betsy found herself smiling. "So, when did you know you were going to be a SEAL?"

"When Johnny Hart's dad came on career day in seventh grade."

"He was kind of a bastard."

"Yeah, he was. But I'd already caught the bug. From then on, it was what I always wanted to do."

"You say that like it's a virus."

"I guess it kind of is. You're useless to the corps until they break you down, but after they reform you in the image they want, you're useless for anything else."

"You're not useless, Jack."

"Yeah, I'm learning. I've been swimming at the community center. Working out a little more."

"I noticed." She could help trailing her hand over his chest.

"Oh you like that, do you?"

"I won't complain."

"I'll keep that in mind."

Betsy liked the idea that he would do that to please her. It was a heady sensation, made her feel just a bit powerful. "I used to think that if you wanted to have sex with your best friend, that was true love."

"And now?"

"Now I think there's something more. Some vital spark that when people talk about it, they say it's sexual attraction, passion. But it's not. They don't know how to quantify it. So they chock it up to sex appeal."

"Is that what you think we have? We're the best of friends who like to be naked together?"

"What would you call it?" Betsy answered his question with another question in the vain hope he'd say what they had was the stuff of fairy tales. Even though Betsy knew there was no such thing, that didn't stop her from hoping.

He didn't answer. He just stroked her back and she surrendered to sleep because it was easier than waiting for a truth she didn't want.

JACK DIDN'T KNOW why he couldn't tell her that he loved her. He opened his mouth and the words just wouldn't come out.

She'd made her decision about what she wanted and she'd chosen a life with him. Betsy deserved to know how he felt, but for some reason, he still couldn't say the words.

Maybe he thought if he said them, it would be like a dare to the world to take her away from him. That was completely illogical, but there it was, glaring and ugly. That was the only explanation.

Seeing her in his shirt had always turned him on, the way it clung to her perfect breasts and brushed the tops of her thighs, being just modest enough to be presentable, but oh so enticing. Everything about Betsy turned him on. Now she was nestled against him soft and warm, and he knew he'd probably spend the night with a hard-on, but Betsy needed to feel safe and secure. Jack had no doubt that if he kissed her, or started stroking his hands through her hair, down her back and— He turned his thoughts away from all the things he wanted to do to her. They'd have plenty of time for that. She was his.

He still wondered if maybe she'd given up her dreams for him. Jack had been listening when she said what she wanted was Glory, but she was alone and afraid, and Jack knew he'd always been her safe place. She needed that now more than ever. Maybe he should have talked her into staying in France, but he'd have an easier time cutting off his own hand than he would telling her no about anything. The noble part of him wanted to make her stay, but his heart wanted to believe this—him—was everything she wanted.

Getting married wasn't just what was best for the baby; it would be what was best for Jack, too.

But was it what was best for Betsy?

He looked down at her drowsy face, lashes slowly fluttering down against the cream palette of her cheeks. Her bow lips were parted and her fingers flexed and released against his chest in a soft succession, almost as if she was checking to make sure he was still there.

Jack rested his chin on the top of her head.

Just let me keep her.

He knew some men would be afraid of the situation he found himself in, and Jack wouldn't deny he was afraid, too. He doubted his abilities to be a good husband, a good father, but he wanted the chance to try.

After the navy, he'd thought he didn't have a future. His career had been his life, but none of that mattered now. His career would be whatever would best support Betsy and their children. He would find a way to give her the fairy tale. No matter what it took.

He used to be afraid of the way she looked at him. The wonder in her wide eyes as she watched everything he did. It had always made him want to be better, want to be worthy. Jack knew that Betsy, whether she knew it or not, had made him the man he was and gave him hope for the man he still wanted to be.

Jack still didn't know what she'd ever seen in him to warrant that kind of devotion, but he couldn't imagine living without it or without her.

This might not have been what either of them planned on, but now that he had it, he wasn't going to let go. As he watched her sleep, Jack swore he'd find a way to make her understand what she meant to him.

The soft kneading of her fingers had ceased and her breathing was deep and even. "I love you."

There, that wasn't so bad. In fact, it was a release to finally say what he'd felt for so long—to admit it out loud to himself. He finally realized that when he'd given her his tags that night all those years ago, what he'd really given her was his heart.

He let himself enjoy the quiet moment, just holding her. This was what he'd gone through hell for, and Jack decided that every second of it was worth it.

Jack must've fallen asleep, because the next thing he knew, she was digging her nails into his shoulder and whimpering.

"What's wrong?" His arms tightened around her instinctively.

"I don't know, but it hurts, Jack."

Fear shot through him hot and sharp. "Where does it hurt?" He kept his voice calm, but on the inside he knew all the pretty pictures he'd just painted were about to get smeared with turpentine.

"I can't explain it. Just…inside."

He never thought he'd have to use his training like this. Everything he'd just allowed himself to feel, he flipped it off like a switch. Betsy needed him to be strong and he wouldn't fail her.

"It's going to be okay, Betsy. Stay calm."

"Don't leave me."

"I won't. I'm right here." He pushed away the walls of their makeshift fort and reached for his phone, but decided he'd make better time to the hospital himself. He stood first, then leaned back down. "Okay, Bets. Hang on tight." He kept saying her name, using small endearments to get her to focus on the sound of his voice and to stay calm.

Inside, he was dying. Jack knew the only reason she had to stay with him was gone and the fey bubble of hope in which he'd seen their future together was gone. He'd wanted this baby, this life.

Her fingers were claws, twisted with her pain as they dug into him.

"I'm sorry."

"That's okay, sweet thing. I can take it." He kissed the top of her head. "Ride the pain any way you have to. Let it roll through you."

"I'm scared."

"Everything is going to be fine," he lied.

He cradled her close, grabbed his keys and drove her to Glory General.

BETSY WAS NUMB.

After a multitude of tests, and hours of waiting, the doctor told her that she'd never been pregnant. It was just a cyst and it had given her a false positive on both tests, as well as mimicking the other symptoms of pregnancy. The cyst had burst and along with it Jack's reason for marrying her.

Just a cyst.

Just the end of everything.

She'd fallen in love with her child and all the wonderful things she was going to do in the world. Those hopes and dreams were all ash and dust.

Just a cyst, and if you'd lose a few pounds, you wouldn't get them.

Betsy didn't know how she managed to keep her mouth closed when the doctor had said that, but she did. Maybe it was the expression on Jack's face. It was stoic and stony, but she could see the fury in his eyes.

His grip on her hand was gentle, but she could feel the strength there. He reassured her, comforted her and kept telling her it was okay.

But it really wasn't, was it? It wasn't okay at all.

He'd asked her to marry him. She'd said yes. Only there was no longer any need, nothing tethering him to her, and she supposed that was just as well. She'd said that she didn't want to be that woman, the one who used a child to keep a man.

The universe had heard and answered.

A dark chasm opened up inside her, and even her bones felt brittle and hollow.

"Don't worry," the nurse said as she handed Betsy her discharge papers. "You can keep trying." She gave them a well-meaning grin and closed the curtain so Betsy could change back into Jack's T-shirt in privacy.

They could keep trying. It sounded tinny and false to her ears and Betsy wanted to crawl under a rock and hide away from it all. She couldn't look at him. He was sitting right next to her, had stayed with her through all of it without complaint, and she didn't even want to look at his handsome face.

Betsy didn't think she'd be able to stand to see what was there in his eyes, the set of his jaw.

"I'm sorry," she managed in a choked voice. "I had a blood test to confirm, I swear."

"If you said you did, Bets, then I know you did. Don't worry about that now. I want to get you home and resting like the doctor said."

Home.

That wasn't going to be with Jack anymore.

It would be back to her little apartment above the bakery. It was home and there were a lot of good memories there.

"I need to stop by your place and get my things."

"My place?" He tilted her chin so she'd face him. "Nothing has changed. I asked you to marry me. You said yes. It's your place now, too."

"Jack." She swallowed hard. "We both know the only reason you asked was that we thought I was pregnant. There's no reason to get married now."

"No reason?" he parroted, as if the words made no sense to him. "How about I love you and want to spend my life with you? How about I wanted to do this with you, have our family?"

"No, you don't. You are physically incapable of breaking your word because you're a good man.

You'd rather spend your life chained to me than hurt me. But you know what? Not only do you deserve better, but I do, too. I deserve to be married to someone who is in love with me. Who thinks the sun rises and sets in my eyes. Someone who feels about me the way I've always felt about you. And I know you don't."

"How do you know that? You're not me. You don't know what I feel."

"Yes, I do know what you feel. Or what you don't feel, rather. Because if you did, you'd have done something besides push me away. Well, I got the message, Jack. Loud and clear, and it's okay. It really is. Just like you said. You promised it would be okay, and it is." Betsy couldn't believe the things she was saying. Every word was a sword that had to push its way through her heart to get to her tongue, but they were right and true, and so had to be spoken.

Her lip quivered, but she refused to cry. "I know you care about me. That's never been up for debate." She worked up her courage to finish. "You're not breaking your word to me and you're still part of the Lewis family. Whatever has happened between us, that will never change. So, now you see, there's no reason to keep up the farce."

Jack's jaw clenched and unclenched. "I'm sorry I didn't tell you before. I should have. But I do love you, Betsy. I'm in love with you. I have been since I gave you my tags. I just didn't know it."

"How do you not know you're in love with someone? It feels like a comet burning you up from the inside out. That's not something that happens and you just…don't notice. Let it go. It's over." She turned away from him. "I want to go home."

"I'll take you wherever you want to go, sweet thing. But I'm also going to prove this to you." He squeezed her hand.

"I don't think I want you to take me home. I need to be alone for a while."

"I know you don't believe this right now, but something was taken from me today, too. You're not the only one who hurts."

"Just go." Tears pricked behind her eyes, that pins-and-needles feeling in her nose. She didn't want him to see her cry.

"If that's what you want." He stood and leaned over her, the scent of him wrapping around her like a blanket. Jack brushed his lips against her cheek.

And for a second, part of her wanted to tell him to stay. It wanted to believe that she was more than an obligation. She wanted to curl against him and let him take care of her. She wanted to talk about all their hopes and dreams together. She wanted—so many things that were in truth out of reach.

She knew she'd done the right thing.

CHAPTER TWENTY-FIVE

AFTER A FEW DAYS, Betsy managed to get back into
the routine of her life in Glory. A routine that didn't
include Jack. She baked. She decorated the shop for
Christmas, and she baked some more. The townspeople were happy to have her back and she had
more work than she knew what to do with. Marcel
and Abelard both called to check in on her and she
put on a happy face.

Jack seemed to take her at her word when she
said that she didn't want to see him, and she was
both mollified to be right and even more heartbroken. She knew that she couldn't be angry with him
for taking her at her word.

But there was still some part of her dreamer's
heart that hadn't been crushed and it kept hoping for
a grand gesture. Or any gesture, but there was nothing. She made herself right with it as best she could
and threw herself into work.

Christmas Eve Day dawned bright and clear.
Betsy was disappointed because she wanted snow.
There was something infinitely magical about
Christmas snow.

Her mother called as she was getting ready to send out the last of the Christmas orders.

"I'm trying to wrap it up, Mom. I'll be over as soon as I'm done to help with the preparations."

"That's actually why I called. You don't need to do anything but look pretty and bring some of those wedding cake samples that your father likes so much. He'll be home for Christmas Eve dinner."

A thrill shot through Betsy. Her dad was coming home. She hadn't seen him or heard from him in months. He'd been on some secret squirrel mission for the Department of Defense and had an alias and everything. He couldn't have any ties to home. "That's great, Mama. I can't wait to see him."

"So, are you bringing the samples?"

"Yes." Betsy found herself smiling.

"And look pretty. Like, pretty pretty. For-strangers pretty."

"If you're trying to set me up with someone on Christmas Eve—"

"I wouldn't dream of it. But we're going to take a family picture. We haven't done that in years."

Betsy hadn't actually told her mother everything that had happened between her and Jack. She didn't want to hash it out a hundred times and she didn't want to see that look in her eyes when she watched them together. It made it more bearable somehow that she'd only shared it with India and Jack himself.

God, she missed him. She missed him so hard it was a physical ache.

She hoped someday it wouldn't hurt so much to love him.

"Okay, Mama. But I mean it. If there is one person there who shouldn't be, I'm leaving."

"No one who's not supposed to be? I can definitely promise you that. I know your heart is firmly and forever in Jack's keeping. I wouldn't interfere. I know you two will work it out."

"I don't want to talk about Jack," she grumbled.

Well, why not? It's not like you think about anything else but him. You might as well talk about him, she chastised herself.

"Okay, okay. We'll see you in a little bit." Lula hung up without waiting for Betsy to say goodbye.

Betsy finished packaging the last of the orders and closed up the shop. She trudged up the stairs to get ready for the family dinner and remembered what her mother said about pictures. The dress she'd planned on wearing had a 1960s comic book print. That wasn't exactly Christmas picture festive, so she grabbed her favorite red cashmere sweater, black leggings and boots. She thought she looked very Betsey Johnson, a designer she loved for more than the obvious reasons.

She applied her makeup carefully and when she was satisfied with her look, she grabbed the box of wedding cake samples that her father loved so much and drove to her parents' house.

Betsy might have accidentally taken the long way so she could drive by Jack's house. It was as close as she was going to get to him and she promised herself that after today, she'd never do it again.

She felt like *that* girl—Stalker McCrazy. It was ridiculous. She was the one who'd told him to go— she had to stop obsessing and get on with the business of living her life without him. She should've done it a long time ago.

His car was parked on the street, and there was a wreath with silver bells on his door. She wondered which neighbor had brought that to him.

Betsy depressed the accelerator and drove faster, determined not to think about Jack at all.

WHEN SHE WALKED into her parents' house, the smells of Christmas ham, eggnog and cranberry-orange candles washed over her. It smelled like happy memories, and Betsy was determined that tonight would be another one.

She inhaled deeply before taking off her coat and hanging it up. Betsy let herself enjoy the momentary silence and peace before the rush of hugs, chatter and face-stuffing that was about to commence. Food was a big part of any celebration in the Lewis household, and every holiday involved feasting.

Betsy loved that about her family. The traditions, the noise and especially the way there was always a place at the table for anyone who didn't have one of their own—be it family or tradition.

People like India, like Jack, who were now part of the family.

She remembered what her mother promised: *No*

*one who's not supposed to be? I can definitely prom-
ise you that.*

Only Jack was supposed to be there and instead,
his car was still parked in front of his house. So much
for not thinking about him.

"Is that you, honey? Come into the living room.
We're about to start pictures," her mother called.

They wouldn't start without her father. She ran
into the living room and launched herself at Anthony
Lewis. He caught his daughter easily and squeezed
her tight. It felt as if she hadn't seen him in years.
She turned her face into his shoulder and inhaled
the familiar scent of him. He looked the same as
when he'd left, maybe a few more wings of gray at
his temples, a sharp contrast to his dark hair. The
lines around his eyes were more pronounced, his job
having taken its toll.

"I'm so glad you're home."

"God, Bets. Leave some Dad for the rest of us,"
Caleb said.

Betsy hadn't seen Caleb, either, since being back.
Her anger at him had been justified, but she realized
it wasn't worth going so long without her big brother.
She yanked him into the hug.

India shifted uncomfortably in her seat. "You
guys are so weird."

"Oh you're not getting out of the love." Lula
hugged her hard and India allowed it. "Merry Christmas, India."

India mumbled something in return, and that was
when the door opened again.

Caleb pulled her in tight for another hug before she could turn to see who it was. "I have to get another one of these before you stop speaking to me again."

"You're not sorry at all, are you? What did you do?" she asked, knowing without looking who stood in the door.

When Caleb released her, Betsy turned oh so slowly, like a doll on a carousel, toward the figure in the door.

Jack.

Of course it was Jack.

The sight of him was welcome and warm, but sharp and painful, too. He'd grown out his hair a bit, long enough so it feathered back behind his ears and curled at his collar like chaffs of wheat tipped with gold. He wore a black sweater that accentuated the width of his shoulders and biceps.

She wanted to fling herself into his arms, press her lips against his hard mouth; she just *wanted*. He had a bag of presents in his hand and he smiled at her as though nothing had changed between them. She could see the boy he'd been in that smile.

"Hey, Bets. Merry Christmas."

She pursed her lips and forced breath into her lungs, commanded her voice to be steady. "Merry Christmas."

Lula embraced him and kissed him on the cheek, and her dad shook his hand and then drew him in close for a man hug that consisted of backslapping and other rough affection.

He did belong there and even though it hurt to see him, Betsy was glad he'd come. Not only so she could quench her thirst for the sight of him, but because he was part of the family. Her parents loved him like their own son. It was only right he spend Christmas with them.

A hot flush crept up Betsy's neck. She felt eyes on her, hot and intense. She looked up to see Jack watching her. He gave her that same devastating smile and she crossed her arms over her chest, as if that would stop her body's reaction to him. The need that seared her from inside out—heart, soul and between her thighs.

"Okay, Jack was just in time. Everyone line up in front of the Christmas tree." Lula directed traffic. "Betsy, I want you in front of Jack. India with Caleb and Anthony— *Anthony!* If you eat those wedding cake samples before we take this picture, homecoming or no, I'm going to—"

Betsy didn't hear the rest of what her mother said. Instead she was standing too near him and he had his hands on her waist and the solid wall of his chest behind her. He smelled like bay rum aftershave, and the scent always made her think of hot nights and even hotter sex. She wet her lips and she didn't know how she was going to make it through dinner. She was torn between trying to get closer to him and running away screaming.

The camera clicked in rapid succession, snapping pictures to commemorate the holiday, and when it finally stopped, Betsy was seeing spots, but the whole of her awareness had narrowed to the tiniest pinprick of light and the heat of his hands burning through her sweater.

"Okay, now you can go stuff your face with those cake samples," Lula relented. "But you better have room for dinner."

On the surface, this holiday dinner was much like any other. Fussing at Anthony was her way of shedding the skin of his other life. It was instant immersion back into the world. It was familiar; it was comfortable.

"What's your favorite, Betsy?" Anthony asked her. "It looks like there are some new ones." He eyed the contents of the purple box.

Her favorite? "The mocha hazelnut, I suppose."

Anthony smiled. "Okay, we'll order one of those."

That brought a smile to Betsy's face. "When do you want it, Dad?"

"That's up to you, honey. Brides get to pick their wedding dates, don't they? I'm just supposed to pay for it." He grinned.

"What are you talking about?" Her eyes narrowed and her heart leaped up into her throat.

Jack went to his stack of presents. "I have two presents for you, Bets. Which one do you want first?"

She shook her head. "No, don't. Don't do this to me." He said he was going to prove it to her, and now here he was, determined to prove, in front of her family, that he did love her. This was the grand gesture.

But it was only his sense of duty, wasn't it?

She didn't have a choice about the hope that

bloomed like a winter rose in the soil of her still-broken heart. If she had, she would have rooted it out like a weed. But no, there it was, bright as the star on top of the tree in front of them.

"Choose." He held up a big box that had been wrapped in red foil paper, and it gleamed as it reflected the hundreds of tiny white lights from the Christmas tree. In his other hand, he held a small blue box that could only be one thing.

"The red one."

Jack's lip curled in a smirk. "Good. I knew you wouldn't take what's in the blue box without what's in this one."

She found herself ushered to the sofa, where she sat down, and Jack placed the shiny box on her lap and her family watched expectantly.

"Are you going to open it or look at it?" Caleb nudged.

"Look at it," she said easily. But with trembling hands, she carefully released the points of tape that held the meticulously folded and sharp-edged paper together.

Inside, there was a white box. Nothing out of the ordinary. Just a plain box that could hold anything from CDs to a shirt.

Jack's sharp eyes took in her every movement and she suddenly felt very awkward and shy. She was afraid of what was inside.

"It won't bite you, I promise."

And Betsy knew Jack's promises were made of gold, so she opened the box.

There, nestled among a sleeve of tissue paper, was her red-checkered blanket. The one that held so many of their memories together. The one where she'd said she loved him. The one where they'd said goodbye.

The one she'd thrown off the embankment in the hopes that the river would carry it away after Jack told her he wasn't in love with her.

A single tear escaped from her closed eyes and she could feel it streak hotly down her cheek. Suddenly it was all crystal clear. He'd kept the blanket because it meant as much to him as it did to her. He'd sacrificed what he wanted so she'd reach for her dreams. His love was deep, passionate, unselfish and forever.

"I think you screwed up, bro," Caleb whispered.

"Shut. Up," India directed.

"No, I didn't," Jack answered with confidence. "I did just fine."

"It's a blanket," Caleb said, as if everyone hadn't seen what was in the box.

"Will you take the other box now, Betsy?" Jack asked, his voice still as sure as it had been.

"Yes. I'll take the box." She held out her hand, her eyes still closed. Betsy was still afraid to look.

This was everything she'd ever wanted, and it was happening right now. Jack was in love with her. He really wanted to spend his life with her. This was what the road to happily ever after looked like— surrounded by her family, bawling, on Christmas Eve with the man she loved making the grandest gesture of all.

Her eyes fluttered open when the box touched her

hand and she saw him kneel slowly, gracefully. She was so proud of him, how he never doubted himself or his own strength as he bent—something he couldn't do when they'd started this.

"Will you marry me, Betsy?"

"Yes. A million times, yes."

"She didn't even look at the ring," Lula whispered.

"I don't care about the ring."

Jack flashed her a grin. "Wish I would've known that before I spent hours trying to choose the right one."

Betsy melted off the couch, down on her knees, and wrapped her arms around his neck, the ring box still in her hand. "It could be a piece of string for all I care."

"I love you, Betsy. And I swore I'd prove it."

"And you always keep your promises." Betsy kissed him.

"Okay, that's enough of that. I don't need to see my best friend pawing my sister," Caleb growled.

"I thought I was your best friend," India interjected.

"You know what I mean," Caleb answered.

"Can I get the blackberry cordial now?" Lula asked.

"As long as there's some left for the wedding," Betsy said when she finally broke their kiss.

"I remember the taste of cordial on your lips." He grinned and eased her away from him and took the ring from the box and slid it on her finger. "On that very blanket."

"I swore that night that we'd drink it at our wedding."

"We will."

Outside, fat flakes had begun to fall, blanketing the world in white, and Betsy was reminded once again that there was definitely something magical about snow on Christmas Eve.

"Is it time for the cordial?"

"Yes, Mama. Get the cordial."

* * * * *

*Be sure to look for the next romance in
Sara Arden's sizzling new trilogy.
And now for a sneak preview of
UNFADED GLORY, please turn the page.*

CHAPTER ONE

BYRON HAWKINS HAD an ear worm.

Most people got them at one point or another—a Top 40 hit they couldn't escape, a catchy ad jingle, a children's song heard one time too often. Byron had such a loop, but he wasn't so lucky as to have anything as innocuous as the last song he'd heard on the radio. He had the screams of his team as they died.

Their terror and pain were always with him whether it was a damning whisper or a roar that sounded like the army of hell.

He knew it was no less than he deserved for his failure. If he hadn't given the order to pursue the guerrillas, they'd have all made it back to camp. They'd have gone home to their families at the end of the mission.

Instead they were ambushed and tortured.

Instead he was the only one who went home.

The voices were especially loud tonight—they always were before a mission, but here in the darkness, he silenced the howls of his fallen brothers, He drowned out that song in his head as he moved through the darkness toward his target—the Jewel of Castallegna.

The jewel was being kept in the Carthage National Museum. It would be no easy feat to get in and out with a national treasure, but breaking and entering was a skill he'd acquired in his delinquent youth.

He didn't ask his betters how a gemstone could serve the DOD; that wasn't his job. His job was to acquire the item and bring it home.

Byron entered through the front door. Security rolled in staggered shifts, and there were only three officers since the museum was closed to the public. He'd tranqued one officer in his car before he came on duty, and had taken his keys. Easy as his granny's pecan pie.

Until he heard voices coming from the first chamber. He flattened himself against the wall and peered through the door.

Two men had cornered one of the most beautiful women he'd ever seen. She was petite, but he could tell from her stance that she could hold her own. She'd been trained. Krav maga, perhaps. She was poised for a fight. Her eyes were the most curious shade of blue, but her skin was dusky and golden. It was too bad so much of it was covered by her black fatigues. She looked ready to do battle, and Hawkins had to admit it didn't get much hotter than a gorgeous woman with a thigh holster and a utility belt.

"You know the jewel should never leave Castallegna," one of the men said.

He swore under his breath. There would be bodies to dispose of. Byron wouldn't be much of a ghost if he couldn't get in and out without a trail of blood a mile wide in his wake, and he could tell this guy wasn't going to let the jewel go without the fight.

He hoped he wouldn't have to dispose of the woman, but he would if she stood between him and his mission.

"The jewel *isn't* going back," the woman answered.

"I can't kill you yet," the man said with a sadistic glee. "But I can hurt you."

Byron knew he had to act. The woman had the jewel or she knew where it was. He launched himself from his hiding place and snapped the big man's neck with a single motion. He dropped like a stone and the other would-be jewel thief sprang to action. He launched himself toward the woman, and when Hawkins would've saved her, she saved herself. As he watched her fluid movements taking the other man down, he realized he'd been right in his assessment: krav maga.

Hawkins was impressed.

Even though she'd subdued the other man instead of killing him, he wouldn't make the mistake of underestimating her.

She didn't seem afraid of him. In fact, she looked almost happy to see him.

That didn't bode well, not at all. If she thought he was someone else, he could use that to get her to hand over the stone.

"Thanks for the assist," she said.

Her voice was melodic and sweet with an accent he couldn't place. She wasn't Tunisian; it was almost Greek. The dossier said the culture and the people of Castallegna were a blend of the two. He wondered if she was a rebel or a patriot. He could tell from the fire in her eyes that she burned with one cause or another.

It would be easier if she was just a jewel thief, an unscrupulous antiquities dealer. One of those could be bought off—not so much when it was a cause.

"Don't thank me yet, sweetheart. I'm here for the jewel."

She smiled, baring all of her straight white teeth at him. "You're looking at it."

"You're shitting me." There was no way, no way that this woman was the Jewel of Castallegna.

"No, Mr. Hawkins. I would never do that. I'm Princess Damara Petrakris, also known as the Jewel of Castallegna. We better get moving. The last thing we need is to get caught with a dead body on our hands."

She knew his name. She had been expecting him. Damn it. This screwed up all of his plans. "That's going to be a problem. I only made provisions for one."

"They didn't tell you the jewel wasn't a stone?" She arched a dark eyebrow.

"No." And Hawkins knew why. As a private contractor, he could decline an assignment, and his handler, Renner, had known that Byron would decline this one if he'd had all the information. Damn him. Damn him to hell. Renner knew what he'd been through in Uganda. Knew why he'd left the army.

He knew it, and he hadn't cared. The DOD wanted this woman on American soil whatever it took, whatever the cost to him.

He swallowed hard. Hawkins was a soldier to the marrow. He knew how this worked. But he couldn't be responsible for someone else's safety. Not again. Not after Uganda. If Renner had dispatched him to kill the two men on the floor in front of him, he would've accepted that gladly, but this… He couldn't do it.

"Whatever is going through your mind, you can't leave me here," she whispered, and put her hand on his arm.

It was so small, so delicate, but he knew she was fierce.

"You don't understand. I planned a water exit in a small fishing boat that's only big enough for one. It's hours from Tunis to Marsala on the water. How long before there are others looking for you? Castallegna is in the Ionian Sea. That's close enough that they'll be watching the airports. I only have papers for one."

"Your Mr. Renner already provided me with documents. I won't complain about the accommodations." She looked down for a moment. "Please. My country—"

"I can't be responsible for you. That's how people die," he confessed. Even though he'd never see her again, for some reason, he needed her to know that he wasn't leaving her behind to be cruel. It was the only kind thing he could do for her.

"I'll die or worse if you don't take me with you."

She cocked her head to the side, and one lock of her hair had come free from her long braid. "And of course you're not responsible for me. I'm not a child. But you can help me. That's what you do, isn't it?"

"What I do is kill people," he said, as if that wasn't clear.

"And for that, I am grateful." She nodded, wearing an earnest expression.

He scrubbed his hands over his face. She wasn't giving up; she wasn't afraid. So why was he? He'd only ever failed one mission before

If he left her behind, this fearless princess, it would be Uganda all over again. He kept seeing her beautiful face bloody and beaten.... He'd heard her attacker. *I can't kill you yet, but I can hurt you.*

Byron Hawkins supposed there was some decency left in him yet.

Knowing what lay in store for her if he didn't take her, well, he just couldn't have that blood on his hands.

For one horrible moment, Damara thought her savior was going to leave her behind. She could see his eyes harden with what must have been resolve, and then they were filled with so much pain. Something had happened to this man.

Yes, he was definitely a killer. He'd snapped Sergio's neck with the swift and easy brutality of a predator. She hadn't been lying when she said she was grateful—Sergio was her brother's head security adviser. A pretty title for what amounted to head tor-

turer. She needed this Byron Hawkins to make her
escape, and in doing so, to save her country from
Abele.

But she knew there was more to this Hawkins
than this machine he'd made of himself.

Damara found herself intrigued by him, by his
pain. It didn't hurt that he was handsome and strong.
He dwarfed her, a giant, deadly wall of lethal power.
What woman wouldn't find that attractive?

Damara had to remember she wasn't just a woman; she was a princess. In her heart, there was only
room for her people—her country. She understood
what it was to live a life in service.

"It's ten minutes to the port of La Goulette, but I
plan to make it in five. Let's go."

Relief flooded her. He would help. She followed
him outside and he led her through some well-
groomed shrubbery to where he'd hidden a Ducati.

He handed her the single helmet and she took it
gratefully.

"It's a Panigale 1199 R. Wish I could take it with
me."

"Did you steal this?" She eyed him.

"What do you think?" He mounted the bike, swing-
ing one long, powerful leg over the side.

She supposed that didn't matter. Damara had more
pressing problems. The seat was tiny. Given his size,
she didn't think there was any way she was going
to fit on the thing. But Damara had said she wasn't
going to complain about accommodations, and she
wouldn't start now.

Especially not when he could still change his mind. "Don't be shy now, Princess."

She'd never heard anyone say *princess* in that way before. It made her shiver. She wasn't sure if she liked it or not.

His arm snaked out and wrapped around her waist as he hauled her onto the front of the bike. As he revved the engine, he said, "Hold on."

She was barely aware of the speed or even the scenery as it melted into swirling colors at the edges of her vision.

The man holding her dominated all of her senses.

He was a solid wall against her back—his body was immovable like a marble statue, but he exuded heat like a bonfire. Even when she'd been surrounded by bodyguards in the royal palace, she'd never felt as safe as she did right at this moment. It was insanity; they were tearing through the streets barreling toward even more danger. Damara was about as far from safe that she could be.

Only she was almost out of Abele's reach and that felt amazing, too.

She breathed deeply, centering herself and pushing down all of her fear. Damara could smell the salt and the sea, something that never failed to ground her. Strangely enough, it seemed to be coming from him more than the air around them.

Their bodies swayed and twisted with the bike as it shot through the streets and alleyways, and for a moment, Damara could swear she was riding the wind.

The colors and scenery slowly untangled into

recognizable things as Hawkins decelerated the machine. They emerged on a small, hidden beach. Damara had been to Tunis and La Goulette numerous times, but she'd never known anything like this was here.

Well, what had she expected? To leave a secured international port from a monitored dock?

She saw the boat that would be their mode of transport. He wasn't kidding; it was going to be a tight fit. She bit her lip. It was true that she'd trained hard for the skills that she had, but she wasn't used to hardship or discomfort.

You can do this.

She could do anything she had to do to stop Abele and save Castallegna.

"Get in and lie down. I'll cover you with the tarp until we're clear."

Damara did as she was told. The boat stank like old fish and she pulled her shirt up over her nose. The roar of a small motor soon rattled the hull and Damara didn't know how long she lay there under the tarp as still and quiet as she knew how to be until he pulled it back from her face.

The first thing she noticed was the sky. The stars were big and bright, like glittering holes burned out of the pitch—breathtakingly beautiful. She could smell the salt in the air again, and the ocean around them seemed so black and fathomless in the dark, except for the pale ribbon of moonlight that shone down like a winding road over the inky waves.

"There's no way we can make it together to Marsala in this, and even if we did, it would blow our cover. There's a cargo ship anchored just over there that's headed to Marseille. It'll be close quarters, dirty and dank for about twenty hours, but I think it'll do the job."

She turned her attention from the sky to where he gestured. "How are we going to get aboard?"

"Captain is a friend. I got in touch with him before I dumped my cell. You're not carrying any electronics, are you? Phone, iPod…"

She shook her head. "No, I knew they'd be able to track me."

"Smart girl."

Pride swelled and bloomed at his praise. She didn't even know him, and after this, she'd never see him again. It didn't matter what he thought of her as long as he got her to the States.

"He's going to linger there for the next twenty minutes and we have to get aboard and down in the cargo hold before any of his crew sees us. So I need you to do exactly as I say when I say it. Can you do that for me?"

"Yes," she agreed easily.

He maneuvered the boat up next to the cargo ship, the sound of the small motor drowned out by the idling growl of the giant engines of the ship. A rope ladder had been left hanging down the side for them.

She grabbed hold of the ladder, the rope abrasive on her palms. For all of her training, she still had the hands of a princess. Damara wouldn't complain; instead she would just do as he instructed. She tried to be as quiet as she could, remembering her ballet lessons and balancing her weight so she didn't flail and clang against the side like some alarm alerting everyone to their presence.

When she pulled herself to the top, she heard voices and she ducked her head, still clinging to the rope ladder. She looked down at Hawkins.

What's wrong? he mouthed.

She made a talking motion with her hand and then held up three fingers to indicate the number of voices she'd heard.

He put his head down for a moment and then he began to climb. When she would have shimmied back down the ladder and back into the boat, she saw it had already been set adrift. They were well and truly stuck.

Damara made herself as narrow as possible while still holding herself steady and he started moving up the ladder behind her, his feet and hands on the outside of hers.

Even though Damara was used to warm temperatures and to heat, she wasn't used to his heat. His body was so hard and hot that, even with the layers of clothes between them, his skin seemed to burn her.

She tried not to think about it—the way she fit against him, the way the hard planes of muscle pressed against her, how small and safe she felt, even dangling off a rope ladder hanging over dangerous waters.

As he moved higher, she became very aware of

another part of his body that was just as hot, hard and insistent as the rest of him. Her cheeks heated and she knew that even in the dark, her face would be scarlet.

He didn't stop to apologize or make excuses, or even acknowledge all of the intimacies that were now between them. This was just a job to him, and his arousal was just another bodily function.

Damara didn't know him, but she knew his kind. He might be there to help her, but he was still a mercenary. Still a man paid to kill. She rather imagined a man like him would have to be cut off from attachment to anything. Even himself.

She exhaled heavily and pushed all of those thoughts out of her head. She didn't have the time or the luxury to think about anything but escape, if the muffled sounds of a struggle were any indication.

Damara bit her lip to keep from calling out to him.

Every second dragged on for what felt like hours as doubt and fear filled her until he reached over the side and grabbed her arm to help her up. His knuckles were bloody, but he was otherwise unharmed.

The image of his hands, though, it burned itself into her brain like a brand. They were broad and strong, already scarred, purposeful. They were the hands of a man who'd had to fight for everything he had. The way he moved, helping her, still using those hands even though he'd split his knuckles open, it was as though he didn't even notice the pain, if there was any.

Damara found that impossibly noble.

And it made her blush hotter.

She had to stop thinking of him as a man and think of him as what he was—a means to an end.

Another echo of voices spurred him to action and he lifted the cover off a lifeboat so they could crawl inside.

She could barely see him in the darkness, but the moon was bright enough overhead that a tiny bit of light shone through the canvas tarp. He held a finger up to his lips to indicate she should stay quiet.

Something sharp needled her back and hip. Damara wanted to stay still and silent, but it quickly became agony. Hawkins seemed to know and he pulled her tight against his body.

Time stopped again, just as it had on the ladder. She was stiff and frozen, but this time his fingers pushed her hair out of her face.

Those same bloody, damaged hands touched her gently, soothed her. This man said so much without saying anything at all. It was all there in that one simple gesture.

You're safe.

I'll protect you.

And she believed he would.

There was a part of her that didn't want him to help her. Part of her that wanted him to be a bastard. She didn't want to get caught, but she couldn't stop thinking about his hands. What they'd feel like on the rest of her body, what they'd look like.

Her face was so hot now she was sure that her cheeks would explode. She was embarrassed by the direction of her thoughts. It was all just fantasy anyway. She'd read too many forbidden books and been denied reasonable human contact for too long, all in the name of purity. Her body might be untried, but her mind certainly wasn't.

Damara shifted carefully to make herself more comfortable, but she was at a loss for what to do with her arm. If this was a lovers' embrace, she'd have clung to him, but he was a stranger. It was as if her own arm was this awkward part of her that didn't belong on her body.

"It's okay." His breath tickled against the shell of her ear. "You can touch me. There's nowhere else to go." His voice was so low, she could barely hear it.

Heart hammering against her chest, she did as he suggested and wrapped herself around him.

The hard length was still there and it occurred to her that it might be a gun instead of—she was such a silly girl. She'd been so caught up in the fairy tale of being a princess he had to save that she'd imagined this whole attraction between them like some stupid movie. She'd even romanticized his indifference. Another reason why she had to get her head back in the game. She couldn't afford to be a princess now. She had to be a leader. Damara had learned there was a big difference.

Except he went through the motions of pushing her hair out of her face again. It was a caress, a touch for the sake of touch.

"Sleep, Princess. It's a long ride to Marseille."

She didn't bother to tell him that there was no

way she'd be able to sleep. Not with his nearness, his heat, the adrenaline still coursing through her veins from the events of the day. Or the possibility of being discovered.

But she was wrong, because it was some time later that she was startled awake by gunfire.

* * * * *

Don't miss UNFADED GLORY by Sara Arden, coming only to HQN in November 2014.

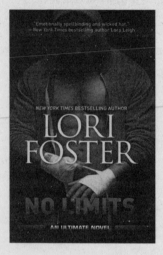

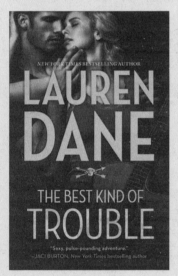

REQUEST YOUR
FREE BOOKS!

2 FREE NOVELS
FROM THE ROMANCE COLLECTION
PLUS 2 FREE GIFTS!

ROM13R